Books By Lily Thomas

Giant Wars Series
Loving His Fire
Grounded By Love
Melted By Love
Wicked Flames of Desire

Galactic Courtship Series
Xacier's Prize
Claiming His Champion
Captivating the Doctor
Escaping the Hunt
Abducting the Ambassador
Wicked Prisoner
Seducing the Enemy
Cuff Me Now
Challenging the Arena
Dark Desires in Space
His Fallen Star

Ice Age Alphas
The Sabertooth's Promise

The Sabertooth's Promise

Lily Thomas

This book is a work of fiction. Names, characters, places and incidents either are products of the author's imagination or are used fictitiously. Any resemblance to actual events or locales or persons, living or dead, is entirely coincidental.

Cover created by SelfPubBookCovers.com/ KimDingwall

www.lilythomasromance.com

ISBN: 9781720242048
ISBN: (ebook)   B07HJDJMNM

Chapter 1

Aiyre shook her body out as she stamped a hoofed foot, fluffing the thick brown fur, knocking the snow from her fur. Then she shifted out of her pronghorn form before she entered the village in her human form. The freezing winter air rushed over her, prickling her bare skin, and she quickly grabbed her fur clothing from where she'd taken them off when she'd left the village earlier in the day.

Her body heat quickly warmed up the furs, as she walked further into the village. Winter was one of her favorite seasons because of the beauty, but it had a cruel side, and the cold was relentless.

Their village wasn't the largest, but it was where she called home. She glanced at all the fur huts dotting the snow-covered area. Smoke trickled out of the center of each tent, personal fires burned brightly within each tent, and she couldn't wait until she could warm herself back up around a hearth.

She could taste the tension hanging in the air, and it ruined the peaceful look of their small village. There were guards posted in the village and the surrounding area around the village. The sabertooth shifter clan was making noise again, but this time it seemed like they might be a more serious threat than usual.

It made her skin crawl with goosebumps just thinking about it. Every day she left the safety of the village to go hunting, she wondered if it could be her last. Just the thought of a sabertooth ripping her throat out made her want to duck into a tent to hide and never venture out. Unfortunately, a tent wouldn't be much shelter when it came to those terrifying claws and teeth which they wielded with deadly accuracy.

She walked into the clan leader's hut. "Good day, Bhirk and Naru." She greeted the leader and his wife, as she ducked inside the warm hut leaving the cold winter outside, where it belonged. *she's already come inside!*

"Good day, Aiyre. Where have you been?" Naru looked up from where she sat on a pile of furs near the fire pit in the center of the hut. Her soft hazel eyes gazed fondly at Aiyre over the flames of the cooking fire.

Aiyre took a seat beside their fire pit and let the heat flowing off of it warm her some more. Shifting from form to form in winter wasn't the most pleasant experience with the cold always lurking in wait for exposed human skin. "I went out to look at some traps we have set and brought a few of the guards some food."

"No luck then with the traps?" Naru looked at Aiyre's empty hands.

"No luck." Unfortunately, she'd found the traps empty thanks to the deep snow they'd been experiencing. The traps had been buried before any animals could be caught, but Aiyre had reset them. Hopefully, the next time she went out, she'd come back with some animals.

Her eyes skimmed over Naru who was developing more wrinkles and spots on her softening skin. Journeys out into the cold were harsh on her, so Aiyre had tried to relieve Naru of some tasks, like feeding the guards posted around the area.

"How were the guards holding up under this impossible weather?" Naru asked as she flipped a few small fish near the fire.

"They were doing fine. A little hungry, but that should be expected. Now that I've brought them some dried meat, they should be good until they are switched out with other men from the clan." And none of them had spotted any sabertooths, so that was a bit of good news. They didn't need the sabertooth shifters sniffing around their village.

"Would you like some?" Naru offered her a small fish she'd cooked over the flickering flames of their cooking fire.

"Thank you." Aiyre accepted the hot fish eagerly. It would help to warm her from the inside out after her trek in the winter wonderland that was their life.

"What news did the guards have, if any?" Bhirk folded his long legs as he sat beside the fire pit, and Naru handed him another small fish that had finished cooking.

Aiyre balanced the hot fish on the tips of her fingers. "They've seen no sightings of the sabertooth shifters." She reported with relief.

Every day was tense with unease as they waited for the sabertooths to attack. Life was already difficult in winter without having to worry about the sabertooth clan causing chaos. Recently, there'd been a lot of unrest as they waited for the mammoths to come.

Naru nodded, pleased with the news. "Hopefully, this means we won't see much of them."

"It doesn't mean they've calmed." Bhirk took a bite of his fish, as he thought on the matter.

Naru frowned, not liking what Bhirk was implying. Just because they hadn't seen the sabertooths in a while, didn't mean they weren't still out there waiting to pounce. The sabertooth leader was blaming their clan for the lack of food in the area this winter.

Aiyre plucked the little fish bones from the flesh of the fish. She tossed them into the fire where they sizzled.

"We have to hunt before winter sets in fully, but need to do it without bothering the sabertooth shifters. Their leader has grown weary of our presence." Bhirk continued.

That was putting it politely. They couldn't venture outside of their village without worrying what the sabertooths would think.

"If only we could stay in our pronghorn forms and move south where the snows would be less severe, and we didn't have another clan breathing down our necks." Aiyre wished it was something they could do.

"It would make it easier," Bhirk agreed. "But some of the clan wouldn't be able to shift for such an extended period of time. The old and the young wouldn't be able to shift easily, if at all." He shook his head. "We would lose too many of the clan if we tried to move now."

Aiyre eyed Naru as she nibbled on her fish. She hadn't even seen Naru shift into her pronghorn form in the past year. She studied the woman who had been close to a mother to her since her own mother had died long ago.

"I still don't understand the cause of the upset." She shook her head. "Our two clans could live near each other in harmony, but this leader just seems to desire a fight with us."

Everyone in the tent nodded their heads sadly.

Bhirk had done his best to try and speak to the other leader, but the man was unpredictable and unbudging in his views. He was adamant the pronghorn shifters were the reason prey was so limited this winter. It didn't bode well for their clan, and she feared what the outcome might be as aggressions grew.

Not that it would be much of a fight. Their pronghorn clan would have a hard time fighting against a larger clan that could shift into sabertooth cats. It would just be a slaughter.

She forced herself to finish her fish, even though her stomach was reeling at the thought of what might come if they couldn't make peace with the other clan. They kept trying, but there was no way for them to please the sabertooth cats.

Naru and Bhirk were like her parents, and she didn't wish to see any harm come to them. They'd been so good to her after her parents had been killed by a bear while out hunting. She hadn't even been old enough to know her parents. They were just faceless people in her memories, and it saddened her.

Thankfully, Naru and Bhirk had been able to tell her about her parents and were kind enough to raise her as their own. They'd been nothing but doting, and she couldn't have asked for anything better, but recently there'd been a bit of pressure about finding a man in the village to combine her furs with. She knew which man they thought she should choose. She just wasn't sure he was the right man for her.

"I will assemble our hunters and head out to gather some meat." Aiyre nodded her head as she watched the flames of their cooking fire dance gleefully, unaware of the danger they were all in.

Aiyre hadn't ever wanted to be a burden on the clan that could have done away with her. She'd only been another mouth to feed, and a few of her clan-mates had pointed that out while she'd been younger and unable to help with hunts.

Now though, she was proud to say she participated in hunts on a regular basis, and she was a reasonably decent hunter. Her clan had been so kind to her, even if there had been some rough patches in there. She'd wanted nothing more than to pay them back for their generosity and kindness.

"Avoid any known hunting grounds the sabertooth clan might think they have a claim to so we don't irritate them anymore," Bhirk warned her gently.

Two words

"You could try the southern valleys," Naru suggested as she began eating her own fish. "They can't possibly think they have a claim to those hunting lands."

Naru was probably right. The southern valleys lay almost a day's journey from the sabertooth village.

Aiyre nodded. "I'll go and gather the hunters then."

"Go." Bhirk waved her on probably just as eager as the rest of the clan to see their meat hut filled to the brim before the worst of winter blew in.

Recently, the sabertooth clan had been making it hard for them to hunt their normal hunting lands, so they relied on ice fishing the frozen lake right beside their village. Unfortunately, the lake wouldn't provide them with enough food for the rest of winter.

Rising from her seat, she found herself reluctant to leave the warmth of the fire, but she had to go hunting to help their dwindling meat reserves. The harsh winter was far from over, and it would only get worse.

As she exited the tent, the cold didn't take long to rush up and smack her in the face. She let the tent flap fall back into place behind her before she let out all the warm air. She slipped on some fur gloves to keep her fingers from freezing off.

Now she had to find herself some hunters to join her.

Slowly, she walked through the village, her fur boots crunching in the thick layer of snow that covered the ground all around them.

She spotted Girk stepping out of a hut. She watched as he paused right outside the hut and stretched his arms above his head, before throwing his fur-lined hood over his head.

She smiled. Now there was the man she needed on a hunt with her.

"Girk!" Aiyre raised a gloved hand in greeting eager to get his attention. He would be an excellent person to have in a hunting party. He had the skill and drive to make a hunt successful.

A smile spread over his face, as he began to stride over to her. "Aiyre! You're back already?"

She shrugged. "It didn't take me long to get meals to the guards."

He draped an arm over her shoulder, his grin going ear to ear. "I'm glad you're back. I'm not sure what I would've done without you nearby." Even though his hood covered his head, she could still see his blonde hair peeking out. *blond. 'Blonde' is the feminine form.*

"Oh!" Aiyre blushed. "You can be such a flirt." She rolled her eyes. Everyone knew Girk wanted to join with her, but he had yet to ask, and she was glad because she wasn't too sure what her response would be. He'd been more of a brother to her than a potential suitor.

"Only for you, though." His brown eyes danced in amusement as he wiggled his eyebrows at her.

"Pfft. Stop distracting me." She smacked his chest playfully. "We need to set up a hunting party and get some more meat for the clan before we run out and starve."

Girk nodded, his lips drawing down into a serious line. "Gather your supplies, and I will gather the hunters."

She sent him a smile, as he took back his arm and let her go. The sooner they got this done, the better, and they had to make the hunt count.

Aiyre glanced at the hunters Girk had gathered for their outing. They were some of the best, and she couldn't wait to set out. They were going to come back with plenty of meat. She was positive about it.

"Where are we to hunt?" Girk folded his arms in front of his massive chest, which was only accented by the large fur coat he was wearing.

"He's right. The sabertooth clan seems to be everywhere we look." Another hunter complained. "Every time we round a tree, there's a sabertooth shifter waiting on the other side ready to slash our throats open."

"I'm not sure that's what I said." Girk scowled at the other hunter.

"We will go to the southern valleys. Hopefully, they won't be out hunting while we are. Those hunting grounds are far from their village, and I'm doubtful they will be there." Aiyre informed them. It wasn't like they could bury their heads in the snow and hope everything would be alright. They'd starve this winter if they didn't get some more food in their meat hut, sabertooths or no sabertooths.

The hunter who'd offered up the complaint grumbled a bit under his breath, most likely wondering why she, a woman, was leading their hunting expedition. There were maybe three women in the clan who hunted but never before had any of them decided to take charge of a hunting party. Only Aiyre was that daring.

Yanking the butt of her spear out of the snow, she led the grumbling group of hunters away from the village and towards a hunting ground where they might find something to hunt without another clan breathing down their necks.

Or worse, coming to blows with them.

Aiyre shared her companions' fears, but they had to hunt if they wanted their clan to make it through the long cold winter. They trudged through the snow-covered ground, first heading south, and then turning to go slightly east.

"Perhaps we should move our village." Someone said from behind her.

"That doesn't sound like a bad idea."

"This close to winter?" Aiyre scoffed. "It would be the same as not hunting. Most of our clan won't make it." She followed Girk through the snow, using his footsteps in the deep powder to make her trek over the ground easier.

"We still might not make it through winter. It might be in our best interest in losing a few to save the rest."

"I can't believe you suggested that." Aiyre glanced over at Friu who was walking next to her.

"We might all die if we stay here," Friu reasoned, looking for someone in the group to agree with him.

"We can't abandon some of our people." Girk stepped in. "We will stick together until the end. We are a clan, and we protect each other like family."

"I'm hoping it won't come to that." Aiyre grimaced. She didn't want there to be an end to their clan.

"I hope the same, but I'm not sure we'll be that lucky." Girk sent her a sad smile.

"Maybe we should take the fight to them," Friu suggested as he thrust a spear in the air.

She wasn't going to let Friu bother her with his stupidity, and instead gave the hunter a stern look hoping to shut him up once and for all. This wasn't something she wanted to talk about. "This is a time for hunting, not wasting time in pointless conversations that will lead nowhere and only result in scaring the prey away."

They went silent, the only sound the crunching of the snow as they trekked onwards. Every once in a while they'd pass a white long-furred rabbit, who'd scurry away in a panic. They were searching for something more substantial, and the rabbits had nothing to fear from them unless they got themselves trapped in one of the snares she'd set earlier.

Once they arrived at the hunting grounds, Aiyre and the rest of the hunting party crouched low in the snow and crawled over the hill. With each movement, more snow built up in front of her, and she used her fur-lined sleeve to move the growing mound of snow.

As they crested the hill, they spotted a herd of horses grazing below. Their shaggy brown coats blew around in the chilly wind, and Aiyre smiled at their good fortune. The wind was working in their favor, blowing their scent away from the herd. This might just be a good hunt, and she could feel the excitement of their small group grow.

If they could manage to take a couple of those horses, it would significantly increase their ability to make it through the winter. That much meat would go a long way and give them some much-needed hope which her clanmates were losing with every day that passed.

Looking to the hunters near her she gave a subtle nod of her head, and a couple of them melted away into the snowy terrain their white fur clothing blending in seamlessly to the background of fresh snow. They would go around to the other side of the herd and kill the horses as her group chased them in the correct direction.

She brushed her hair out of her face, as the wind picked up slightly.

Pausing she sniffed the air. A scent trickled through the cold.

What was that scent? Aiyre felt like she should be able to place a name to it, but she was having a hard time figuring out what it was. Her pronghorn side allowed her human side a little better ability at smelling, but if she wanted to smell even better, she'd have to be in her pronghorn form.

Right now, was not the time to be shifting though. It could startle the horses below, and they needed this hunt to be a success.

Her attention focused back in on the herd of horses meandering below them. They had to concentrate and make sure not to mess this hunt up.

She gave the signal, with a flick of her hand, and her group of hunters leaped up from their position in the snow. As they began to sprint down the hill, her heart stopped in her chest.

"Stop!" She hollered at the top of her lungs.

All the hunters froze in their tracks and looked up at her surprised by her sudden outburst. Their brows were drawn down above their eyes, wondering why she was halting their hunt. All she could do was point soundlessly over their shoulders.

The men in her hunting party turned, and their eyes widened as they finally understood. Sabertooths were sprinting across the snowfield, their tan coats streaking across the white snow in a blur of color. They'd come to this valley to hunt!

Aiyre and the rest of the hunters scrambled back up the hill and out of sight of the oncoming sabertooths. If they were spotted, there could be trouble, and they wouldn't come out on top.

"What are they doing here?" One of her fellow hunters hissed in obvious irritation.

Aiyre shook her head confused herself. "I have no idea why they would be hunting this far south."

Were they trying to start a fight? This hunting ground was well out of the way of their village. She got the horrible feeling that the sabertooths were doing their best to get rid of their pronghorn neighbors.

They watched on as the cats barreled down on the herd of horses. A couple of them sprinted around the herd, throwing the whole herd into a mass of panicked chaos. Then several of them tackled a horse, bringing it down with little to no effort, and then one of them latched onto the throat. It was like the sabertooths were taunting them, showing them that they too would be just as easily dispatched.

"Maybe we should fight them," Someone uttered.

"Don't say such things," Aiyre hissed back. "Our hunters might be able to bring down horses, but we'd have no chance against the sabertooth clan. They are born hunters and have two forms in which to hunt," Aiyre said harshly, her breath coming out in white puffs.

"It's too dangerous to stay out with the sabertooths roaming the area. We should return to the clan." Girk and the other hunters who'd split off rushed back over to them.

"I agree. We can always come back out at a later time." Aiyre guided the men back to the village. Her heart sunk. Everything had been going so well until the sabertooths had shown up. It was like the gods were teasing them.

Walking into the village without anything to show had been the downside to Aiyre's whole day. The eager looks on her clanmates' faces had turned to dismay when they realized there would be no meat to add to their already dwindling supply.

As much as Aiyre hated to admit it, this might be the last year for her clan. The meat they had wouldn't last all winter. Perhaps she would suggest a split of the hunters for tomorrow. Each group could go to a different hunting ground. Then they'd have a better chance at getting in some kills without the sabertooth clan interrupting them.

Aiyre settled down next to the village campfire. The orange and red mix of flames soared high into the black night sky. She watched some embers take flight, flying high into the sky, where they burned out and then fell back to the snow, dull and grey. 'Seconds' were unknown at this time - it's before people had clocks!

The stars shimmered brightly in the dark sky, and for a couple of seconds, she let a moment of calm wash over her. Even with death staring them right in the face, she was going to enjoy the small joys in the land around her.

The clan had all gathered around to share food and talk. It warmed her to be sitting among them, even if they might be dealing with desperate times.

"Hello, Aiyre."

"Ezi." Aiyre smiled warmly, as she looked up. "How was your day?"

shone A blush filled Ezi's cheeks, as her jade eyes shined brightly in the firelight. "Drakk has claimed me." She plopped down on the log Aiyre was already sitting on.

"Drakk?" She glanced over to where the hunter sat in front of the enormous village campfire. Ezi was a lucky woman indeed. He had to be one of their finest hunters. "I'm sure you both will be very happy and have lots of children." She wiggled her eyebrows.

Ezi sent her a timid smile. "I'm surprised by his offer, to be honest."

"Why?" Aiyre leaned in towards the fire, placing her gloved hands near the warmth.

"I just never thought anyone would notice me."

"You're beautiful, Ezi. Someone was bound to take notice and desire you to be their woman."

"Thank you." Another blush crept up Ezi's face and neck at the compliment.

Aiyre felt a pang in her chest. She wasn't jealous that Drakk had claimed Ezi, but she was saddened that no man had claimed her yet. Where was the man for her? She was starting to get on the older side, and there were still no offers for her to accept or decline.

Laughter erupted from the other side of the campfire. At least, her clan was able to enjoy themselves in such trying times. It showed their ability to get through this together. And it was a good sign that Drakk and Ezi were joining their furs together. No one here was about to give up hope over what the future might hold.

"Don't look so down." Girk plopped a seat next to Aiyre and Ezi.

"It's hard not to worry. I love everyone here," she swept her arm through the air, "yet I fear I might not see some of their faces come spring." Aiyre worried.

"We will find a way. We have always found a way." He wrapped an arm around her shoulder and drew her close to his sturdy frame.

He was definitely the most kind-hearted man they had in the village. He'd been nothing but sweet with her, and she was thankful for that.

"I don't understand how you can be so positive," Aiyre grumped over at him. She was glad people were looking on the bright side, but she didn't want anyone thinking it wouldn't take effort on their part to make everything work.

Ezi's eyes darted between them. "Should we be concerned?"

Aiyre looked over at her friend. The sparkle in Ezi's jade eyes had dimmed. "You should only worry about your first night with Drakk."

The blush returned to Ezi's cheeks, as she forgot about the worrisome topic of their survival.

"He's put a claim on you?" Girk asked his eyebrows nearly shooting off his face.

"No need to sound so surprised." Ezi's eyes flashed with a bit of hidden steel in her small frame.

He raised his hands. "He will make a lot of men jealous is all."

"I've already said that." Aiyre nodded her head in confirmation.

"Someone say my name?"

Aiyre peered over her shoulder to see Drakk standing behind Ezi looking protective, and she couldn't help but smile at Ezi's good fortune. "Just commenting on how lucky you are to have claimed Ezi before anyone else could get the chance."

A smile spread over his lips. "Indeed. I look forward to our night together after we are done with the joining rituals tonight."

A deeper blush tinged Ezi's cheeks, and Aiyre smiled at Ezi's obvious discomfort. It was amusing to watch her friend's emotions play out across her facial features so easily for the world around her to see.

"Don't fool us, Ezi. You are as eager as he is." Aiyre gave Ezi a slight push on her shoulders to get her off the log. "Now go, prepare yourself, and give us something to celebrate tonight." It would get all their minds off the horrible hunt.

Drakk took hold of Ezi's hand and led her back to her hut where he would leave her before going to his own hut.

"We are starting to pair off." Girk gave her a meaningful look, and this time it was her turn to blush.

Aiyre had never been with a man before, and Girk hadn't been on her list of potential suitors, only because she never thought he would be interested in her. "You'd have to ask Bhirk's permission." She told him.

"I already have." Girk smiled at her. "I know you're like a daughter to him."

"And he said yes?" Aiyre wouldn't be surprised. Girk was a man who could provide for her and any children they had together. It wouldn't come as a complete surprise that Bhirk would give his blessing, but she would've thought he would have asked her how she felt about Girk.

Girk nodded.

Did he want her because of her position? Since Bhirk, the clan leader, had taken her in as his daughter, any man who married her would become the leader, once Bhirk got too old or died. Naru and Bhirk never had children. The gods hadn't blessed them with that joy, so Aiyre had been doted on since she was a small child.

Girk could make a good leader. He was stubborn for sure, but he also listened, and he had a compassionate heart. He would make an excellent choice for her. And there was the fact that he was incredibly handsome. He would make her a great partner in life.

But her heart wasn't into the idea as much as her mind, despite all the reasons to pick him. Aiyre didn't know what she wanted in a man, but was he really it?

The firelight reflected off his blonde hair, as his brown eyes watched her intently. He was definitely one of the most attractive men in the clan, but that wasn't enough for her. She needed to know they would work together. Once joined, they would be expected to spend the rest of their lives with each other until one of them died.

"I'm not ready to leave Naru and Bhirk," Aiyre blurted out, before she rushed to her feet, and fled the campfire area in a rush, not giving him a chance to say anything more to her.

Aiyre burst into the hut she shared with Naru and Bhirk and flung herself on her pile of furs. She had so much to think about, sabertooths and now Girk who unexpectedly wanted to be joined with her. She hadn't seen that coming.

"Did Girk speak with you?" Naru's voice rang out of the semi-darkness from the other side of the fire that warmed the inside of the tent.

"Yes," Aiyre muttered against the soft strands of fur she was laying on.

"What did you say?"

Aiyre shrugged in the darkness and rolled over. "I can't leave this tent yet."

"You will have to leave us someday. We won't be here forever, and then you will need a tent of your own with a man and a family." Naru's voice was soft but also firm with the truth she spoke.

Aiyre's heart broke at the very thought of Bhirk and Naru dying one day. She refused to think about it. It wasn't their time yet, and she still had time to figure out what she wanted out of her life.

"Don't think of his interest if you don't wish to, but you will need to get yourself ready for Ezi's journey into womanhood." Naru sounded thoughtful. "Perhaps, it will help you to understand what you are looking for in a man when you see her go through the ceremony."

Aiyre nodded as she jumped to her feet. She would think about Girk's offer at a later time. He'd surprised her was all, and she was sure after some time to think about it, she would be able to give him an answer.

"I would love to see you wear the dress I wore when I joined with Bhirk," Naru said softly from the other side of the fire.

"I would like that." Aiyre's heart soared into the skies. Naru might not be the woman who gave her life, but she wasn't sure she would want it any other way.

Walking around the dark interior of the tent Aiyre picked out a pack of dried meat, some herbs, and some paints in wooden jars. She'd worry about her proposal after Ezi was joined with Drakk.

Naru and Aiyre left their tent together and joined a group of women heading to Ezi's hut. It was time for them to get her ready for her joining with Drakk.

They stopped in front of her tent, chatting until Ezi came out dressed in elaborately-decorated clothing. Beads of wood and small stones stood out against the light brown fur. A cloak of white fur draped from her head to her feet. It was a cloak that all the women in their clan had worn and would wear in the future. Her dark hair had been braided alongside her face with little bone and wooden beads.

She was stunning.

Aiyre stepped forward, took Ezi's arm, and guided the group of women to a nearby cave that was only for the women of their clan. This was where Ezi would prepare herself for her new start in life as a wife and hopefully, if the gods were kind, a mother.

They were able to hear the men's group chanting off in the distance as they proceeded to their own cave. The men would be preparing Drakk for his joining with Ezi. Soon the men would come to this cave to leave Drakk and Ezi alone, but first, the women had to prepare her and ask the gods of fertility to be kind.

This cave was for the women, and for couples who were going to be joined for the first time. It would be the only time a man would see the inside of this particular cave. Here they celebrated the woman's ability to create life, and they found it to be the perfect setting for joining ceremonies in hopes the gods would grant the couple many children.

They ventured deep into the cave. Their branches dipped in animal fat burning brightly, lighting their way down the long rock corridor.

"I'm nervous," Ezi whispered in the flickering dark.

"Of course, you are, but Drakk will guide you. There's no need to worry about anything." Aiyre knew Drakk would take care of Ezi. Their joining had only been a matter of time. Those two had been meant for each other. Whenever Drakk knew Ezi wasn't paying attention, he would sneak glances her way, and Aiyre had caught Ezi doing the same on a few occasions.

"We are here." She whispered as the group of women emptied out into a large chamber.

All sorts of symbols and drawings decorated the rough walls surrounding them. Mats of fur were laid out for each woman. Aiyre took her seat, lit the firewood that had been waiting for them and watched the smoke spiral up to a hole in the ceiling of the cave.

Then she took out her paints and placed them around her, preparing herself for the beginning of the ceremony. Each woman did the same, except Naru who set out her paints in front of Ezi, and then helped Ezi out of her clothing. The cave had warmed considerably since they'd entered it and lit the fire.

As the partner to the leader, Naru would lead the women in this ceremony, and then someday that privilege would land on Aiyre's shoulders. Thank goodness Naru and Bhirk still had plenty of years left in them, it meant she wouldn't have to take on this role anytime soon.

Aiyre quickly dipped her fingers in the assorted paints sitting before her, spreading designs up her face and arms. She swirled the cool paint over her skin, loving the feel as the paint hardened on her skin, trapping the small hairs on her arms like the bog in the summer trapped unsuspecting animals.

Once she was done tracing images over her skin, she found Naru had finished with painting Ezi's naked body. Red circles had been drawn around her nipples, and a red line went down her chest all the way to her belly button. Lines decorated her arms and legs with dots interspersed in the design.

Then Ezi walked around to each woman in the cave, and each woman painted a design onto Ezi's body. Some symbolized fertility while others symbolized long life.

Ezi glided over the smooth stone flooring of the cave to Aiyre. Generations of clan members had worn these floors smooth. Then Ezi bent down on her knees in front of her, drawing her attention back to the ceremony.

Dipping her finger into the red paint, she lifted her finger and drew a line from Ezi's throat down between her breasts. This line was a way of asking the gods to bestow Ezi with a long life.

Before Ezi could walk away, she reached out and gave her friend a quick reassuring squeeze of her hand. Ezi rose and went to sit before Naru once more. Naru grabbed a bundle of dried herbs and lit them with the fire. Smoke filled the cave.

Relaxing, Aiyre breathed it in. As the herbs took effect, she watched the paintings on the cave wall come to life. The image of a woman with her thighs spread, welcoming a man into her body. Heat rushed up inside Aiyre. Then the images of animals distracted her, as she watched them prance around the cave walls as the firelight played over their forms.

It didn't take long to hear more footsteps echoing down the corridor they'd all come in through just moments ago. Drakk was on his way to claim Ezi. She felt excitement enter her for her friend. Someday she would also welcome a man in here. Perhaps it would be Girk.

Aiyre glanced around the cave in the dancing firelight. She loved being inside these caves, where her ancestors met, and now she waited with her clan to welcome the future of their clan.

Someday she would be in this cave receiving her man. A flutter bounced through her insides as she tried to imagine the man she would choose to share this night with.

Drakk entered the cavern in all his naked glory. The firelight caressed his toned muscles, and the painted designs on him made him look that much more dangerous.

Aiyre couldn't help her eyes dropping lower to where his member stood proudly between his legs. She bit her bottom lip. Ezi was indeed a lucky woman, and it looked like Drakk was more than excited to join with Ezi.

She turned her gaze over to her friend. Ezi's jade eyes had glazed over with desire as she appeared transfixed on the image Drakk presented at the chamber's entrance.

Good. The herbs had helped to calm Ezi's nerves. It wouldn't have done them any good to have her trembling in a bundle of nerves.

The women slowly filtered out of the cave, leaving Ezi and Drakk alone for the night. Aiyre expected they'd be back to camp at some point, whether it was tonight or a couple of nights from now. She'd made sure to leave the dried meat behind, in case the couple forgot time and needed something to eat. No one would blame them. This was their time to come together before the gods.

Aiyre felt the drug still racing through her system by the time they reached the village campfire. The orange flames danced in front of her, forming images of wild animals.

"Have you thought more about my proposition?" Girk walked up behind her, his warm hands landing on her shoulders, massaging the tension out of them.

"I have."

His head dipped to the juncture of her shoulder and neck, he took a deep breath and placed a soft kiss on her exposed skin. "What do you say, Aiyre? Will you join with me?"

"I'm not ready." It was semi-truthful. She wanted to say yes and start a family, but her heart wasn't into it as much as her mind was, because she still wasn't sure they would be the right fit for each other.

Girk let out a heavy sigh as he removed his hands from her shoulders. "Is there any way for me to convince you otherwise?"

Aiyre turned and faced him. "I don't think so." The drug pulsing through her system demanded that she initiate something with him, but she couldn't. She couldn't give him any false hope for a future joining.

His blonde hair was tousled, and there were several designs painted over his bare chest, and she marveled at the fact that he wasn't shivering in the night air.

"Don't think this means I will give up." A glint of determination entered his dark eyes.

She smiled up at him. "I would be insulted if you didn't at least try a little longer to win me over." She wasn't quite sure why she'd just said that. She was giving him hope, and it was cruel of her, but she did enjoy their friendship.

He smiled back down at her before he left to speak with others in the clan. Aiyre watched his back as he strode through the village. He was everything she should want. He had broad shoulders, plenty of strength to carry the weight of the clan, and he got along with everyone. Girk would make the perfect fit for the leader of their clan.

Naru came to stand beside her. "Don't worry about it much." She watched Girk as well as he joked with their clanmates. "You will find the right man in time. It took Bhirk several moons to finally convince me to join with him." She confided.

"Truly?" Aiyre looked over at her. She'd never heard this before, and it surprised her. Bhirk and Naru had always seemed like they would've jumped at the chance to be with each other.

Naru nodded. "I wasn't sure about being joined with a clan leader. This role comes with so many responsibilities, and they scared me at first." She turned her soft eyes over to Aiyre, before wrapping an arm around her and drawing her in close to her side.

"It's not the position that scares me." Aiyre continued to watch Girk interact with the people around him with ease. "I fear choosing the wrong man."

"Forget about it for tonight and enjoy the merrymaking. You needn't give him an answer anytime soon."

Aiyre smiled. "You're right." She wasn't being asked to choose a man right now. There was plenty of time for her to continue to toy around with the idea of joining with Girk.

Naru released her, and Aiyre quickly joined in on the celebration of the new union.

Once she let herself enjoy the celebration, there was no stopping her. It seemed like they would go on all night long celebrating the joining of two of their clanmates, but eventually, they all found their huts for the night and settled down.

Chapter 2

Screams penetrated her dreams, and Aiyre cracked open her sleepy eyes. The screams still sounding around her full of terror and pain. Aiyre leaped up from where she'd been sleeping and grabbed her hunting spear that rested near her bed of furs.

"What is it?" Naru rose from her sleeping furs blinking away the sleep on her eyes, with Bhirk quickly following suit.

"I don't know." Aiyre grabbed her fur gloves and bolted outside, only to freeze in her tracks. The overwhelming scent of sabertooth cats assaulted her nose, and they weren't wild cats. They were from the shifter clan.

Bhirk ran past her, his spear gripped tightly in a hand and joined in the fighting that was going on all around them. Most, if not all, of the shifting sabertooths, had to be attacking their village. Dread filled her stomach. This might very well be their last day alive!

Fear raised its ugly head causing her to want to shrink back into the hut she'd just left.

Aiyre shoved her fear down. She had a task at hand, and there was no place for jitters when she needed to have a firm hold on her emotions. Hoisting her spear, she joined Bhirk in attacking a sabertooth shifter.

They had him backed up against a couple of huts. Bhirk jabbed his spear point from the left, and Aiyre thrust hers from the right. The cat was only able to dodge the first spear, which presented an opening for her spear tip. She thrust the long wooden shaft into his side with all the pent-up resentment she had in her towards the sabertooths.

The spear tip sunk deep into the sabertooth's flesh, ripping a horrendous roar from the beast as it sunk to the ground. It gave a couple of final twitches and then died, blooding pouring from the wound she'd delivered it. Slowly, the sabertooth faded into a man, who was now scrunched up around his gut, where the spear had pierced him.

Aiyre had no sympathy for the man. It had been their decision to storm the pronghorns, and she would do whatever she had to when it came to defending her people from this unprovoked attack.

"Have Drakk and Ezi come back from their night together in the cave?" She glanced over at Bhirk, her eyes wide in panic as she thought about Ezi in this skirmish.

"Let's hope they haven't," Bhirk tossed over at her, not giving her much hope.

She prayed they'd stayed in the cave instead of coming back to the village. This way, at least someone would survive from their clan because it wasn't looking like they would come out on top.

Not to mention, she'd hate to see either of them die after only one night together. They deserved to have a lifetime.

Grabbing the hilt of her spear, she placed a foot against the dead man's side and yanked, dislodging her spear from the dead man lying at her feet.

She and Bhirk moved on to the next sabertooth, which was stalking a little girl from their clan. Aiyre didn't even think about it, she leaped onto the sabertooth's back, distracting the shifter away from the girl.

He bucked under her, trying to dislodge her, but she wasn't going to let go without a fight, not when a child's life was in danger. She couldn't even believe the sabertooth would be so cruel as to stalk a child. It was a child! What harm could she possibly pose to him?! - ? only

Bhirk used her distraction to their favor and rammed his spear into the side of the sabertooth's neck, downing the shifter in one move. He too slowly faded back into a man, the light quickly fading from his brown eyes.

Aiyre unwrapped her arms from around the man's neck and jumped onto her feet. Glancing up she saw the little girl disappear behind a hut.

"You should leave with the women, Aiyre." Bhirk grabbed her arm and tried to usher her away from the fighting.

"I'm staying." She shook his arm off. "We need every hunter available to fight off the sabertooths." And she knew he couldn't argue with that.

A pained holler sent chills running down her spine, and when she turned to look behind her, she saw Girk had one of his legs captured in a sabertooth's mouth of razor-sharp teeth.

Drakk ran up to her. "Run, Aiyre! Follow the other women. Do not stay and fight." His eyes darted around as he looked around the village. "We won't win this one!"

"You didn't stay in the cave for the night?!" Aiyre panicked as she thought about Ezi being in this chaos and blood. That woman wasn't a hunter, and she couldn't help but worry about her friend.

"I couldn't wait to bring her back to my hut and my furs." Drakk shook his head, his eyes wild with the fear they all felt. "Now go!" He shoved her, causing her to stumble over her own feet.

Her heart sank knowing Drakk was in the village, but it did give them one more fighter. She just hoped Ezi made it out of the village alive since she wasn't a skilled hunter and there were too many sabertooths running around to count.

She looked back over at Girk who was still doing his best to dislodge his leg from the mouth of the sabertooth and panic seared through her.

"I will see to him. Run!" And then Drakk and Bhirk ran to assist Girk their spears ready.

One look in Drakk's eyes had convinced her she'd be no help to them. That man was as fearless as they came, and she knew their odds were terrible when he thought they'd all die. If they were fighting a losing battle here, there was no reason for her to die here.

She hefted her spear and rushed out of the village. Her feet sank into the deep snow, but she attempted to keep up her speed, knowing she'd need distance. She felt like such a traitor by turning tail and running, but she'd only get killed with the rest of the clan's hunters. Everywhere she looked the sabertooth shifters outnumbered them two to one, maybe even more.

Maybe she could catch up to the rest of the women and help get them to safety, but finding tracks in the dark was too difficult. She was running around blind, and her pronghorn form wouldn't be much help with the night.

Naru! Did she make it out of the tent?

Aiyre stopped as her heart thundered away in her chest and looked back at the village. The village campfire had been kept burning all night long, and it illuminated the surrounding huts. She watched on as fur huts were toppled over, and it looked like the fighting was almost over. There wouldn't be time to go back and check on Naru. The sabertooths were sure to spread out and try to find any survivors.

She felt her heart cry out, as she forced her feet to carry her away from the village. Her fur boots dug into the thick snow, as she pushed herself as fast as she could go through all the build-up of snow on the ground.

This gap shouldn't be here

Aiyre gave up on trying to follow any of the fleeing women and turned in the direction of a nearby hunting cave she knew of in the area. Some of their hunters would use it if they found themselves too far from the village when lousy weather hit or night fell. And none of the sabertooths would know about it unless they tracked her.

Some of the women in the clan knew of it as well, and Aiyre hoped it might end up being a meeting spot for any surviving clanmates. She could only hope, but right now it was the best plan she could come up with when her mind was racing faster than she could process.

A growl ripped through the cold night air, right as she entered the nearby forest of towering pine trees. Twisting around she found herself face to face with a sabertooth shifter.

"There's no reason for more blood." She didn't know why she was talking to a sabertooth, but she was hoping she could find one of them that had a heart beating in their chest.

It raised a paw, preparing to attack her.

She pointed her spear in its direction. "Leave me alone!" She jabbed the point in its direction. On her own, she wasn't sure she'd be able to defeat the sabertooth, but she wasn't about to admit that. "I will defend myself." She jabbed the spear tip towards it again.

Its mouth opened, showing her its massive canines which reached well below its lower jaw. It was close enough to allow its foul breath to wash over her, and she felt her stomach roll in disgust.

They'd be visible with its mouth closed, then.

The shifter lunged, and Aiyre dodged to the side, forcing herself into a roll. Leaping to her feet, she bolted through the trees hoping to gain some distance before the shifter could collect himself and come after her. She had to leave this shifter in the dust, or she wouldn't live to see the sunrise in the morning.

But she heard the sabertooth cat following close behind her. Its large paws crunched into the frozen snow, leaving no doubt in her mind that it was gaining on her.

Her breath puffed out in front of her, as she pumped her arms at her sides. The enormous pine trees surrounding her had helped to prevent the ground from being burdened by snow.

Two words   A sharp pain clamped down on her left arm, and she swallowed her scream. She couldn't alert anymore of the sabertooths to her presence. One sabertooth was already one too many for her to handle.

Using her spear point, she twisted around and used it to slice the sabertooth's face. It let go of its hold on her arm and backed off with a howl of pain, only to come leaping at her once more.

Bracing herself against the ground Aiyre hugged the spear tight and aimed it at the cat's heart. It tried to avoid the spear but saw her plan too late. The cat crashed down on it.

Her eyes widened as she saw the jaw full of deadly teeth right up in her face. Her eyes met the cat's piercing gold eyes, and she watched as the light slowly dimmed in its speckled depths. Then its dead weight shifted the spear, allowing the large cat to land on her.

Slowly, it shifted into a man.

Letting out the breath she'd been holding, she shoved him off her with just a little bit of a struggle. Aiyre laid there in the snow for a couple of seconds. She could barely grasp how her life had changed so suddenly. This was the first night she'd used her spear to kill anything other than an animal, and she'd already killed three men. After tonight, her life would never be the same.

Rising on an elbow in the snow she kicked the man's body with a foot to make sure he was really dead. He made no sound. She pushed herself onto her feet, braced a foot against his chest, grabbed the shaft of the spear with two hands, and yanked her spear out. She grimaced as her injured arm protested, but she fought through the pain.

A wetness built up in her eyes, but she swiped at it with her fur sleeves. Thoughts of her clanmates raced through her head, and now that she was out of the village despair was entering her. She hoped some of them would survive this. She wasn't sure what she would do on her own. Would it even be possible for her to live on her own during winter?

Her freezing fingertips drew her back to the matter at hand, her survival. Her fur gloves had been lost during the fighting in the village, and she had to get to the hunting cave and retrieve some of the fur-lined gloves they had stashed there before she lost her fingers to the cold winter air.

Space not needed

Turning on a fur boot, she left his body there and rushed to cover the distance between her and the cave, but making sure to take a slightly longer path, doubling back over her same tracks, and trying to confuse her scent in case another sabertooth wandered across her scent. She didn't need anyone coming after.

As Aiyre approached the fur-covered entrance of the cave, hope swelled in her chest like the roar of a waterfall in spring. Would any of the women be in there? Her eager fingers peeled back the fur covering. She popped her head inside and took a look inside. Disappointment settled heavily in her stomach as she found it empty, dark, and cold.

Maybe the women would arrive in their own time. It was early yet. She wasn't ready to give up hope. She'd escaped, and she hoped that meant others would as well.

Turning to take a look behind her she found the forest quiet. From here, she couldn't even see the village fire. Images of Girk with his foot caught in a sabertooth's grip haunted her. She wanted nothing more than to run back and assist her clanmates, assuming they were even still alive.

By now, there was a high probability her clanmates had been finished off, and the only thing she'd see when she got there were sabertooths.

Fingers trembling from the cold and terror vibrating through her, she rushed inside and found some gloves to shove onto her freezing fingers. A fire would be nice, but the smoke and light could attract some unwanted attention. There was distance between her and the attacking sabertooths, but they might search the area, and she wasn't sure how far they might look for survivors.

Grabbing all of the furs stockpiled in the cave she bundled them all up around her.

Then she took a look at her injured arm in the murky darkness of the cave. She'd lost some blood, but it appeared to be scabbing over from what she could feel in the dark. Now she'd just have to worry about infection, but there was nothing she could do until morning when she could actually see the wound.

Thankfully, as she felt her arm, she only discovered just a couple scrapes on each side of her arm. Her arm had fit perfectly between his sharp canines, and he hadn't crushed the bone of her forearm.

She grabbed a sharp obsidian knife that had been in the cave and used it to cut a fur into long strips. Then she tightly wrapped the pieces around her forearm to make sure it didn't start bleeding again.

Shivers ran through her body. Without the warmth from a fire, she might not make it until morning. She'd been hoping a pile of furs would keep her warm enough, but she wasn't so sure about that now.

Glancing at the dark fire pit, she debated the options inside her mind. The fire might attract some unwanted attention, but she needed to risk it. Even with all these furs at her disposal, she might not stay warm enough on her own.

She could change into her pronghorn form, but even that form would eventually succumb to the penetrating cold that surrounded her. And there was still the possibility she might accidentally shift back into her human form while she slept, and then she could wake up shivering and naked in the cold cave.

Flinging the furs off of her, she rose and grabbed some of the wood stacked against one of the cave walls. The logs clunked against each other as she gathered as many as she could carry. Then she struggled them over to the fire pit at the mouth of the entrance and found some flint in the cave. Striking the stones together, she got a spark to light the tinder. The warmth wrapped around her cold body pushing the cold from the cave and eased her shivering.

Now that Aiyre was out of direct danger, she thought back to what had happened. The attack seemed unprovoked in her mind. Had the sabertooth hunting party seen the pronghorn hunters and reported back? She had no idea. Although this attack could have been planned a long time ago.

A shiver rocked through her, and she scooted closer to the flames of the fire.

All the men in her clan were probably lying dead in their village. There was no way they'd won that fight. They'd been taken by surprise and outnumbered. Her heart felt like it would burst from her chest with her heartache. It had been just last night that everyone had been joking and laughing around the village fire. Ezi had just accepted a claim from Drakk, and life had seemed almost perfect. *couldn't. 'could' makes no sense.*

Maybe she should have said yes to Girk's proposal. He might've died thinking she could care less about him. He was a good friend and a great hunter, and she should've been honored to be his.

Aiyre knew she shouldn't feel any guilt, but she couldn't help the way it was eating her from the inside out. Girk had deserved better, but it wasn't like she'd known their lives would be cut so short.

She just hadn't thought about him as any more than a friend and needed some time to think on it. Aiyre just hadn't realized how little time she'd have to think on his proposal. But it didn't matter, because he'd probably been killed. The image of him with his leg caught in the saber's mouth still wounded her deeply.

This hunting cave was well known in her clan. Hopefully, that meant any survivors from her clan would gather here, assuming they were in their right mind and not running around aimlessly in fright or lost in the dark night.

For now, she'd try to get some rest, and just tend to the fire through the night, and hope she didn't attract too much attention.

They don't know what hours are yet.

The frigid morning brought nothing but disappointment for Aiyre. No one had shown up during the long hours of the night. Had no one survived or were they too scared to come back to any areas they were familiar with? She dearly hoped it wasn't the first reason.

Bundling up the furs around her Aiyre stoked the fire with a stick and threw on a few more chunks of wood. Sparks flew in every direction, and the flames leaped in excitement at the new tinder to burn.

She had to travel back to the village and see if anyone survived. If not, she'd salvage what she could and figure out what to do after that. At this moment, she had to start thinking about her survival. She was alone, and she'd never faced a more uncertain future.

There was the strong possibility there'd still be sabertooths prowling around the area, but she would just have to risk it. This cave had enough to keep her alive for a few days, so she'd need to get more supplies from the village.

Shoving her animal skin gloves over her hands, she threw off the furs and grabbed her spear as she headed out into the snow-covered world she called home every day. She trudged through the thick layer of snow. She passed through the forest with ease and without any sabertooth sightings.

Space not needed

The only companion on her journey were the creaking of the tree boughs as they strained under the weight of all the snow they'd received. Every once in a while a branch would snap under the weight and Aiyre would jump out of her skin, spinning around to double check she wasn't about to be pounced on by a sabertooth. If she hadn't seen so much death and gore last night, she would've enjoyed the peaceful walk more, but all it was doing was putting strain on her frayed nerves.

Once she reached the edge of the forest, she watched her village from behind a tree trunk. Any sign of movement and she would turn tail and bolt.

Nothing moved as she continued to watch the area intently, her eyes continuously skimming over the village. Sucking in a steadying breath, she decided it was time for her to get her feet moving and see what was left of her life.

It took her no time to reach the village. The moment Aiyre was greeted by the sight of her village her shoulders drooped, and she felt an emptiness enter her chest. There were very few dead sabertooth shifters, but a lot of her dead clanmates littered the ground. Bodies were strewn all over the place.

Tears filled her eyes as she searched for familiar faces and stumbled upon Bhirk's familiar form. Rushing over she dropped her spear and flung herself onto the ground beside his body. Her gloved hands shook, but she continued to reach out, took hold of his shoulders, and flipped him over.

"Bhirk!" The cry tore out of her throat, as she choked back a sob. One of the sabertooths had ripped out his throat. She felt like she heard his deep voice trying to soothe her hysteria, but she couldn't stop the tears from pouring out.

Glancing around through the tears she saw Drakk's lifeless form entangled with a dead sabertooth shifter. She walked over and pushed the unknown man's body off of Drakk.

"I'll find Ezi for you. If she's alive, I will see to her safety. You have my promise." Aiyre placed a hand against his frozen cheek. His face gone blue from the cold. Minutes haven't been inserted yet.

She hated to leave them where they'd fallen, but she couldn't do anything about it. There were too many bodies for her to move on her own. A proper burial would have to wait... if it happened at all.

Several minutes of stumbling around the village passed before she wandered upon Naru's lifeless body. It was no surprise that she hadn't made it far with her age and inability to shift, but it didn't make the loss any less painful.

Aiyre knelt down by Naru's body. She took one of her stiff hands into her own. "Thank you for everything. I'm sorry I couldn't have done more for you after everything you gave to me."

She swallowed the lump in her throat. She was afraid she wouldn't be able to let go of Naru's hand if she held on for too long, so she released the hand that had reassured her so much. Aiyre let Naru's hand slip from hers.

There were some bodies she had yet to find, like Girk and Ezi, but that didn't mean they couldn't have been killed further away from camp while fleeing.

Aiyre was still alive, and she had to keep living. Digging through the camp for supplies, she did her best to ignore all the sightless eyes watching her every move. Chills spread down her spine when she came across a little girl. The same girl she'd done her best to save last night.

Were the sabertooth shifters born without a heart? To kill a little girl over nothing more than their leader and his inability to sit down and talk with her clan! She was sure this could have been solved without so much bloodshed.

Pulling her fur coat closer around her body, she grabbed the bag of supplies and continued around the camp looking for any more weapons she could stash back at the cave. There was no telling how long she might be on her own, and she needed to prepare herself for the worst.

Chapter 3

Daerk crept deeper into the forest, his golden cat-eyes picking up on the slightest movement in the snow-covered trees around him. He intended to bring back something for his clan to eat if it was the last thing he did. He'd already been gone for a few days because deep winter was coming and prey was becoming a bit on the scarce side.

Their leader, Brog, thought killing off the pronghorn shifters would fix their problem, but Daerk knew better. This was a matter of it just being a scarce year, nothing more. They had a large clan and a lot of mouths to feed, and it didn't help that Brog was quick to demand the most meat from each kill for his own hut. Brog had taken several wives and had too many children to count and was overstretching the winter supplies.

Now Daerk was left to hunt on his own and sneak meat to members of the clan that needed it more than their selfish leader. If Brog wasn't careful, he'd have a revolt on his hands. Daerk would lead it if he knew people would follow him. Unfortunately, Brog led his people with fear, so he wasn't too sure others would join an overthrow of their ill-tempered leader. Not unless he did something really heinous.

Freezing, he let his tan furry ears twitch back and forth. Hunting in his sabertooth form had always been his preference. His hearing and eyesight were far better, and he didn't need to bother with cumbersome clothing or weapons. His sabertooth form came equipped with everything he could possibly need.

The crunch of snow caught his attention, and he spun around to see two of his clanmates tearing through the trees at high speed. He recognized their scents to be that of his two closest friends, Tor and Rir.

Both of them stopped in front of him huffing and puffing. They seemed agitated, but he couldn't ask them what was going on without changing into his human form since communication in their sabertooth forms was limited.

He led them back to where he'd placed his clothing and weapons. He wasn't about to change into his human form without his clothing nearby when the air was frigid, and snow coated the ground. Hunting would just have to wait.

Daerk shifted out of his sabertooth form, and the winter air prickled his skin. He rushed to throw on his fur clothing, threw the hood over his head, and some gloves onto his hands.

"What brings you all the way out here?" Daerk asked with a growl irritated at the interruption in his hunt when he hadn't found anything.

"Don't be angry at us." Rir held up his hands as he shifted and began vigorously rubbing his hands over his arms.

"You interrupted my hunt. Why shouldn't I be irritated?" He glowered at the two men standing in front of him.

Tor spoke up after he shifted. "While you were out hunting, Brog led an attack against the pronghorn clan."

"What?!" Daerk strode towards Tor ready to smash his fist into something, but Rir stepped into his path.

"It wasn't our decision to attack the pronghorns." He held his hands up in the air. "Don't take your anger out on us."

"Did you go?" Daerk hoped his friends wouldn't have participated in such a heinous act.

Rir shook his head, his long brown hair swaying with the motion. "We came to find you, once Brog left with his men. We have no idea how the attack went... or if any pronghorns survived." Rir continued to rub his hands over his exposed skin.

"Not well for the pronghorns." Tor guessed. "How could they have any chance against our numbers and skill. In our animal forms, we would dominate them easily." He shivered in the cold air, looking like he wanted to change back into his sabertooth form.

"They weren't our problem." Daerk grumped. "Killing them will gain us nothing but a reputation by the time the next clan gathering happens in spring."

Every spring, all the clans in the nearby area would gather together and trade. They'd also celebrate another year of surviving the cold of winter.

"Brog only wanted a battle, whether or not the pronghorns are our problem." Tor shook his head and scrubbed a hand down his beard. "We all know he's been waiting until the clan was desperate enough to believe his lies. But it couldn't have been a fair fight for the pronghorns."

"Did any other hunters stay behind?" Daerk wanted to know how many men sided with him on this subject. If he ever decided to take control from Brog, he needed to make sure he had the numbers on his side. Otherwise, he'd be torn to shreds.

"Brog only took a select group of hunters with him. You might have some willing to back you, but just because they stayed behind doesn't mean they want to overthrow Brog."

They had several female hunters who would definitely be an asset should they be needed, but could he convince them to join the cause? Only time would tell, he supposed.

"Are you thinking of challenging Brog?" Rir asked intrigued, a slow smile spreading across his face.

"I've thought about it." It sounded appealing, and Daerk was considered the best hunter in the clan. If anyone was going to challenge, he supposed it would be him. "I'm just worried I might not be the best to lead us or that no one will support my leadership."

Brog had plenty of supporters who were just as bloodthirsty as their leader. If he lost the challenge, he wouldn't just be banished. He'd be ripped to pieces.

"We believe in you," Rir said as his teeth clinked together from the persistent cold.

Daerk frowned at him. "You two aren't the whole clan. I need to know how they feel before I make a move and find myself banished from the clan." Or worse.

"I doubt that would ever happen." Tor frowned as he shook his head. "You've been feeding them, ever since we realized our meat hut wouldn't last us all winter."

Tor was right. The clan wasn't about to throw him out when he was the only one interested in keeping them alive.

"Head back and act as though I'm still hunting. I'll go check on the pronghorn clan to see if there are any survivors." He didn't need Brog breathing down his neck, because Brog wasn't foolish, he knew Daerk wouldn't condone his actions.

It was time their clan moved on from this area and found better hunting grounds. The mammoth migrations had changed, so they couldn't stay here and expect to live the same life. Killing the pronghorn shifters wouldn't bring prey back to their land. It would only make them monsters.

Daerk quickly shed his clothing and shifted back into his sabertooth form. His face elongated, fur sprouted from his skin, and his fingernails extended into long curved claws.

The distance to the pronghorn village would be covered quicker in his animal form than in his human form. In some ways, he'd prefer to stay in this sabertooth form all the time, but his human side demanded to be seen every now and then.

There was still the possibility that Brog hadn't gone through with the attack. Tor and Rir hadn't been back to the clan since Brog left to attack the pronghorn clan. Daerk could only hope Brog hadn't gone through with it, and that it had only been a bunch of bluster.

Sprinting off in the direction of the nearby pronghorn clan, his large paws allowed him to glide over the snow with minimal effort. He just wished he could enjoy the air whipping past his fur coat, but he dreaded what he might see when he arrived at the pronghorn clan.

It didn't take him long to reach a cliff overlooking the pronghorn clan's village. He sucked in a deep breath, preparing himself for what he might see.

As he popped over the edge of the cliff, his heart dropped. Brog had seen through on his threat. Daerk hoped it'd been bluster, but here was the proof in front of him that it wasn't. There were barely any huts standing, and bodies dotted the pristine landscape of snow.

A few furs flapped uselessly in the wind, but it was the only movement he picked up on. It was a shame. He hadn't known any of the shifters in this village, but the loss of life for no reason just appalled him.

With one last look at the decimated village, he turned to leave. Another movement in the village caught his attention, and he focused in on it. His cat eyes zoomed in on the area below him. At first, he wondered if he'd just seen a fur waving in the wind, or if he'd truly seen someone.

Then he saw a shadow moving near the trees of the forest.

Someone was alive down there!

As he sniffed the wind, Daerk picked up the scent of a pronghorn woman somewhere below him. He watched on as the shadow crept out of the forest, and the woman walked hesitantly through the destroyed village, collecting items and mourning over her dead.

Was she the only survivor or where there more walking about in the area?

A growl rumbled up his throat, and an itch started under his skin. As the woman bent over to grab something off the ground, his eyes fixated on her shapely behind. Even under all those furs and from this distance, he could tell she had some curves to her body.

Every time the wind shifted and brought her scent wafting towards him, he felt his cock stir. It was an addictive scent that drew him in, yet he resisted the urge to make any movements. A pronghorn shifter wouldn't welcome him after the attack on her people by sabertooth shifters.

Sensing his presence, she turned and her hazel eyes collided with his. She froze in mid-reach, and then took a defensive stance. She was a pronghorn with spirit that was for sure. Both of her forms would be nothing compared to him, yet there she was acting tough.

She had nothing to fear from him though.

Daerk decided it was time to leave. There was no reason to make her panic even more. He turned and left the area, leaving her to her own devices. She had enough to worry about without him freaking her out even more.

✴ ✴ ✴

When Aiyre felt eyes boring into her back, she'd swiveled around to spot a sabertooth watching her from a hill. There was too much distance for her to know if it was a shifter or just a wild animal looking for an easy meal.

Their eyes collided. Its golden cat-eyes skimmed over her, and shivers flew down her spine causing the fine hairs over her skin to stand on end. Would it attack? Or would it just pass by?

It turned around, and she watched as it disappeared over the crest of the hill. Once it left her sight, she decided it was time to get out of the village. She'd gathered as many supplies as she would be able to carry, and she didn't want to test her luck with the gods. Predators were sure to sniff down all the blood and death, and she wouldn't want to be in the village when the predators came looking for an easy meal.

Heading out, Aiyre made sure to take a long, convoluted path back to the cave. If that had been a sabertooth shifter, she didn't need him following her back to her cave. She still found it unbelievable that they'd been attacked. It all just felt like a horrible dream.

She would never be able to get that night of screaming and blood out of her mind.

As Aiyre approached the hunting cave, loneliness settled in her chest once more. Aiyre wished someone else from her clan would join her, but when she peeled back the fur cover, the cave was still empty. Hefting the supplies onto the floor of the cave, she prepared herself for a lonely day.

Grabbing hold of some firewood, she placed them inside the fire pit, knelt beside it, and began to blow on the hot coals, until the tinder caught fire. Backing away, she sat back on her bottom and watched the fire catch the larger logs.

This was the last safe spot for her.

Now all Aiyre had to worry about was food stores and getting herself to another pronghorn clan, or even a human clan. She wouldn't be able to shift around a human clan, not because humans didn't know about them, but because it might cause them to toss her out. They might take her in for the winter months if they thought she was just human though.

She was a great hunter, and she could help provide them with enough meat to take care of the share she ate. She just needed more than herself in a hunting party. Otherwise, rabbits and other small game would be all that she would be able to hunt by herself.

Aiyre settled in front of her fire and wrapped a couple of thick furs around her shoulders. Now that she was settled down with nothing more to do, the horrors of the past few hours rushed back to her.

Everyone she'd known was either dead or wandering around out there in the frigid cold. She felt like she should search for them, but traipsing through the snow alone could be dangerous if she ran into any animals… or any more sabertooth shifters.

But at some point, she would have to leave.

Daerk followed the pronghorn shifter as far as he could, but the snow seemed to be against him. It fell in waves, covering her scent and preventing him from finding out where she hid away.

He'd be back at some point, and hopefully, he would find her again. She'd stirred something inside him, and he knew he had to find her and explore his drive to see another glimpse of her. There was something in her scent that was drawing him in.

With one last sniff to the shifting snow, he turned back, heading towards his village. His thoughts wouldn't forget the sight of her though. She plagued him. Those hazel eyes of hers. He'd seen the sorrow in those lovely depths. She lost her whole clan in one night. He couldn't even imagine not having his clan nearby.

She wouldn't be able to live out the winter on her own, and he wondered what her plan was, like how she'd hunt enough food for herself... and keep herself sane. Being alone all winter would be hard on her emotionally.

His large paws crunched against the snow, allowing him to keep from sinking into the deep snow as he traveled through the forest.

The village rose up before him. The fur huts scattered around the snow, smoke rising from each hut. It was nice to be back, but it came with its problems.

"Where have you been?" An irritated voice rang out behind him.

Daerk turned his head towards the voice, and his fuzzy ears zeroed in on the source of the sound. Talking of a problem, the biggest one in the village was striding straight towards him with a dark look marring his face.

If Daerk wished to speak, he'd have to change forms, but he was reluctant to do so because he hated speaking with Brog. If he didn't shift, he'd also piss off Brog and getting into a brawl would do no one in this clan any good.

Daerk shifted and instantly regretted it as the cold air puckered his bare human skin.

"Where have you been?" Brog repeated baring his teeth slightly like Daerk needed a reminder he was in charge. *Reins haven't been invented yet!*

"To visit the pronghorn village that you decimated." Daerk did his best to rein in his anger. No need to get himself or Brog all riled up.

"They were starving us," Brog growled, no hint of remorse in his voice or eyes.

"They were not." Daerk gave Brog his back and strode into the village. The cold was puckering his skin, and his feet demanded he get off the freezing snow before they fell off.

"The pronghorns were taking all our food and invading our hunting grounds. You will see, Daerk, you will see. Now that they're gone we will see better times." Brog promised him.

comma Daerk shook his head. Brog had killed all of the pronghorns for no reason, and soon the clan would realize this when winter kept going on as poorly as it had before. Brog just wanted a reason to shed some blood, and he'd gotten his chance.

He would challenge Brog, but he had to bide his time. Soon more of their people would realize Brog was a selfish leader, only looking out for his own needs. All he needed to do was sit back and wait while Brog dug himself further into a hole.

If he challenged too early, Brog might have more supporters than he did. Time. He needed to wait and be patient. There was no need for him to challenge Brog right now.

Daerk pushed open his hut flaps and found a welcoming fire burning brightly in his hearth. Thank goodness. One of the women in the clan had been kind enough to see to his fire while he'd been out.

He quickly grabbed some new fur clothing and covered himself. He'd have to go out and retrieve the clothing he'd left in the forest, but it'd have to wait.

"Brog destroyed them then?" Rir poked his head inside Daerk's hut.

"He did." Daerk sighed.

"I hoped his men were bragging about nothing." Rir meandered inside the hut and stood in front of the fire with his hands held out to the warmth.

"Unfortunately, not." Daerk still couldn't forget about the people strewn about in the pronghorn village. "It was a sight I never wish to see again."

"Will you take the leadership?" Rir whispered his eyes darting up to look at Daerk.

He shook his head. "No. It's not my time. I first need everyone to realize his actions did nothing to save us from starvation. Then I can make my move, and our people will support me."

"You're more patient than myself," Rir smirked. "It's good I just follow your lead, or I would have challenged him for such an act. I can only imagine what you saw."

"You would get yourself killed," Daerk scoffed and led the way out of his hut.

"Thanks," Rir grumped.

"I'm not saying you couldn't battle Brog and win. I'm just saying he has a lot of allies who'd team up on you." And that was one of Daerk's fears. That he might be outnumbered.

"True."

"We need to go out and hunt something to bring back for tonight. Those last couple of horses didn't get us far." Which was what he had been doing until he had to go see if Brog indeed had attacked the pronghorns.

"I will find Tor." Rir headed off deeper into the village.

Daerk smiled as a couple of women passed by giving him open smiles. He was a fine specimen, and there were plenty of women he could fill his nights with, but then he'd be just as bad as Brog.

Taking several wives just because he hadn't found his mate was disgusting. Daerk wouldn't do such a thing, because if he found his mate, he wanted to make sure there was nothing uncomfortable for her here in his village.

Brog was too desperate and greedy, and it was the same reason why he ruthlessly murdered the pronghorn clan.

Still the pronghorn shifter he'd seen earlier pestered him. Her scent had been delightfully irresistible as it tickled his nose. Daerk snorted as he shoved the thoughts of the pronghorn away. A pronghorn and a sabertooth shifter would be a farfetched match. far-fetched

Their children could be either shifter, and he wasn't sure he'd know how to raise a pronghorn.

Daerk shook his head. He'd smelled her from a distance, and that distance could've confused his nose, even in his sabertooth form. A pronghorn as a mate would definitely be a stretch. But some hunting with his closest friends would help ease his mind, both from the pronghorn female and Brog.

"I found him." Rir and Tor strode towards him.

"Then let's get going. Anything we can bring back will do us good." Daerk led his men to the edge of the village, where they stripped off their clothes so they could shift without tearing their clothes to shreds.

As he pulled off his thick fur shirt, he noticed a flock of women gathering at the edge of the village to watch.

"They're here to see the mighty Daerk." Rir teased.

"And yet a few of them appear to have eyes for you as well." Daerk tossed back. They did indeed have eyes for Rir and Tor. Three fine men who had yet to find their mates. Of course, they would attract the attention of unmated females.

Daerk shed his pants and boots and let the shift overtake him. It was a quick process that only took the blink of an eye. Daerk shook out his muscled body, his fur fluffing with the movement. He loved his sabertooth form. He let his claws slip out from his toes, the long nails scraping the snow below him.

He turned to see if Rir and Tor were ready.

They both had shifted. They each gave a shake of their massive bodies after their change. Rir yawned, his long pink tongue rolled out between his large canines.

They were ready to go, so Daerk bounded into the forest leading them away from the village. It seemed like he spent more and more time outside of the village if only to gain some peace and quiet away from Brog.

The snow fell, obscuring their view, but they had their trusty noses leading the way. As long as the wind assisted them and the snow didn't fall too thickly, they'd come back successful. He only hoped they'd be lucky enough to land a larger animal, something that would stock their stores for most of the winter.

A rabbit skittered through the forest, as they snuck through the undergrowth. Not large enough to really care about, but Daerk couldn't resist the chance for the chase. It would allow his mind to relax.

He launched himself, scattering snow on Rir and Tor who were trailing behind him.

Puffs of white air surged out of his nostrils, as he pushed himself. The rabbit zagged, and Daerk zigged, opened his mouth, but the ball of fluff managed to get another zag in and his mouth closed down on empty air with a snap.

He heard a chuff from behind him and found Rir and Tor giving him toothy grins. Their ability to communicate in these forms was limited, but he knew they thought him silly for giving chase after a rabbit. The rabbit had one thing over him, the ability to turn without a moment's notice.

But it'd been fun and got his mind off Brog, so he didn't really care what they thought.

With a few more minutes of prowling around, they left the forest and broke into a snowy meadow. In the distance, they saw the dark forms of horses trying to find grass below the snow. Their hoofed feet dug at the snow, trying to expose any nibble of grass that they could. *Sabretooths had short tails*

Daerk twitched his long tail, sending Rir and Tor off in another direction. They'd worked together many times before, and words weren't necessary to communicate. He would spook the horses and drive them towards his waiting friends. With any luck, they would land a horse.

Crouching low to the ground he prowled around the grazing horses, careful to stay out of sight. The falling snow helped to hide his massive form, and he allowed it to build up on his shaggy tan coat.

The horses snorted, plowing the snow with their hooves, too distracted by the search for food to notice him getting closer.

Daerk waited in a crouched position when he was close enough. He wanted to make sure Tor and Rir had enough time to position themselves.

Once he determined enough time had passed, he launched himself, growling for good measure.

The herd of horses snorted and turned tail, galloping directly towards where Rir and Tor waited. A few horses broke off of the main group in their panic, but he ignored them. He just needed the majority of them to go in the correct direction.

When the stallion started to stray from the path, Daerk charged him to get the stallion to lead his mares back to the correct path.

The stallion runs at the rear of the herd — he doesn't "lead".

It worked.

Rir and Tor jumped out of nowhere. Rir latched onto the neck of a horse, and Tor onto the neck of a second horse. Tor's horse went down without much of a struggle, but Rir's horse was still standing and trying to dislodge him with sharp hooves.

Daerk jumped onto its back, and his razor-sharp claws dug into the horse's flesh. He clamped his large canines into the back of the horse's neck, while Rir held steady at the front of the neck. *This would risk them breaking on contact with bone.*

The horse slowly went down.

Daerk let loose and stepped off of the horse, once it ceased moving. They'd killed two horses. This would be an amazing amount of meat for their clan after the last two horses they'd taken down. It wouldn't last them all winter, but it would relieve them for long enough for them to hunt some more.

Now all they had to do was get the kills back to the village. It would take some time and effort, but it was all well worth it in the end.

He butted heads with his companions to celebrate their success. Rir tackled Tor, and they fell into a ball of fur as each of them tried to get the upper hand over the other one. He let them celebrate, and then he grabbed Rir by the scruff of the neck, pulling him off Tor.

Then he grabbed a hold of one of the horses with his mouth and began to drag it back to the village. Rir took hold of the second kill, and Tor trailed behind until either of them needed help.

There was nothing for him to do but think as he dragged the kill across the frozen ground.

That pronghorn's scent still pestered him, and he felt the need to go back and see how she was getting along. Where had she disappeared to in the forest? Had she found a safe place to hide? Was she able to gather enough supplies from the decimated village to survive in the cold winter climate? Would she be able to gather more food for herself as the winter set in? Questions swarmed in Daerk's mind, and he felt oddly responsible for the woman, as though it was his fault that her clan had been destroyed. After Brog's attack, she wouldn't be likely to accept any help from a sabertooth. He couldn't blame her, if she ended up hating him.

But first, he'd have to find her and make sure Brog didn't learn about her existence. The moment Brog heard he'd found a living pronghorn, it would be the same moment Brog would kill her just to spite Daerk for his opposition. It was no secret Daerk didn't agree with killing off an entire neighboring clan.

They finally arrived at the edge of the village and shifted back into their human forms.

"Good hunt." Rir smiled triumphantly.

comma "Brog will be pleased with it, but unhappy with you." Tor pointed out. "He only leaves the village to attack others, instead of hunting for the clan. You make him look bad with every kill you bring back."

Daerk knew that. "I'm not about to let my clan starve just to please Brog. I can handle Brog and any irritation he might throw in my direction."

People flowed out of their huts and rushed over to take apart the two horses. Everything would be used, nothing wasted. And tonight, they would give thanks to the animals for their generous donation to their people.

"Again, you are our great hunter." Brog's voice rang out, venom dripping on every word.

Daerk turned to find his leader staring at him with contempt glowing brightly in his dark eyes.

"Just needed a way to ease my boredom and hunting seemed like a good idea." Daerk did his best to brush off the successful hunt. "Rir and Tor were the ones who brought down the horses."

"Just as long as you remember who the greatest hunter among us is." Brog glared over at him. "I'm the one who took care of the pronghorn problem."

"Always."

Daerk wanted nothing more than to rip the man's throat out with his canines,but now wasn't the time. He needed Brog to keep proving himself an unfit leader so that Daerk would have enough people standing behind him when he took control.

"We will harvest the meat, and then celebrate our good fortune in the caves!" Brog announced to the rest of the clan, which had gathered around to listen in to the conversation.

Daerk left, unable to bear any more from Brog. Grabbing his clothes from the ground, he proceeded towards his hut.

***

Daerk dipped his fingers into the red paint and drew lines going down his face. He'd given Rir and Tor the privilege of carrying the horse heads to their cave for the ceremony of thanking the gods for such a great hunt. It would help keep Brog off his back, and they had been the ones who targeted those two horses in the first place. All he'd done was chase them in the correct direction and help finish them off.

He rose from in front of his hut's fire. He glanced around. Every year that passed had him longing more and more for his mate. She was out there. Somewhere. Just waiting for him to discover her. Once he found her, he would be able to fill his hut with more than just himself and his weapons. He was ready to wake up to a warm female, and maybe even the crying of a child who wanted to be fed.

With a sigh of unfulfilled longing, he left his tent.

His clanmates chanted past, and he stepped into line with them. They were making their way to the sacred caves, with Rir and Tor leading the way. They held the horse heads above their own heads proudly. Large grins plastered all over their faces.

Everyone's face was decorated with paint, and Daerk couldn't help the smile that spread across his face. It was good to see his clan having such a good time. They didn't celebrate every kill, but getting two horses had been a gift for them.

The gods hadn't given up on them quite yet. Now it was time to thank the gods and hope many more hunts like this would happen throughout the winter.

Within minutes, the dark mouths of the caves could be seen not too far ahead of them. As they entered the stone corridors, their torches lit their way as they weaved through the inside of the hill.

They arrived at a spacious center cavern, and Brog took his position near the shaman, Eron.

Daerk glanced around at all the drawings on the walls. Their shaman was skilled. Perhaps Daerk might have the honor of seeing them drawn someday, or even have the chance to draw some of the paintings himself.

The flickering light of the fire showed scenes of their clan in their sabertooth skin chasing down prey or finding their mates. This cave meant everything to them. The smoke lined walls showed just how many generations had used this very cave for the same ceremonies.

The horse heads were brought up to the shaman, and then Rir and Tor took their position back in the crowd of clanmates. The shaman took a couple of large bowls and walked around to each person of the clan to allow each person to sip from its contents.

The shaman ambled up to him, and Daerk looked down into the bowl of blood which had been harvested from the horses they'd killed.

He took a sip from the bowl, dipped his finger into the blood, and drew a line down his nose.

The shaman moved on to the next person and the next until everyone in the clan had taken a sip. Then the shaman made his way back up to the altar and poured the rest of the blood over Brog.

Only the clan leader was allowed the privilege to have the blood poured over him, and he would be the only one to stay the night in the cave and ask the gods for good luck for their clan when it came to hunting.

The shaman hummed for a bit, and then dismissed them with a wave of his hand. The rest of the ceremony would be finished by the shaman and the clan leader. No one else knew what transpired inside the cave between the two and the gods.

But Daerk hoped to one day find out.

Chapter 4

Aiyre shivered, waking herself from her deep sleep. She glanced over at the fire pit, which had gone dark. It must've fizzled out during the night, and she wasn't sure she wanted to keep it burning all the time.

She'd been afraid the sabertooth she'd seen last night would find out where she lived, but thankfully the weather had been on her side, and fresh snow had covered her tracks. She'd known venturing close to the village this soon after the attack would be dangerous, but at least she now had some more supplies, in case she found herself alone for the long winter.

As she grabbed a bag of dried meat, shivering overtook her body. Even in her fur clothing, the cold reached its icy fingers around her. Aiyre would have to start a fire and keep hoping her luck stayed strong.

Leaping up she grabbed an armful of wood and threw it onto the fire pit, arranging it properly. Then she dug around until she found a still lit coal, coaxing it back to life, she lit the tinder. Within minutes, she had a pleasantly crackling fire.

Aiyre put her gloved hands closer to the fire, warming them up a bit.

She had to decide what to do for the day. What she needed was more food, in case this was her home for the winter. Thankfully there were some traps nearby that her clan had placed out before being attacked. If her luck was running high, there might just be a rabbit waiting for her.

After stripping off her gloves, she packed up a small bag with some dried meat and headed out of the cave.

The cold air smacked her in the face the moment she walked past the fur cover of the cave, and she pulled her fur gloves back on, tightening them down with a couple of leather straps.

Aiyre trudged into the snow, which came to about mid-calf. The snow had done its job in hiding her tracks from the previous day, and her scent.

It would make her search for the traps a little more difficult as well, but as long as she wasn't found by any more sabertooths, then she was fine with it.

She found the first trap not too far away, but it was empty. She reset it on top of the fresh snow but made sure it wasn't too obvious to any passing animals.

Aiyre trudged her way to the next trap she knew of in the area. It only took her a couple of minutes, and she smiled as she closed in. A white rabbit hung from the leather rope. She was glad no predators had found it first.

Taking a stone knife out of her pocket, she cut the rabbit down, grabbed it by its feet and moved on to check the other traps.

It didn't take her long to find the rest of the traps, and none of the others had caught anything, so she reset them.

As she headed back to her cave, she kept her eyes open for any signs of sabertooth shifters or any of her fellow clanmates. Aiyre still refused to believe that all of them had been killed. If she'd survived, then she was sure others could have as well.

But she saw no sign of them by the time she got back to her cave. Pushing the fur cover aside she looked inside cautiously, just in case any unwelcome visitors had come calling while she'd been out.

It was empty.

Sitting down in front of the fire she placed the rabbit in front of her. Taking off her gloves she grabbed her stone knife and used the knife to slice the rabbit down the belly, making sure to not break into the skin of the abdomen.

First, she took off the fur, slowly, making sure to keep it intact. She still didn't know how long she might be on her own, and she needed to make sure she had plenty of backup furs in case she got injured or sick. She could deal with hunger, but the cold could kill her in the blink of an eye. *back-up*

Then she set it aside as she prepped the rabbit, making sure to put all the innards into a wood bowl. She placed the bowl over the fire so she could cook the innards for a quick meal. *She'd discard the stomach and intestines, at least.*

The task of cutting the rabbit meat into long strips was a slow process, but nothing would go to waste. She hung the pieces above the fire so that they would dry. Then she stretched out the rabbit fur near the fire pit so the skin would dry as well.

Grabbing the bowl, she dug in eagerly, using her fingers to eat the hot meal. It would be some of the only fresh meat she would get her hands on. Everything else would be dried out for future use so that she could stretch it out for as long as possible.

The moment the warm meal plummeted into her stomach, she felt herself relax a little bit.

When she finished, she strode out of the cave and washed her hands in the snow. She wished there was more, but a rabbit was only so big.

Aiyre returned to the cave, threw on some more wood and glanced around.

If she could, she needed to find another pronghorn shifter clan or at the very least a human clan. With a human clan, she wouldn't be able to shift, but at least she'd have a better chance at survival.

But before she went anywhere, she needed to search the surrounding area for any survivors of her own clan. She couldn't leave without first searching the surrounding area. It would bother her for the rest of her life if she didn't at least search.

She gathered some dried meat she'd found in her decimated village, stuffed them into her pockets, put her gloves back on, grabbed her spear, and headed back out into the snow-covered world that was her home.

Time to go hunting, but this time it was for her own people.

If she couldn't find anyone today, she'd head out to find a human clan or any clan that wasn't the nearby sabertooth shifters.

The snow picked up again as Aiyre circled the area. She grumbled at it since it felt like the snow was opposing her search for any missing clanmates. But she pushed through, squinting into the thick falling white fluff.

Aiyre passed by her village, close enough to see if any survivors had shown up, but not close enough to be seen herself. She didn't want to chance that any sabertooth shifters would be lurking nearby and spot her.

There was no movement in the village, and she didn't have the guts to go back in only to see her clanmates were still dead.

Aiyre weaved her way through the trees, trudging through the deep snow. She circled around the camp, but there was nothing. There were no tracks other than her own and those of small animals.

It was a setback, but she wasn't about to give up on her people. Maybe they'd be further out. She tugged the hood of her coat closer around her face until the fur lined hood tickled her cheeks.

Aiyre walked towards a favorite hunting ground of theirs. The whole clan knew about their hunting grounds, and in their fear, they may have fled to a place they knew.

She crested the hill and looked over the vast expanse of snow. Unfortunately, she wasn't able to see too far because of the sheet of falling snow, but she pressed on.

A few minutes passed until she found a sign of hope. Aiyre had stumbled upon some tracks. She squatted down and took a look at them. They were fresh since the snow had yet to cover them up, but they weren't animal tracks. They were definitely human, and they were small, so they had to be from a woman.

Aiyre rose and quickly stumbled through the snow after them for a few more minutes until she saw a dark figure lying prone in the snow.

Her heart stopped in her chest, and she flew through the snow, her knees twisting out sideways so she could hop over the deep snow.

It had to be someone from her clan, and her heart soared into the cloudy sky above her. Who could it be?

"Ezi?" Aiyre called out as she neared, but there was no movement in front of her.

She dropped to her knees, the snow layer cushioning her when she got to the figure, who was face down. Grabbing the figure's shoulders, she flipped the person over and was greeted by Ezi's blue face.

"Ezi?!" Panic soared through her when Ezi didn't say anything. Aiyre rubbed a gloved hand against Ezi's face. "Wake up, Ezi. Wake up!" She couldn't lose another one of her clanmates.

Ezi's mouth moved, but Aiyre was unable to hear what she said, but she was alive!

Aiyre leaned in, putting her ear close to Ezi's mouth. "What did you say?"

"I'm... cold." Ezi's teeth clinked together.

"Of course, you are. I'll get you back somewhere warm, but you have to help me because carrying you will be difficult." Aiyre pleaded with Ezi. She'd do whatever it took to get Ezi back to the cave, even if Ezi was unable to help her.

But Ezi surprised her as she stood with Aiyre's help. "Good. Good. Now keep coming with me. Imagine that nice warm fire." She coaxed Ezi forward who moved with stiff, jerky movements.

She had to be frozen solid, and Aiyre's heart went out to her. Did she know Drakk was dead? Aiyre wasn't about to tell her any time soon. First, Ezi needed to recover from her frozen solid state, and then Aiyre would deliver the bad news.

"Are you limping, Ezi?"

Ezi just nodded.

"Push through it. I will see to your leg when we get back to the cave, but I can't do anything for you out here."

Ezi gave her another nod, but her eyes stayed clamped shut.

Aiyre feared that her friend might not live, but she wasn't about to give up on Ezi.

Were more of her clanmates still out there? Wandering around? She supposed she wouldn't ever know. Coming across Ezi had been pure dumb luck. Nothing more.

"Have you seen anyone else?" Aiyre asked hoping beyond hope that Ezi would say yes.

Ezi shook her head.

So much for that hope, but at least she had Ezi. She was thankful to have one of her clanmates alive.

They made it a few more steps, and then Ezi's leg gave way, and they both landed face first in the snow.

Aiyre came up sputtering and patting the snow from her face with the fur mittens that covered her hands.

"Here." Aiyre stripped off her extra layer of fur clothing and wrapped the fur around Ezi. She had plenty of clothing on to spare a layer.

"You… need this." Ezi chattered out, her teeth clicking together. She tried to refuse the furs. Aiyre placed them over her shoulders anyway.

"I will survive. You need it more than I do." Aiyre put her arm under Ezi's shoulder and helped her back up. "We're getting closer to the cave." She coaxed Ezi onwards.

Every step seemed like an eternity, but she'd make sure they both made it there. Aiyre didn't want to live out the winter alone, and Ezi was her closest friend.

"Here we are." Aiyre guided Ezi into the welcoming warmth of the cave, which still had a roaring fire in the fire pit. Good thing she'd thrown more wood onto it before she left.

Aiyre let Ezi sit, but stripped the clothing off of Ezi. All the snow on her clothing would melt in this heat and then freeze her. She spread out Ezi's fur clothing so that it could dry.

Taking a small spare fur she ran it over every inch of Ezi's skin, drying her off. Then she covered her with spare dry clothing.

"Thank you," Ezi whispered.

"Don't thank me. I'm your clanmate. I'll always be here for you." It was only the truth. She'd do anything for another clanmate.

"Where… is Drakk?" Ezi's eager jade eyes rose to meet hers.

Aiyre could hear the desperation in her voice, and it broke her heart in two. She wished she had better news for Ezi.

"Don't worry about that right now." Aiyre patted her hand. When she felt how cold Ezi's hands were, she helped her closer to the fire. "Just relax and let the fire warm you. I'll brew something to warm you from the inside out. You should be feeling better in no time." Both things that haven't been invented yet.

The wind blew viscously outside their cave, blowing some snow past the fur covering. The storm was really starting to ratchet up. Aiyre stepped up to the fur covering the mouth of the cave and peered out. The snow fell so thickly that she could only see a couple of inches in front of her face.

"Winter will be harsh this year." And now she had another mouth to feed. Ezi wasn't a hunter, so it would be up to Aiyre to see to their stores of food. She let the fur covering fall back into place. She didn't want to let too much hot air out of the cave.

Aiyre went to get some water boiling. She had to see to Ezi. She'd worry about surviving winter when she was done saving Ezi's life.

Grabbing a stone pot from further inside the cave Aiyre filled it with snow, and then placed it above the fire. While she waited for the water to boil, she stripped off her own shirt and the strips of fur to take a look at her wound.

Her arm was looking fine, but she'd give it a rinse anyway.

Grabbing a small fur, she dipped it into the pot of water and rinsed off her wounds. Then put her fur shirt back on.

When she heard the water boiling, she grabbed a handful of dried leaves, threw them in, and waited. Once a couple of minutes passed, she got a horn cup and poured the liquid into the cup.

She bent down next to Ezi, wrapped her arm around her shoulder, and brought her up to a sitting position. Ezi let out a hiss, and Aiyre's attention was drawn to her leg.

"Sorry." She repositioned Ezi so that her leg laid straight out in front of her. "Drink this slowly, but try to drink it all."

Ezi took the cup from Aiyre and brought the edge up to her lips. She took a small sip and let out a pleased sound.

"You look much better." Ezi's color was returning, and her eyes had finally opened fully, and the frost had melted off her lashes.

"I owe everything to you." Ezi took another sip of the hot liquid. "Where is Drakk? Have you seen him?"

Aiyre didn't want to tell her anything, but she couldn't keep the secret for long. "I visited the village, the day after the attack."

"Were there any other survivors?" Ezi looked up at her, her eyes full of gleaming hope.

Aiyre bit her lip. She had to tell Ezi at some point, and it was better to get it out now. "You are the only one from our clan that I've seen alive."

Ezi's eyes teared up a bit. "And Drakk?"

Aiyre shook her head, her braid wagging behind her.

A sob choked Ezi, as she buried her head in her hands and wept.

Sitting down beside Ezi, Aiyre wrapped her arms around her friend. One night with Drakk was all she'd gotten. With time the pain would ease, but Aiyre doubted Ezi would ever forget about Drakk. All it would take was time. Maybe she'd even find another man who would lay claim to her, and she could start again.

"I know you need to grieve, but I need to see to your leg." Drakk may have died, but she didn't need Ezi dying.

Ezi nodded her head, tears still pouring down her cheeks.

It broke Aiyre's heart to see her friend shredded over Drakk's death. Why did he have to die? She felt anger towards those sabertooth shifters. They'd done an irreversible act that was worse than evil. It was insane.

Aiyre rolled Ezi's pant leg up and poked and prodded her leg until Ezi let out a pained cry and winced.

"I think your ankle is twisted and you have a deep gash on your leg."

"Can you heal it?"

Aiyre shrugged. "I'm not a healer, but I can try my best." They might need a healer for this, but could they find one?

Rising she grabbed a couple of pieces of wood and tied one on each side of the foot. "This is all I know about healing a twisted ankle." Grabbing a fur, she dipped it into some water and cleaned away the blood from the gash on Ezi's leg. Then she tied a fur strip to help stop the bleeding.

"What should we do?"

Aiyre shrugged her shoulders. "We will have to find another clan to join."

"I want to see Drakk before we leave."

Aiyre paused her eyes flickering over Ezi and the vulnerable image she presented. "Are you sure?" It could traumatize Ezi to see her recently deceased partner more than just the knowledge of his death.

"I have to say goodbye." Ezi pleaded.

"We will see him before we leave then if there is time and you are well enough." Aiyre could only promise so much.

"Thank you."

"Don't thank me yet. We have to survive."

Aiyre grabbed a couple of slices of the drying rabbit meat. "Have some food. We will need energy for the journey ahead of us."

Ezi munched down on her piece and looked around the cave. "Where is this?"

"A hunting cave near our village," Aiyre told her, not at all surprised Ezi hadn't known of it, since she wasn't a hunter.

"How close?" Ezi's hand trembled.

"We are well hidden with the heavy snowfall outside," Aiyre reassured her. "No sabertooth shifters will find us. We should get some rest." She redirected the conversation. "I have no idea how far we might have to travel to find another clan, and it will require us to be well-rested."

"A human clan?"

"Perhaps." Aiyre sat back letting the warmth of the fire wash over her. "I'm hoping we can find another pronghorn clan, but with it being winter we can't be picky about who takes us in."

"Sorry, I'm not more useful."

Aiyre let out a laugh. "Not everyone can be a hunter. We need more than hunters in a clan if we want to survive."

"I suppose that is true," Ezi mused.

"Get some rest. You'll need it." Aiyre urged her.

"See you tomorrow." Ezi sent her a smile before she settled down beside the fire.

"I'll be here." Aiyre watched Ezi as she rolled over, giving her back to the fire and pulled a fur over herself.

Good. Ezi was going to need some rest.

Aiyre walked over to the fur covering the mouth of the cave and took another look out. The snow was still falling too thick to see anything. It would hide the light and the smoke from the fire, which meant they shouldn't have any unexpected nighttime visitors.

Still, she grabbed her spear and laid it down next to where she was sleeping. If someone came into their cave, she was going to react before thinking. She had more than herself to keep alive now.

As she settled down, Aiyre heard Ezi start to sniffle and weep again. Her heart broke, knowing Ezi's pain. She too had lost people she'd loved.

A couple of tears trickled down her own face. She would never see Naru again. Or Bhirk. She rubbed the tears away.

She wanted nothing more than to take revenge against the sabertooth shifters, but she couldn't do anything by herself. And it wasn't like she was about to march into their village and take them alone.

With a sigh, Aiyre did her best to tune out Ezi's weeping and tried to focus in on the crackling of the fire. She needed to get some rest as well.

"Thank you for doing this," Ezi said as they made their way out of the mouth of the cave.

"I understand why you want to see him, but I fear it might only make you more miserable." Aiyre worried.

Ezi nodded. "It might. I just need to see him and say goodbye."

"I wish we could hold a burial ceremony for them all," Aiyre muttered. It felt disrespectful just to leave their bodies to the animals, but two women would struggle to perform a burial ceremony for so many clanmates.

"We can do something." Ezi insisted. "Maybe burn incense and say some prayers for them. We might not be able to do anything about their bodies, but we can ask the gods to take care of them in the Eternal Hunting Grounds."

"Neither of us are a shaman." Aiyre wasn't sure it would do much.

Ezi shrugged inside her thick fur clothing. "Does it matter? It has to be better than nothing. We need to make sure they get to the Eternal Hunting Grounds."

Aiyre pictured the Eternal Hunting Grounds in her mind. It had to be better than this eternal frozen ground. The Eternal Hunting Grounds were filled with endless game and always warm. At least their clanmates were in a better place where they didn't need to worry about starvation, being hunted down, and would be able to shift as much or as little as they desired.

That sounded nice to her. She wished she could shift more often, but being mistaken for a prey animal by a hunter would be a horrible moment. She didn't need a human hunter to throw a spear into her pronghorn form.

They trudged their way through the deep snow, making their way slowly through the forest of towering trees. Ezi leaned on her, keeping most of her weight off the other leg, but she'd still suck in sharp intakes of breath every time her leg caught on a thick mound of snow.

It was eerily quiet like it always was during winter. The only sounds were the creaking of the tree limbs under the immense weight of the wet snow. The animals had either gone further south to warmer weather or were waiting it out. Only a few were brave enough to face the thick of winter.

They broke out of the forest, the snow-covered village straight in front of them.

"Will you help me find him?" Ezi asked, her voice gone wobbly.

"Of course. He was near the village fire the last time I saw his body," Aiyre informed her.

The two women made their way into the village, Aiyre helping Ezi to keep her weight off her leg. The snow had done a good job of covering everything up, and they were careful of where they stepped. They didn't want to accidentally step on a clanmate's face.

Aiyre bent over when she found a lump in the snow and used her gloved hand to brush off the snow. A female face greeted her. It was Heria. Her heart went out to the woman. Those damn sabertooth shifters.

She rose and moved on to the next lump under the snow. Brushing off the snow she was greeted with another woman's face. It was Naru. Her heart sank.

Footsteps crunched on the snow as Ezi neared, and Aiyre could hear the pain she was enduring just to say goodbye to Drakk. "I didn't think she'd be able to get out quickly enough. It hurts me to see it was true though."

Ezi knelt down with Aiyre's assistance and placed her hand against Naru's frozen face. "She was a mother to every woman in the clan."

Aiyre nodded, her own eyes clouding up with tears.

"I know she was more a mother to you than us." Ezi reached out and squeezed her shoulder. "We will give her a proper ceremony as well." Ezi hugged Aiyre's shoulders.

"Let's find Drakk." Aiyre didn't want to be out here longer than they had to be. Who knew if the sabertooths would come back? She'd already seen one the last time she visited the village. "Whatever we do, let's be quick about it."

Her pulse began to race a bit as she thought about running into another sabertooth. Ezi was in no condition to run, and Aiyre wasn't sure how many times she could successfully kill a sabertooth.

Ezi nodded, and they continued to search around the village and brush off lumps of snow until they finally found Drakk.

His face had gone blue, but the cold had prevented any decomposing. He almost looked peaceful in his snow tomb. She was almost surprised he was dead.

Ezi let out a hiccup of a sob, tears pouring down her face.

Aiyre walked away, giving Ezi some time and space. It was unfair of the world to have taken Drakk away when they'd only had such a small amount of time together. One night, and then it had all been over.

Aiyre made her way over to what had been Naru's tent and went inside. It was empty, of course, and just as cold as the outside. The fire pit was black and unlit. Aiyre shivered and walked around the tent until she found the stash of herbs.

Some would be useful for when they traveled, and the others could be used for the burial ceremony. Aiyre had never performed one, but she'd give it her best without the help of a shaman.

Taking a second to take a last look at what had been her home, she felt a pang enter her chest. It would be hard just to move on, but she and Ezi were still living and needed to continue to survive.

She pushed her way out of the tent to see Ezi still knelt over Drakk's body. She'd uncovered more of his large frame.

"I have the herbs that we can burn for the dead." Aiyre came to stand beside Ezi. "Have you had enough time?"

"No." Ezi dashed tears from her eyes. "But I know we can't stay here long. Let's perform the ceremony and put everyone to rest." Ezi rose and took some of the herbs Aiyre had found. "Do you have some flint on you?"

"Yes. Here." Aiyre gathered some cloth and wood from around the camp and made a small fire.

Ezi threw the herbs on, and they watched the small wisp of smoke spiral into the air, getting lost among the background of grey clouds.

"I wish we could stay longer, but we really need to keep moving." Hopefully, these herbs would do their dead clanmates well and help them to the Eternal Hunting Grounds. It was the best she could do.

"I know." Ezi heaved a sigh and then sent her a trembling smile that was ready to fall off her face at a moment's notice. "It all seems like a dream."

Aiyre knew exactly what she meant. "All we can do is live and give their deaths a purpose."

"Never thought of it like that." The fragile smile stayed planted on her lips.

"Come." Aiyre guided them out of the village, hefting her bag which they'd packed before leaving the cave, and then let Ezi use her other shoulder. It was time for them to find another clan to join.

Chapter 5

Daerk couldn't seem to get the pronghorn shifter off his mind. Last night his dreams had been filled with her distant, but pleasant, figure. He needed to see her up close and get a better whiff of her scent. Even in sleep, she'd been pestering him, causing his slumber to be restless.

Her village had been decimated. He just had to figure out how to keep her safe until he could get rid of Brog. Brog wouldn't allow Daerk to keep a pronghorn here in their village, not when his leader thought all pronghorns were better dead than alive.

Yet here they were stuck feeding all of Brog's children. Not that Daerk would suggest they do anything else. The children were not to blame for their sire's actions. Maybe it was a good thing Brog hadn't found his mate. It could be difficult for him to explain why he had so many wives... and so many children. He should be more patient. Daerk almost felt bad for him.

Daerk shook his head. The man still made him want to vomit with disgust. Taking so many wives when he was from a mated shifter species. He shook his head. It was deplorable.

He made his way out of his tent and slipped on his fur gloves. The snow had stopped falling, but the skies were still grey with displeasure.

"What are we doing today?" Rir bounded out of nowhere, his white fur clothing blending in with all the snow between the fur huts.

"*We* aren't doing anything. *I* am doing something though."

"What is that?" Rir looked over at him with interest. The man was more curious than anyone else he knew.

Thankfully for Rir, Daerk was eager to tell someone he trusted about what he may have discovered. "I think I found a pronghorn who was still alive."

"When?"

"When I went to see what happened to the pronghorn shifters."

Rir's eyes popped wide.

Daerk mused. "She's been plaguing my mind. I feel I should do something for her. There's no possible way she can survive the winter on her own."

Rir scoffed. "You best stop thinking about bringing her here. She wouldn't be safe." Not needed

"Of course, I wouldn't bring her here. Brog dislikes me already, and I couldn't imagine what he'd do if he found out I'd discovered a pronghorn was still alive and hadn't killed her." Actually, he had a few ideas what Brog might do, and none of them were good.

Rir nodded.

"Still… we should do something for her." Daerk just couldn't stop his inner sabertooth from pestering him to go find her. "She might even be useful in swaying some of the clan to back me. Once they see and meet a pronghorn, they might see the error of Brog's ways."

"Have you considered there might be another reason this pronghorn is pulling you in?"

"What are you talking about?"

"Tell me that your sabertooth doesn't purr every time you imagine her image." Rir waited for him to refuse it.

Tor strode up, to Daerk's relief. He wanted to put an end to these musings that he and Rir had gotten into. And that last statement Rir had uttered? He wasn't even sure how to answer.

Though it might be a good point. He'd been thinking an awful lot about that pronghorn. She shouldn't interest him, yet her image was burned into his mind. A pronghorn as a mate? It was almost impossible to fathom.

"What are we doing?" Tor asked his hand coming up to stroke his beard.

"Finding Daerk's mate." Rir filled him in excitement gleaming in his eyes.

Daerk glared over at Rir who was jumping to conclusions. He was only being drawn in by the pronghorn because he wanted to do something to make up for the actions of Brog's men.

Tor let out a small huff of a laugh. "Wouldn't that be hard? Some go their entire lives without meeting their mate. It's not like we can just sniff her out."

"He found her, but he didn't do anything about it." Rir scowled at Daerk like he might be insane. "Now we have to find her again."

Tor's eyes widened. "You found your mate, and then didn't bring her back?"

"He's worried about Brog." Rir filled him in some more before Daerk could even speak.

Tor nodded his head, his long black hair swaying around his bearded face. "If him attacking a neighboring village doesn't churn the stomachs of our clanmates, then him trying to kill your mate definitely will."

Tor was right, but Daerk still wasn't sure Rir was guessing right about this pronghorn. "I'm only being pulled towards her because she is alone and needs help now that her entire clan has been wiped out."

"You're in denial," Rir persisted.

"Who is she?" Tor asked.

"You can meet her once we find her," Daerk told them giving up on convincing them she wasn't his mate. Whatever they needed to think. He knew it was impossible. A sabertooth and a pronghorn couldn't be mates.

"Should we take any supplies?"

"You and Rir can pack a couple of small bags, but I can't. I know Brog will have men watching my actions. He's getting more afraid that I will make a move against him."

"He should be worried," Rir growled with a slight bare of his teeth.

"We will meet you in the forest then," Tor said as he and Rir headed further into the village.

Daerk glanced around. He didn't see any obvious signs he was being watched, but it didn't mean that someone wasn't keeping track of him.

He made his way away from the village slowly, doing his best not to attract any attention from the people milling about by acting too eager.

"Going somewhere, Daerk?"

Daerk spun around to find Mira standing behind him.

"Just out to stretch my legs." His eyes narrowed. He wasn't too surprised to find her lurking nearby but knew it would never be good.

"Want some company?" She purred as she stepped closer.

He knew she wanted something from him, and he may have accepted her offer, but his sabertooth protested it, loudly. Not to mention he wasn't fond of her either. It was well known she'd been sleeping with Brog. "Looking for some peace and quiet."

She sent him a pout and prowled even closer to him. "I know something better than peace and quiet." Her hands worked their way up and over his shoulders, but he sidestepped and backed away.

"Perhaps another day."

Mira threw him a displeased look her lips forming a tight line, but he didn't stay long enough to see what else she might say. For all he knew Brog had sent her to keep an eye on him. Then again, she was known to sleep around in the village, so maybe she had deemed it his turn.

How lucky for him.

He brushed it off. He'd take a longer path to their meet-up point just in case Brog was interested in him today. He could call off the search for the pronghorn, but hadn't he waited long enough? Daerk was trying to be patient. He just couldn't resist the small taste he'd gotten of her smell. His sabertooth purred in agreement.

Daerk worked his way through the forest, trying to leave as little evidence of his movements as he could. It was hard with how much snow there was covering the ground. His footsteps would be a dead giveaway.

He wondered how hard it would be to find the pronghorn. The snow had prevented him from finding her the first time, and he wondered how much she would be moving around. If she were smart, she'd find somewhere like a cave to stay safe.

Neither of her forms would allow her to protect herself from wild animals or from anyone that might want to cause her harm.

Rir and Tor had been right to be surprised that he had just left the pronghorn to disappear into the snow storm when she'd drawn him in so much. For all he knew she wasn't even alive anymore. Daerk had no idea if she'd had any cover for the storm that blew through the area.   Two words

The gods could be cruel, but they wouldn't be unfair to him. His sabertooth growled at the thought of her lying dead under a sheet of fresh snow, and he told himself it was just because she could be a great asset to bring down Brog.

Daerk stopped at the meeting spot, a tree with a couple of scratch marks on its thick bark from so many years ago when he went through his first shift. He brushed his covered fingers over the marks. He would love to share the first shift with his children. He just needed to get his hands on his mate so that he could have those children, wherever she was.

His father had been there for him during his first shift, and it was the only reason he'd stayed sane. He just wished his father was still around. A pain entered his chest as he remembered the day he'd been told of the hunting accident that'd killed his father.

Rir and Tor had yet to arrive. Daerk only hoped they were both able to get out of the village without drawing too much attention to themselves.

Footsteps crunched through the snow, and he whipped around to confront whoever it was coming his way.

Rir and Tor popped out of the thick forest.

"Anyone see you?"

"Not that we know of, and we don't think we were followed," Rir informed him.

"Good." Daerk smiled. "Let's go find the pronghorn then."

"Your mate you mean," Rir teased him, and he rolled his eyes.

"I'm next."

Rir punched Tor's shoulder. "You don't even know where your mate is. At least, Daerk has an idea of where to search."

"She's somewhere out there. We just have to find her." Tor smiled, his dark eyes filled with glee.

"Yes, but at least I have a starting point." Daerk sided with Rir even though he still wasn't convinced the pronghorn was his mate. He just didn't want to wander around for a lifetime trying to find Tor's mate. "Be patient. She'll find you at some point."

"Says the man who was lucky enough to find his mate, and then left her in this dangerous world alone."

He scowled at his friend. "I still don't believe she is my mate, and I had no choice but to leave her. It was the briefest of scents that I picked up on." Daerk turned his attention to the packs they brought. "What did you bring?"

"A little food, for emergencies. I figured we could easily hunt down some small game if needed." Rir filled in. "Flint and some fur clothing. I wasn't sure how you came across this pronghorn and if she might need some warming up," Rir said, trying to get Daerk to tell him some more about her.

Daerk gave in. "I encountered her when I went to visit the pronghorn village. She appeared to be by herself and was scouring the village for supplies. She disappeared on me before I could find out anything more."

"I can't wait to meet her," Tor said eagerly as he rubbed his hands together. "One of us is finally getting a mate, and maybe some children." Tor winked over at Daerk.

If she was his mate, what would their children be like? He had yet to meet anyone who had bred outside of the sabertooth shifter clans. Maybe some would be pronghorns, and some would be sabertooths. He'd never met a sabertooth shifter who'd mated to a pronghorn. He hadn't even thought about it, which was part of the reason why he doubted she'd be his mate. It seemed farfetched.

"Looks like you have everything we might need," Daerk said as he finished looking through the bags they'd brought. They'd even brought some herbs for healing. Good. Who knew what her condition might be. "Let's head out before someone comes looking for us."

Daerk liked his friends, but they were a bit on the chatty side. A couple of hours had passed, and he couldn't recall even one second of silence. The main rambling of their conversations revolved around mates, and what they hoped their mates would be like.

It had him thinking back on the quick sniff of her scent. Every time he thought about it her image would come into his head as clear as if she were standing in front of him. His sabertooth purred again. He would admit she pulled at him, but a mate? A pronghorn mate? He wasn't sure how that could work.

"We're getting close to where I saw her last," Daerk informed them, so their chatter would finally cease.

They crested the hill and looked down at the snow-covered village below them. It was eerie with how silent it was. Daerk could just imagine how full of life it had been before their clan had slaughtered the pronghorn shifters.

"It's worse than I could have ever imagined." Rir looked down at the village.

"We should go down and see if there are any fresh tracks to follow. She may have come back after the most recent snow storm."

He looked up at the grey clouds. He couldn't see the sun, but it was getting close to dusk. They'd want to explore the village quickly, and then find a place to stay the night.

He led the way down the hill, sliding through the snow until he reached the bottom.

"Crap!"

Daerk turned around just in time to dodge a flying Rir who had tripped and rolled down the snowy hill. He looked down at the jumbled mess of Rir and his supply bag.

"Having problems?" Daerk raised a dark eyebrow.

Rir scoffed as he rose and brushed the snow off his fur clothing. "Nothing I can't handle."

"We shouldn't have brought him along." Tor hitched a thumb over at Rir.

"I tripped was all," Rir muttered. "It could've been anyone."

"It wasn't even a steep hill." Tor snorted. "I just hope you do that when you eventually find your own mate, and I'm there to witness it. She'll be so impressed."

Rir punched him on the shoulder, and Tor stumbled away with the force.

"Come, children, let us search for some tracks." Daerk made his way into the village, leaving the two of them behind. They were going to drive him insane.

There were lumps under the snow that he assumed were bodies. "Make sure to step around the lumps." He directed the other men.

Then he found a body that had been uncovered. Maybe the pronghorn had come back to say goodbye to her clanmates. This one was a man, and he wondered if he had just been a clanmate or something more to the pronghorn woman he'd seen.

His sabertooth growled at the thought of her with another man. Maybe Rir was right. His sabertooth was never this talkative.

He wasn't going to jump to any conclusions, not that it mattered. The man was dead, and Daerk was still alive. If there had been something between them, there wasn't now.

Daerk moved onto the next uncovered face. This time it was an older woman. A mother or aunt? He bent down next to the body and examined the face. Not needed "Sorry you had to die this way." The poor woman had been defenseless against an attacking force of sabertooth shifters. It'd been unfair of them.

A little pile of burned incense caught his attention. He looked over at it. Was that why she'd come back? To help her people with whatever ritual they needed to get to the afterlife? He'd offer to bring their shaman if she wanted.

Daerk was sure Eron, the sabertooth shaman, would be willing to do a burial ceremony. Eron might even know the pronghorn shifter ceremony, assuming it was even different from what the sabertooths did.

"Find anything?" Daerk stood up and looked over to where his men were dodging lumps under the snow.

So many bodies. It was gut-wrenching.

"Nothing," Rir reported.

Tor looked up and shook his head.

Daerk grumped. Her tracks had to be around here somewhere, unless she'd been a spirit.

Glancing around he found the direction he had seen her moving before he had lost sight of her. Daerk made his way over there. "Follow me!" He called out and soon heard his men crunching through the snow towards him.

"Where are we headed?"

"This was the last direction I saw her moving. I'm hoping there will be some tracks or a scent." Daerk sniffed around. He was in his human form, but he still had a better sense of smell than a normal person.

Rir sniffed around. "I smell a couple of rabbits off to our left, but no scent of a woman."

"I still think this would be the best area to check out. Spread out and let me know if you find anything. Otherwise, we meet back at the pronghorn village."

They nodded and split off from him. Daerk headed straight into the forest, while he searched for a scent or some tracks. There was nothing he was picking up on.

Time to switch forms.

Daerk shed his clothing as fast as he could. He was a built man, but the cold of winter had definitely set in, and goosebumps spread out over his skin. The shift was painless and fast. It was like his conscious slipped into another form that had just been waiting nearby.

He lifted his sabertooth nose to the air and sniffed around. There was a slight trace of something in the air. Was it her? Only one way for him to find out.

Putting his nose to the ground, he followed the trace. It led him zigzagging through the trees. This had to be her scent from when she had been trying to lose him. He'd probably scared her witless in his sabertooth form.

The scent got a bit stronger, and once he broke out of the forest, he looked up to see a fur covering the mouth of a cave.

His heart puttered in his chest. Would she be in there? Should he change into his human form and deal with the cold, so he didn't scare her?

He approached the cave cautiously. His massive paws barely sank into the soft snow, but the scent wasn't indicating that there was anyone inside. So Daerk decided not to shift out of his sabertooth form.

Pushing the fur out of the way with his snout he entered the dark and cold cave. She wasn't here, but her scent was all over the place, as was another delicate female scent. His sabertooth side purred in delight at being surrounded by her sweet scent.

"I have your clothing," Rir's voice called out from behind him.

Good. Now he wouldn't have to go and find it.

Daerk shifted back into his human form. He grabbed his clothing out of Rir's hands as he strode out of the cave and threw it on before the cold froze him. His clothing warmed within seconds.

"We'll camp here for the night and go back out to search for her."

"Someone is going to notice our absence from the village," Rir warned.

"There's nothing we can do about it. I had hoped to find her before the day was out, but I'm not about to give up."

"We at least know her scent now and can help a little more tomorrow." Tor strode into the cave. "Brrr. Let's get the fire started before night falls and the cold freezes us to the bone."

"Please." Daerk motioned him forward.

Tor hopped to it and had a fire roaring into life within a couple of minutes. "There we go." Tor held his hands out to the fire.

"Do we leave at first light?" Rir asked as he pulled some furs out of storage from further inside the cave.

"Yes. I want to find her before she gets herself killed or something kills her. Winter storms can come up unexpectedly, just like wild animals."

"Here." Tor dug into the pack he'd brought and handed out some dried meat.

Daerk took the meat. He wasn't too hungry, more worried than anything else. He wanted to get a hold of his wandering pronghorn. His sabertooth purred in agreement.

Tor sniffed the air. "Is there another scent in here?"

"It seems like she might be traveling with another woman," Daerk commented. He was just glad his friends were here to help him find her. It showed the depth of their friendship.

"Smells nice," Tor commented absently.

Daerk threw him a raised eyebrow, but Tor seemed lost in thought. Whatever.

"Brog's going to be more than just angry when he discovers we went away from the village for more than a day without telling him," Rir commented as he got cozy under some furs.

"He will be." Daerk wasn't trying to provoke Brog, but he may just end up doing that. It was the pronghorn's enticing scent though. He just had to explore it some more and find out why it was drawing him in.

"Ready to face his wrath?"

"For her?" Daerk raised an eyebrow. "Of course. I just hope we find her so that his wrath will make it all worthwhile."

Tor scoffed and scratched his beard. "You haven't even met her, and she has you wrapped around her finger."

"Our clan decimated her village. If we can help her, we should. I wouldn't call that being wrapped around someone's finger." Daerk commented as he chewed on the dried meat.

"I think Rir is right. You may have found your mate." Tor sighed as he leaned back against the cave wall. "I can only hope it will be that easy for me."

"He'll never find her," Rir said from where he was laying down.

Daerk rose an eyebrow. "Why not?"

"She'd take one look at his ugly face and go running in the opposite direction."

Daerk nearly choked on the piece of dried meat, as he laughed.

"Ha, ha. Very funny, Rir." Tor threw him a look.

"Get some sleep, you two, and try not to keep me awake with your bickering. As funny as it might be, it will keep me up, and then I'll have a foul mood tomorrow." Daerk grabbed himself a couple of furs, laid them out, and faced the wall of the cave. He was so close! He could feel the jitters enter his body, his sabertooth thrumming with excitement.

Daerk walked back into the cave and looked down at Rir and Tor. They were snoring soundly, even though the sun had risen about an hour ago.

So much for getting out of here at sunrise. Daerk walked back out of the cave, grabbed a handful of snow, balled it up, then grabbed another handful of snow and balled that one up.

Then he took his two snowballs and walked back into the cave. Taking aim, he nailed Rir in the face with one.

"Oomph!"

He took aim and nailed Tor in the side of the face.

"What the…?" Tor bolted up, scraping the snow from his beard looking thoroughly displeased.

"What part of sunrise don't you two understand?" Daerk folded his arms in front of his chest.

"So, we deserved a snowball in our face?" Rir flicked the rest into the fire, causing it to sizzle and pop.

"Could have woken us up like a normal person," Tor grumped.

"You could have woken up on your own. Come on. I already packed your bags." Daerk was eager to get back on the trail.

The men got up and shuffled out of the cave.

"Still cold."

"Get used to it. We will have several more months of it." Daerk looked out over the snowy landscape. This might be a dismal time for some, but he enjoyed the crisp white that coated everything around them.

They headed back to the pronghorn shifter village, which took them no time at all.

"Now that you know her scent. Help me find it." Daerk was positive she'd come back to the pronghorn village. While the men had been sleeping, he'd tracked it back this way.

The men walked around the village sniffing the air.

"I might have something over here," Rir called out.

Daerk rushed over and sniffed the air. It was faint, but it did seem to be her scent. It gave him some hope that he was still hot on her trail.

"We'll follow it and see if it leads anywhere."

Tor came to stand beside them. "I think I can pick up the second woman's scent." Tor looked around. He bent down and examined the ground. "This looks like a small drop of blood."

Daerk bent down next to him to examine the drop Tor was pointing at. Was it his pronghorn's blood or the mystery woman who'd interested Tor?

He took a whiff of the air, but it all came up as the unknown woman. Not his pronghorn. Relief flooded him.

He glanced over at Tor and ended up seeing a little bit of concern marring the other man's face.

"Something wrong, Tor?"

Tor shook his head slowly, but Daerk noticed his fists clenched at his sides.

"Something could end up tracking them other than ourselves because of this blood. I'm sure predators would be eager for any sign of weakness." His pronghorn was wandering around with an injured woman who was leaving a blood trail for anyone to follow.

"Animals in winter would be eager for an easy kill," Rir agreed.

"We need to find them before something else does." Daerk rose and led the way out of the village.

They traveled for half the day, following blood spots in the snow. The blood spots were increasing not only in size but in frequency.

"Daerk, you might want to see this," Rir called out.

Daerk glanced over to where Rir was standing just a few feet away. He walked over. "What is it?"

"We aren't the only ones following the pronghorn."

Daerk saw the deep tracks in the snow. He bent down and gave the air around the print a sniff. "Bear."

"Shouldn't they be sleeping?" Tor sprinted over to give the print a look. "It does look like a bear print though."

"They could be in danger." Rir met Daerk's eyes.

Daerk got the hint. As he shed his clothing, he told his men, "Come along, but not in your shifter forms. One sabertooth shifter will scare them enough." He stripped off his shirt and pants and let the shift overtake him. It felt refreshing. Both of his skins felt normal to him. He shook out his thick tan fur. Then he shot off across the snow. Who knew what kind of lead the bear had on him, so he had no time to spare.

Chapter 6

"Come on, Ezi, we can do this." Aiyre encouraged her longtime friend as she noticed Ezi beginning to weaken.

Ezi's arm was draped across her shoulder, as Aiyre tried to take weight off Ezi's twisted ankle. She glanced over her shoulder and saw some drops of blood marring the pristinely white environment. Her wound must be worse than Aiyre thought. She cringed.

"I don't… know… if I can," Ezi panted.

"If you give up, we'll both die, because I'm not leaving you by yourself."

"Anyone… tell you… you're stubborn?" Ezi's jade eyes flashed with slight annoyance.

"Every day," Aiyre confirmed. "It might not be the best trait, but it might just help to save your life."

"I'm just slowing us down," Ezi grunted. "I'm going to keep you from finding cover before night falls."

Aiyre shook her head. "Then we tough it out in the open, but I'm not giving up on you. For all I know we are the last two of our clan alive, and I'm not letting you die."

"I still can't believe they are all dead." She could hear the tremble in Ezi's voice.

"We will never forget them. They will live on in us, but we must live to make sure that happens."

A crunch sounded behind them. Aiyre spun around, dragging Ezi in a tight circle.

"Ouch!"

"Shh." Aiyre gazed at the giant bear standing before them.

[handwritten annotation: Ssh]

Its nose was down to the ground, sniffing a drop of blood on the snow. Then its muzzle rose, its loose lips exposing horrible yellow teeth, as it opened its mouth. White air puffed out of its leathery nose as it snorted.

[handwritten annotation: No, she shouldn't — that's acting like prey and could encourage an attack.]

"You should run," Ezi whispered horror shaking her words.

"No." Aiyre would die protecting her friend before she turned tail.

"We'll both die, and then the clan won't live on."

"So be it, Ezi." Aiyre let go of Ezi's arm slowly, allowing her to sink to the ground. "Just stay there and try not to attract the bear's attention."

"I'll do my best."

Aiyre reached a hand behind her and detached her spear from her pack. She hefted her spear. She was glad she brought it, but she wasn't sure it was going to help save them. Taking a bear down with one spear? She'd better start praying for a miracle shot to the heart.

The bear gave another huff, as it eyed them with its beady black eyes. It was probably trying to decide what its chance was when it came to taking them out.

Aiyre met its gaze, not willing to back down. It might be more than five times her size, but she had determination on her side and a desire to live.

"Go away." She whispered, hoping the bear would think they were too difficult for a before-hibernation-snack.

The bear decided they were worth the effort. It started to circle them as it grunted into the cold air, and Aiyre made sure to keep herself between the bear and Ezi. If it wanted Ezi, it'd have to go through her.

It gave another huff, almost like it was exasperated with her persistent efforts to save her friend.

"You should just leave me." Ezi pleaded from where she was sitting in the snow. "My leg will probably kill me anyway."

"Stop talking, Ezi." Aiyre snapped. She wasn't leaving.

The bear kept circling, but the circle was getting smaller and smaller. It was going to come in for an attack.

Aiyre swallowed her fear as her heart thundered away in her chest.

Then the bear charged. Its massive body barreled towards her, and then it stopped and rose up, a paw nearly taking her head off as it took a swipe.

Aiyre lunged with a stab towards the bear's thick hide, but the stone point only slid off all the fur and fat.

They were going to die. Fear rose its ugly head as she gazed up at the massive form of shaggy brown fur.

* * *

Daerk's heart nearly stopped when he came across his wandering pronghorn shifter being attacked by a giant bear.

He plunged forward and knocked the bear in the side with all the force he could. The bear stumbled away from the women as he heard startled gasps sound behind him. He wasn't surprised they'd be startled.

The bear righted itself and took a swing at him. All he saw was a paw full of sharp claws flying past his face, very little room to spare. *long, but blunt*

He backed off, only to launch himself on top of the bear. Daerk's mouth clamped down on the bear's neck, his long canines sinking into the flesh, but the bear didn't go down.

How much fat did this thing have on it?! *? only*

Daerk thrashed a bit to try and get his canines into some flesh. All the bear's thick fur tickled his throat. Dislodging his hold, Daerk jumped off the bear's back. He might need some assistance to take down the bear.

He spared a second to take a glance over at the pronghorn shifter. She was trying to drag the other woman away from the fighting. Good. At least she recognized danger and was smart enough to get out of the way.

Still, he wanted more distance.

Daerk lunged at the bear, and then backed off, trying to get the bear to follow him and leave the women alone.

Unfortunately, his wild bear wasn't so easily swayed. It gave a swipe of its massive claws in his direction and then lumbered back in the direction of the women.

Where were Rir and Tor?

Daerk rushed to put himself between the women and the bear. The bear halted in its tracks and eyed him. Maybe it was finally rethinking this attack. It should go find a couple of rabbits to eat before its hibernation. It just wasn't allowed to eat the pronghorns. *It wouldn't be stupid enough to risk death or serious injury like this.*

It charged him, deciding he would make a tasty snack in place of the women. He dodged the sharp teeth, backed off and then came back in to sink his teeth into the bear's neck. The bear rose up on its back feet, but Daerk didn't let go, even when he saw a paw full of sharp claws coming straight for his side. It would easily slice him open and spill his guts all over the snow. *No chance. A slash or puncture-wound at best.*

Something slammed into the bear's back, throwing it off balance and saving Daerk's internal organs from being freed all over the ground.

Daerk let go before the bear crushed him with its weight. When he backed off and looked up, he saw Rir and Tor had finally arrived and had changed into their sabertooth forms.

Good. Three sabertooths would have no problem taking down this giant bear.

His men started to shred at the bear's hide with their claws, and Daerk went back in for the neck. He bit down where he thought the spine would be, and finally heard a snap. The bear went limp and fell to the ground. *Biting bone would break his sabres. They used a throat-bite to kill.*

The three of them backed away, waiting. Rir moved closer and touched the bear with a paw. Dead. Good.

He looked around and saw his pronghorn was still dragging the other woman across the snow. Time to talk to her.

⁑ ⁑ ⁑

Aiyre glanced up and saw the sabertooths had taken the bear down. That meant they'd probably come for them next. Her grip on Ezi's under pits tightened, as she pulled Ezi across the ground faster.

"Just leave me, Aiyre!" Ezi cried frantically.

"How many times will we have the same discussion?" Aiyre was getting exasperated with Ezi. They only kept going in circles. She wasn't leaving Ezi. It might be a logical decision, but she couldn't abandon her last clanmate.

Glancing back up she met the eyes of three sabertooths. All three were fixated on them. She pulled harder.

"Ouch!" Ezi complained.

"Sorry," Aiyre mumbled as she continued to pull Ezi across the thick snow.

Aiyre looked back up and paused as the lead sabertooth shifted in front of her very eyes. She couldn't look away. He transformed into an impressively handsome man, too bad he was a sabertooth shifter.

Her eyes scanned down his frame, from his brown hair to his golden eyes and then down the rest of his naked body.

The other two sabertooth cats shifted into equally handsome men, but neither of them could compare to the god standing in front of her. Her heart skipped a beat.

"What do you think they want?" Ezi asked.

"I have no idea." Aiyre continued to drag Ezi across the ground. It was a lost cause at this point since the sabertooths would easily catch up to them, but she wasn't giving up. "Maybe they'll freeze to death."

"I doubt it." Ezi sounded just as miserable about their odds as Aiyre felt. "But," she suddenly said with hope blossoming in her voice, "they are in their human forms which might mean they don't mean to harm us."

Ezi had clearly lost too much blood to think clearly. "We'll get through this." She didn't believe a single word she was saying, but it was better than announcing to the whole world that they were about to be killed.

The men strode over to a pile of bags and clothes.

"Aiyre, you can stop dragging me. We aren't going anywhere fast, and they will be on us in a second."

Ezi was right. She should save her energy.

Aiyre reached behind her back and dislodged her spear from where her pack was holding it, as she let go of Ezi.

"What are you doing?" Ezi criticized.

"I doubt they are about to assist us, and I plan on defending us for as long as possible. If I'm going to die, then I'm going to bring at least one of them down with me."

"Maybe we could try to talk? We don't even know if they are even part of the same shifter clan."

"How many sabertooth shifter clans could there be?" She hoped not too many. "I only know of one in the area. They have to be from that clan, Ezi, and I doubt they'll want to talk."

"Be careful. I don't want to see you get killed." Ezi pleaded, her voice breaking. "Not after everything else."

One of the men grabbed a pile of clothing and distributed it among the other two. Once the men were clothed Aiyre sighed a bit in relief. Fighting naked men would be a bit disturbing for her. Even from over here she couldn't help her eyes from skimming over his naked backside.

Her gloved hands tightened on the wood shaft of her spear. She pointed the stone tip towards them as the men picked up their supply bags and made their way towards her.

Ezi could be right. They might just be three bachelor sabertooth shifters searching for women to start their own clan with, but she doubted it. It was a big world and wandering into someone who wasn't from the area seemed unlikely to her.

The men stalked towards them, and Aiyre rushed to put herself between the sabertooth shifters and Ezi.

"Don't get yourself killed," Ezi begged from behind her.

"Don't come any closer!" Aiyre yelled at the three men, who were well-built and so much taller than herself. Their clothing didn't help calm her. It made them seem even larger than they already were.

They weren't armed, but then did they really need any weapons? All they had to do was shift, and they'd be armed with the deadliest weapons nature had bestowed upon them.

The one in the front held up his hands. "We mean you no harm."

"Doubtful!" She called out still brandishing the spear.

"If we meant you harm, we could have let the bear finish you off, but we didn't." He dared her to disagree his gold eyes pinning her to the spot where she stood.

True. "All of you are sabertooth shifters, and we are pronghorn shifters, as I know you can smell. So, what do you want if not to kill us?"

The leader looked to the other two men. "We were searching for you."

"Why?" Aiyre brandished her spear when he took another step towards her. "I will defend myself." She warned him.

"I don't doubt it." His hands remained up. "You have no reason to trust us if you came from the pronghorn village that was attacked, but you will have to take my word that we mean you no harm."

"What could we lose?" Ezi asked from behind her, her voice a bit strained. "I need help, or I'll die, and we need a more than just ourselves if we want to survive the winter. Even you said that earlier."

Aiyre hated the fact that Ezi was making so much sense. She wanted to get rid of the sabertooth shifters, but they might die without help, so what could they possibly lose?

Aiyre lowered the spear. "I keep my weapon and one false move, and you will have a fight on your hands." She warned him.

He nodded. "We understand. I am Daerk, and this is Rir." He pointed to the man on his left. "And this is Tor." He pointed to the other man. Then he looked at her expectantly.

"I am Aiyre, and this is Ezi. We did come from the pronghorn clan that was attacked. I assume you are some of the sabertooths who are responsible." Aiyre accused him unable to keep the venom from her voice.

Daerk took in a deep breath his chest puffing out with the action and let it out slowly. "We are part of the clan that attacked yours, but none of us knew about the attack until it was too late." His golden eyes pierced her. "We were not a part of the attack."

"I can't take your word for it." She met his eyes, unflinching in the face of yet another unknown danger.

He nodded. "Understandable, but allow us to help you." He held out a gloved hand. "Given time we can prove to you we mean neither of you any harm."

Aiyre glanced over at Ezi and then down to Ezi's leg which was covered in trickles of blood. Looking back up at Ezi's eyes she could see her friend was ready to take the risk.

Aiyre bit her bottom lip. "Fine." She backed away, allowing the men to get a look at Ezi who was still sitting on the ground. "You can prove yourself by helping Ezi with her twisted ankle and the wound on her leg." Aiyre glanced over to Ezi who looked a little pale with all her blood loss.

"Rir, you will carry her." Daerk directed one of the men.

"No!" Tor blurted out, making Aiyre jump and tighten her grip on her spear.

Daerk turned in the other man's direction and arched an eyebrow on his well-chiseled face. Couldn't the sabertooth shifters have been ugly instead of attractive? All three of them were exceptional specimens.

"Then you carry the injured one, Tor."

Aiyre eyed them all with skepticism, but the one named Tor approached Ezi slowly and picked her up gently, and Ezi didn't even flinch once.

"Do you need to be carried?" Daerk sidled up close to her and sent her a smirk.

Aiyre jabbed the point of her spear tip under his chin. "Touch me and die, sabertooth." She growled.

Daerk backed away, the grin never leaving his face. "It could be quicker if I carried you."

"I am... was... a hunter in my clan. I can handle myself out here." Aiyre's eyes narrowed on him.

A smile creased the man's lips, almost like he was impressed with her spirit.

Good. She wanted respect from these men since it might help with keeping herself and Ezi alive. She was still dubious about their intentions. After all the sabertooths had done to her people, she wasn't ready to trust them.

"Where are we going?" Aiyre glared at the man who seemed to be in charge. "We won't go to your village." They'd be killed within seconds of entering that village. There was no doubt in her mind.

"We will bring you to a cave we know of near enough to our village so we can provide assistance, but far enough away, so no one wanders into you," Daerk told her.

"There is a small cave near our village," Aiyre retorted. "We'll be more comfortable there."

"Your cave is too close to your village. If anyone from our clan checks for survivors, like I did, they might notice your presence. Our leader... did not like the presence of your clan, and I know he will want to finish the hunt if he finds two of you still alive."

So, they'd tracked them all the way from the cave. It made sense that they should change the area they were hiding in. If these men had found them, then others could also find them.

"Why help us?" Aiyre still wasn't sure about his motivation.

Daerk went silent for a little bit, and she could see him thinking behind those golden eyes of his. "Enough people have been killed. I want to bring redemption for my clan. They've been misguided, and I know they will come to regret their actions."

Aiyre felt like he was holding something back from her, but she'd let it slide now and press him later.

"Lead the way then." Aiyre motioned him forward.

He inclined his head and headed off through the snow. She set off after him with his men trailing behind. She took a few glances over her shoulder to make sure Ezi was fine.

Ezi had a wary look in her eyes but wasn't screaming for help, so Aiyre tried to relax her guard a bit. The men did seem to want to help them. It was odd, but they needed the help.

"If you weren't one of the sabertooths who attacked my clan, then where were you?" Aiyre questioned Daerk as she pulled up beside him.

"I was hunting, and these two," Daerk hitched a gloved thumb over his shoulder, "they were searching for me so that they could tell me about the attack."

"And if they'd found you in time, would you have been able to do anything?" Aiyre was curious to know. Could her clan have been saved by this one man?

"Probably not." His bright golden eyes glanced over at her, and her heart skipped a beat. "I don't know."

She cocked her head to the side. "There was a chance?"

His lips pursed. "A slight one. I would have had to challenge my clan leader. Unfortunately, I'm not sure how many would follow me if I tried to take over."

"Anyone who would allow such a massacre to take place is just as guilty as those who attacked my village." She challenged.

"You don't understand the fear Brog has hammered into my people. He's made examples of people before."

"Why risk the annoyance of your clan leader by helping us?" Because she was sure his clan leader would think he'd lost his mind.

He shrugged. "I don't believe my clan would have done this if they had a level-headed leader. Brog, our leader, needs to have control and does it with terror. He made sure everyone in the clan thought you pronghorns were killing us off."

She couldn't imagine living among a clan full of sabertooths. They had to be violent and unpredictable, and so far, Daerk had yet to change her mind on that. He wasn't ripping any throats out yet, but there was still time for him to turn violent.

Aiyre glanced back at Ezi who had to be feeling better now that she wasn't using her leg.

"Worried about your friend?"

"Yes. Her ankle is twisted, and if that isn't enough she has a deep gash on her leg, and I'm worried about it getting infected." And she was worried about being left alone for the rest of winter.

"We'll see to her." He reassured her. "If she needs something more, we can sneak our shaman over to this cave."

"Your shaman would assist us?" She couldn't help but feel a bit surprised their shaman wouldn't share the feelings of their leader. Usually, a shaman and a leader had the same views and worked as a unit, like Naru and Bhirk.

"Of course he would. Not everyone in my clan agreed with the attack. And some of those who did attack may have feared retaliation from our leader had they not done as he said."

Aiyre looked at him coldly. "That's little comfort when my entire clan lies dead among their tents, slaughtered in their homes." She stalked away to walk beside her friend, fussing over her furs.

Something inside of Daerk gave a sharp pang as she walked away from him. He told himself he only felt guilty that he hadn't been able to prevent the attack, but he was starting to worry that it wasn't guilt that had driven him to find this woman again.

Chapter 7

Within an hour, they arrived at a cave with a fur flap covering the mouth of the entrance. From the outside, it looked very similar to the one she'd been staying in for the past few days.

Daerk stepped up to the entrance and held back the flap with a gloved hand. Aiyre stepped forward. With the light from outside shining in, she was able to see the cave was enormous compared to the one she'd been staying in with Ezi.

She walked in cautiously. Hopefully, the sabertooth shifters wouldn't kill them in their sleep, although this would be a lot of effort to kill two women who most likely would've died in the snow.

The rest of the group filed in, and the one named Rir bent over the fire pit and got a raging fire started in a matter of minutes.

She put her hands out to the fire and enjoyed the warmth that was filling the cave.

Tor placed Ezi down near the fire, and she noticed him hovering over her friend. Aiyre walked around the fire to take position near her clanmate. Aiyre wasn't liking the interest this sabertooth was showing in her friend, and until she knew why, she was going to stay close.

She placed her spear against the cave wall, and then bent down next to Ezi. "How are you feeling?"

"I'm fine, but my leg hurts." Ezi winced.

"The herbs I brewed for you must be wearing off. I can ask them to collect some more for us."

"What do you need?" Tor squatted next to them.

Of course, he would be listening in. Why was he hovering? She glared a little at the overly-interested sabertooth.

"She needs things for her twisted ankle, like herbs to take the pain away and to stave off infection." Aiyre decided to put the hovering Tor to use. This way he might leave the cave and stay away from Ezi.

"What's going on over there?"

She looked up to see everyone was now staring over at the two women. "We just need to see to Ezi's comfort."

"Ezi," Tor mumbled, and Aiyre narrowed her eyes at him.

"We packed some supplies." Daerk grabbed a leather pack and brought it over to her. "Use whatever you need, and if you need something else…" Daerk looked over at Tor. "Get him to help you."

Aiyre tossed him a nod. "I'm going to take off your bandage," she told Ezi, "which means removing your splint. You could experience some pain."

Ezi nodded. "I understand."

Aiyre dug through the bag, found some herbs, and handed them over to Tor. "Get some water boiling, and then throw these in."

"What will they do?" He glanced at the herbs he was taking from her and gave them a sniff.

"They'll take away her pain."

He snapped to once the words were out of her mouth. Something was going on around here, and she still wasn't sure what it was.

Aiyre glanced over at Daerk. His golden eyes were trained on her, even though he was trying to look relaxed by leaning against the cave wall with his arms crossed over his chest. Something was definitely up, and she was going to tread cautiously until she knew what it was.

"Something wrong?" Ezi whispered over at her.

"Maybe not. I'm not sure." Aiyre whispered back. She dug through the pack pulling out anything and everything she might need for Ezi's leg.

"Tell me. I need something to distract my mind." Ezi gave her a weak smile.

"I don't want to worry you about nothing. Let's talk about something else." Aiyre started to unwrap Ezi's bandages and splint.

Ezi let out a hiss of pain, and Aiyre noticed Tor's gaze fly to Ezi's face. She didn't know enough about sabertooth shifters to understand his interest in Ezi, but it concerned her. Each clan had kept their distance from each other. Maybe their clan didn't have enough women to keep the men entertained, and he simply found Ezi fascinating.

Aiyre shivered. Yuck! She couldn't think about one of the sabertooths between her thighs. If they were trying to win them over, they'd have an uphill battle on their hands. She couldn't see Ezi or herself being interested in one of them.

Aiyre packed the new bandage full of whatever herbs Daerk had in his bag, and then wrapped the fur bandages around Ezi's leg. Then she reattached the splint.

"Hopefully this wound heals before an infection sets in, and as for the ankle, I can only hope I'm doing what needs to be done." Aiyre frowned. "Unfortunately, I don't know too much about healing, and I'm doing my best."

Ezi gave her a warm smile. "I'm just happy to have you by my side. When I was walking around out there by myself, all I could think was that I would die alone."

Aiyre gave her hand a reassuring pat. "I was afraid of the very same thing. I'm glad I was able to find you."

"Here you are." Tor tiptoed his way over the uneven floor of the cave with a small wooden cup balanced in his hands and then handed it over to Aiyre.

"Thank you." She blew on the liquid, and then pressed the cup to Ezi's lips. "Drink as much as you can, but don't force yourself."

"I can do it." Ezi took the cup from her hands and drank some of the warm liquid. "Hmmm… it's warm."

Aiyre smiled. She was happy to see pink in her friend's cheeks again. They were going to get through this, with the help of three sabertooth shifters. Their lives had definitely taken a strange turn.

Aiyre stood up, and her smile slipped from her face as she eyed the other men in the cave. She was going to need to get some sleep, but she wasn't sure she should trust these men. She didn't know them, and they were sabertooth shifters, which meant they had two strikes against them.

Keeping an eye on Ezi and Tor, she made her way over to where Daerk stood, still leaning against the cave wall.

"You do know we are pronghorn shifters, right?" She asked, needing to make sure he understood exactly who he was helping.

"We've already had this discussion."

"I just wanted to make sure you heard me earlier. I'm still having a hard time seeing three sabertooth shifters helping us."

His golden eyes skimmed over her, and she saw heat soar through them. Did he find her attractive? Maybe she'd mistook what she'd seen flash through his eyes. She hoped so.

Her eyes skimmed over him. She'd seen him bare naked, and she was still able to think back on that moment with ease. He had a pleasing form, full of toned muscles that he should be proud of. Heat flooded her cheeks as she thought back to that glimpse of his cock. Even when he wasn't hard it'd been hard to miss the cock that had dangled between his legs.

"We need to collect the meat from the bear," Daerk interrupted the direction of her thoughts, "if we're going to have you two live here through winter." Daerk pushed himself off the wall, getting extremely close to her and taking in a deep sniff that she had a hard time not noticing.

Then he turned around and headed for the mouth of the cave. "Come with me, Tor and Rir. We will bring our packs and collect the meat and fur from the bear before another predator comes by."

Tor took a glance over at Ezi but did as the leader of the group bid. Rir was quick to follow.

Daerk turned towards her. "Can I trust you not to run?"

"No."

Daerk huffed in annoyance, but she cut him off. It was true. If she only had to think about herself, she would be on her way as soon as the men left the cave. But she had Ezi to think about. She wasn't going to run if she couldn't take Ezi with her

"I won't leave without her, and she can't run." Aiyre folded her arms across her chest.

He seemed mollified. "We'll see you soon then. Be cautious of anyone else who could show up." And then he was gone.

Aiyre looked over at Ezi, who had her back against the wall.

"Feeling any better?"

"The tea has taken effect," Ezi confirmed a drowsiness to her eyes.

"Good."

Aiyre sat next to her friend, while they waited for the sabertooth shifters to come back.

The men walked in silence, as Daerk kept his eyes open for any dangers. Not just to them but any threats to the women back at the cave. He'd have to check every day to make sure none of his people ventured over here, and if they did, he would have to redirect them without giving the women away.

The pronghorn woman's scent had been even more intoxicating in person. He'd found himself drawn to her at every turn, and her presence in the small cave had nearly overwhelmed him. He'd been glad for the excuse to go back and collect the bear meat, if only to have the chance to clear his head.

His sabertooth begged him to go back to the cave and take her. It bewildered him. He wasn't entirely sure how a sabertooth and a pronghorn were supposed to work. There was no telling what type of shifter the children would be, and Daerk wasn't sure he was up to raising pronghorns. His sabertooth purred at the idea of children with Aiyre, completely unfazed by the idea of pronghorn children.

Challenging Brog was becoming imperative. If he ever wanted to bring her into his clan, he'd have to get rid of Brog. Unless he wanted to start his own clan, but that idea didn't really appeal to him. He wanted to ensure Aiyre's safety, but he also wanted to save his clan from Brog's influence. Brog was going to run the clan into the ground.

The bear carcass came into view as they crested a small hill buried under the snow. There were birds already circling the carcass and fighting over who got first dibs.

Daerk sprinted over the snow, waving his gloved hands in the air like a madman. "Get out of here!" He hollered.

The birds flew up into the air with a tremendous clatter of noises. They were displeased with the rude interruption, but wouldn't risk their own lives to fight him. They knew once he was done, they would be allowed to pick at scraps of meat on the bones.

"Let's get this meat collected before anything larger shows up." He could always shift into his sabertooth form and defend the meat, but he wasn't about to risk his life with his mate so close.

He had yet to even kiss her. Those deliciously full lips of hers called to him. He'd kiss them soon enough though. It was the sole focus of his mind since he'd met her.

"I'll start on removing the fur. You two cut the bear open and remove the innards." Daerk directed his men. He took a stone knife out of one of the packs and started to work on getting the fur off. Nothing needed to go to waste.

Daerk watched Tor out of the corner of his eye. His friend had been acting strange since they found the women, and he was wondering what it might be about.

"Is something wrong?" Daerk finally asked.

Tor and Rir both looked up from where they were working on the bear.

"With you, Tor."

"What do you mean?" Tor gave Daerk his full attention, letting Rir continue with degutting the bear.

gutting

"Ever since we found the women, you've been... attentive to the injured woman." Daerk watched every flicker of emotion on Tor's face. He'd been right. Agitation flashed over Tor's face, and then resignation.

"I think Ezi is my mate." He almost looked like he was ashamed to admit it.

Rir snorted as he looked between the both of them. "Both of you? With pronghorn shifters?" He shook his head.

"Something wrong with my mate?" Daerk challenged, his eyes narrowing. He hadn't expected Rir to have a problem with it.

Rir shook his head, his long brown hair swaying around his shoulders. "I'm just wondering where my pronghorn mate is. Seems a bit unfair you two should find your mates in the same group of women just days apart, while I'm still waiting."

A smile broke across Daerk's face. "Be patient. You will find her in time. Although I can't guarantee she will be a pronghorn."

Rir smiled.

Tor nodded his head as he ran a hand over his beard. "Perhaps she'll be a rabbit shifter."

The smile slipped off Rir's face as he threw a handful of guts at Tor, who had to do some quick maneuvers to dodge the flying red blob.

"We have to get the shaman out here to see to Ezi," Tor said the moment he righted himself. "I can't let my mate die because of an infected wound."

Daerk nodded. "We will get him out here as soon as we can. First, we have to make sure Brog doesn't get suspicious of us leaving the village. If we come back here too often, he is bound to have us followed."

"He's right. Brog isn't the type to tolerate pronghorn blood coming into the clan," Rir confirmed.

"I can't leave her in that state," Tor complained, his face contorting like he was the one in physical pain.

"You'll have to unless you want Brog to kill her in front of you." Daerk wasn't keen on leaving his mate for an extended period of time either, but if it prolonged her life, then he'd do it.

"Do we bring all the meat to the cave?"

"No. We will bring some to Aiyre and Ezi. The rest we will bring back to the village so that we can tell Brog we just went hunting." It would be the best way to prevent Brog from getting too interested.

"Good idea."

Daerk sidled up beside Tor so Rir wouldn't butt into the conversation. "Approach her slowly. Our people destroyed her village, and she was injured in the process. She is going to blame us. They both are going to blame us." And fear them, which set his stomach to rolling. He didn't want his mate to fear him every time he came close or tried to touch her. She might not show her fear, but he would always be able to smell it.

Tor scrubbed a hand over his beard. "I'll do my best. I just wish I could welcome her into my tent and show her she has nothing else to worry about from this world."

"I know exactly what you mean, but if you go too fast, you might just end up pushing her away." He wasn't sure if he was saying all this out loud for Tor or himself. He too just wanted to wrap his arms around Aiyre and breath in her delicate scent.

"Even with the troubles of having a pronghorn shifter as your mate, you two are lucky." Rir's eyes took on a distant look.

Daerk strode over to his other friend and slapped him on the back. "She will come in time. Do not worry about that."

Rir smiled at him before returning to his work on the bear.

Daerk took the time to take a glance around. Everything was pristinely white and so peaceful looking, but if anyone from his clan found the women… there'd be trouble.

"Have you two even thought of your offspring?" Rir laughed. "I wonder if they will be sabertooths with horns." He snorted at the image he'd presented.

"I had been wondering who they would take after." Daerk was worried about it. He'd take whatever offspring she gave him with open arms, but he would have no idea of how to raise a pronghorn.

He wouldn't be able to take them hunting in their shifter form if they were a pronghorn. And how good would they be at hunting in their human form? Daerk couldn't always be there to protect them from the world.

"It is a worry." Tor seemed lost in his own worries as well.

"At least we have each other. You and I will figure out how to raise pronghorns together." Daerk sent him a reassuring smile.

He should feel more appalled at the idea of raising a pronghorn family, but all he could feel pulsing through him was happiness at finding his mate. Now all he had to do was convince her she wanted him as well, but he was sure it wouldn't be easy.

Harvesting the bear meat had taken Daerk and his men the rest of the day, and they were forced to travel at night back to the cave. It wasn't a huge deal for them, but it still presented a possible danger. There were several creatures roaming the landscape that could take them on, like a pack of wild sabertooths or any direwolves. Two words, and they'd be unlikely to attack humans.

When the cave came into sight, and he saw the inviting flicker of light behind the flap covering the entrance he was barely able to contain his excitement. Those dangers wandering around didn't just affect him and his men, but these formidable predators could wander across the waiting women.

His heart picked up speed. Fire usually kept predators away, but the pronghorn shifters would make a tempting meal. Daerk would have to shift into his sabertooth form before he left so he could spread his scent around. The evidence of a sabertooth would make most anything turn tail.

almost

Daerk pushed his way through the fur flap and was greeted with the sight of his beautiful mate sitting in front of the fire. The light spilled over her delicate features, highlighting her subtle beauty. She wasn't the type of woman to knock a man off his feet. Instead, she set a fire burning in him that only she could quench. He enjoyed the slow burn.

Maybe he was biased since she was his mate, but he didn't think anyone could be any more stunning. Daerk was ready to drop to his knees and beg for her attention. Her scent had filled the cave, and he took in deep lung-fulls of the enticing smell. His sabertooth purred.

Rir shoved past him. "You're blocking the entrance." He grumbled.

Daerk moved out of the way so Tor could come inside without barreling through him like Rir.

Aiyre glanced up and her soft brown eyes collided with his. His sabertooth wanted to purr in satisfaction. Then her eyes moved to Tor, and Daerk glanced over at his friend who was sitting down close to the one called Ezi.

He hoped his friend listened to him about going slowly. She was an injured pronghorn shifter who was about to learn she had caught the attention of a sabertooth shifter. It could startle her beyond Tor's reach if he weren't careful.

Daerk shook his head. Tor would listen to his instincts, and instincts never led them astray.

He skirted the perimeter of the fire pit as he made his way over to Aiyre, and then lowered the pack of meat near her. Then he took each slab out and hung it above the fire so it would cook. He kept sneaking glances at her when she wasn't looking, which was easy since she seemed intent on watching Ezi and Tor.

He couldn't wait to undo her tight braid and run his fingers through the silky strands.

Daerk again looked over at his friend who was trying to engage Ezi in conversation.

"You don't have to worry about him making a snack of your friend," Daerk commented as he continued to place the bear meat over the fire.

Aiyre looked over at him. "That's not what I'm afraid of him doing. It's the intent in his eyes that makes me wary."

"What about the intent in my eyes?" He couldn't resist asking her to see what her reaction would be.

Her brown eyes darted up to his, and he saw barriers rise in their rich depths. "The only intention I care about is how far you're willing to go to help me and Ezi survive. If we can make it through the winter, we can find a new clan in the spring."

Daerk's inner sabertooth growled in displeasure to hear her so easily state that she planned to leave him. He tried to shake it off and gave her what he thought was a charming smile, but she frowned at him in displeasure. His mate was going to be a hard one to please, that was for sure. "Do pronghorn shifters have mates?" Daerk asked, changing the subject.

Aiyre looked back over at Ezi and Tor. She shook her head. "No, we do not. We choose who we want to be with and join together in a ceremony before our clan."

That was going to make life a lot more difficult for Tor and himself.

"Were you joined with someone?" He was hoping she would say no. A mate mourning the loss of her man, now that was too much of a challenge. It could take months, maybe even years to win a heart that had already been given.

"I was not, although one man had hoped to join with me. But your clan made sure he didn't have the chance to convince me."

Daerk sat back and kicked his legs out beside her, his task at the fire done. "Did you want to be joined with him?"

A thoughtful look entered her eyes. It was a yes. His sabertooth grumbled in displeasure.

"No." She shook her head. "I don't think we were right for each other, although I could have done much worse than him."

Good. That meant her heart was free for him to win, and his sabertooth once more purred with pleasure.

"And you?"

"Me?"

Aiyre met his gaze as she folded her arms in front of her chest, only accenting her breasts under all that fur clothing. He swallowed hard. What he wouldn't give to see her naked.

* * *

Aiyre didn't know what to make of their situation. The sabertooths had destroyed her village, and now she was sitting around a fire talking to one of the possible killers. He claimed to not have participated, but could she trust the word of a sabertooth shifter after what they'd done?

She just wasn't sure. So far, the men had done nothing to indicate any sort of hostility, but after recent events, she found herself a bit jumpy and untrusting.

Daerk scooted closer to her. His scent washed over her. It was so masculine and strangely comforting, pure leather and man. Aiyre almost felt like she could snuggle up into him, but of course, she wasn't about to do that. Instead, she raised her eyebrows, waiting for a reply to her question.

"I have no one that I am mated to as of yet," He supplied.

"Mated?" The phrase seemed odd to her.

"We sabertooths have mates. We do not get to choose, as you would say." His golden eyes roamed over her.

Aiyre glanced over to where Tor was paying Ezi too much attention. Could it be? She'd do whatever she needed to do to keep Ezi safe from Tor if that was what was going on over there.

She turned her attention back to Daerk who was still watching her.

"So, you're saying that you only... get intimate... with someone once you're mated?" She asked. Maybe Tor was interested in Ezi for a more basic reason. Although in Ezi's current condition, she couldn't imagine someone thinking about her in that way.

Daerk frowned. "There are a few who join with others before they find their mate, but it is generally frowned upon. It can cause... problems after one person in an unmated couple finds their mate. But it does happen, especially as one grows older and continues to go mateless."

Aiyre shifted uncomfortably under his intense gaze. She rose suddenly from her seat and busied herself with a soup she had started over the fire. She ignored Daerk as she poured a bowl for Ezi and then chased a reluctant Tor away from Ezi's resting place.

The three sabertooth shifters left the cave, leaving Aiyre to think in peace while she fed her friend.

Tor's interest didn't bode well for Ezi, one way or the other. They needed to find another clan to take them in before spring, but the journey would be harsh. As Ezi drifted off to sleep, Aiyre decided they would stay long enough for her friend to heal. Until then, she would do her best to keep Tor away.

In the morning, the men took their leave. Aiyre suspected they had spent most of the night outside in their sabertooth forms, leaving enough of their scent around the cave to scare off potential predators.

"We will have to leave you two alone for a while, maybe a day or two, to keep up appearances at our village," Daerk told them.

"Will you two be all right?" Daerk asked his eyes falling on her once more.

"Of course. I can hunt, and we have the cave for protection. And I shouldn't have to hunt with all the bear meat you've provided for us." She waved a hand at the meat that was now stockpiled in the cave.

"Is there anything else you need before we leave?" This time it was Tor who asked, and he only had eyes for Ezi.

Aiyre stepped between them. "We'll be fine." She repeated.

Daerk placed his hand on Tor's shoulder. "We'll be on our way, then. Grab your bags." He said to the other two men, and then they were gone, but not before Tor gave Ezi another long look.

Once they were gone, Aiyre turned to Ezi with a sigh of relief. "I thought they might never leave. Tor unnerves me, lingering so close to you."

Ezi snorted, "He's nothing compared to the way Daerk hangs on your every word."

Aiyre looked at her in puzzlement. "What are you talking about?"

Ezi gave her a look. "Last night you mentioned that we had a small supply of firewood, and not an hour later, that man had enough kindling and logs stacked in here to keep us warm all winter."

Aiyre shook her head. "They all brought in firewood."

"Yes, but it was Daerk who made them do it." Ezi laughed at Aiyre's expression, but in the next moment, she winced as she shifted her leg. Aiyre immediately made her way over to her friend's side and bent down next to Ezi's leg so she could get a look at it. She told herself she wasn't relieved by the excuse to end their conversation. "Is the leg feeling any better?"

"Not really. The herbs don't seem to be working as well as this morning."

That wasn't good. "Let's take a look then."

Aiyre slowly unwrapped the bandage, having to lift Ezi's leg every once in a while. Ezi would wince, but she put on a brave face when Aiyre knew the leg had to be extremely painful.

Aiyre tried to keep her face expressionless as the last bandage fell away. The wound had turned a weird shade of purple around the edges. "Can you feel this?" She gave a light poke to the discolored leg.

"Maybe. I don't know. Did you do something?"

"Let's hope they do bring their shaman, and they don't wait two days to do it." Aiyre couldn't believe how bad Ezi's leg had gotten. It was a weird shade of purple, something Aiyre had never seen before.

"And if they take two days?" Ezi asked her voice barely a whisper, but Aiyre could hear the fear in there.

"Maybe I should head out and see if I can make it to the nearest clan. They're human, but they should have a healer, someone who can help with this. If the sabertooths take too long, you might... die." And Aiyre couldn't handle another death in their clan.

"I should be more scared than I am."

"Because you're brave."

"Or because no matter how you look at our lives, everything seems scary."

Aiyre cocked her head to the side. "It is true. Our lives keep taking unexpected turns."

"In this latest turn, we have two overly interested sabertooth shifters."

Aiyre frowned. She really didn't want to think about Daerk. "Do you want me to do something about Tor?"

"What could you do?"

"I could attempt to kill him." Aiyre would do anything to keep them safe.

"Then the others would just kill you." Ezi snorted, but she wasn't thinking about her leg anymore, and that was all Aiyre was trying to do. True. "I don't know of any other way to get him to lose interest in you, because you're right, he does seem enamored."

"Then don't worry about it for now. Besides, I might be able to convince him to go away." A twinkle entered her eyes.

"How?" Aiyre was curious. Maybe she could use the same tactic on Daerk.

"I could be pregnant."

Or not.

"You only spent one night with Drakk." Aiyre was skeptical. She'd known plenty of couples who waited months, sometimes even years, before the gods blessed them with children.

"But we... a few times that night." Ezi shrugged, a light blush staining her cheeks. "You never know. He may have left a part of himself with me," Ezi rubbed her stomach fondly, "and what other man would be interested in that?"

"You'd be surprised."

Ezi cocked an eyebrow at her.

"Daerk told me about... sabertooth matings. They have mates. As in someone who is destined to be with them."

"So... Tor's interest in me could be more than just thinking I'm pretty to look at?" Ezi bit her bottom lip as she waited for Aiyre to respond.

"Yes."

"I'm not ready for anything. It's too soon." Ezi shook her head and looked like a rabbit who had just been told it was tonight's supper.

Aiyre rushed to calm her friend before she tried to flee the cave in a panic. "We'll explain it to them. They have no idea you were recently joined and just lost your partner. It might make Tor back off, or I can ask Daerk to make him leave you alone."

A new worry entered Ezi's eyes. "But who will make Daerk leave you alone?" She asked.

Aiyre bit her lip and didn't answer, turning back to the task of rewrapping Ezi's bandages.

A couple of hours passed, and when Ezi's condition wasn't getting any better, Aiyre decided they couldn't wait. She was beginning to think she might have to find someone else to help them in case the sabertooths didn't come back soon enough.

Aiyre took all her clothes off as she rushed to her feet.

"What are you doing?" Ezi placed her hands behind her, ready to dart to her feet.

"Seeing if there is anyone else around we can ask to help us." Aiyre motioned her to sit. "You just sit there and don't irritate your leg."

"Don't think the sabertooths will come back?"

"I can't rely on them solely. They may not be able to get away from their village, and your wound is beyond anything I know how to heal." Aiyre wasn't sure Ezi would live, even if Aiyre tried to tend her wound all day and night long.

"Should I expect you back here at some point?"

"I shouldn't be longer than two days. You have plenty of wood in here, and food." Aiyre glanced over to their water bags. "And plenty of water."

"See you soon, then." Ezi sent her a weak smile, and it looked like the color of her eyes were already growing dull.

Aiyre finished ripping off her clothes and let the shift overtake her. Her snout grew longer, her long ears sprang up on top of her head, and fur spread over her skin. Once she was done, she gave her body a good shake.

longer? She wouldn't have one at all in human form!

With one last look over her shoulder at Ezi, Aiyre bounded out of the cave, her hooves clinking against the stone floor, and then she entered the snowy world around them.

Her legs were built for this though. They were long and slender and allowed her to bound through the snow with speed. She'd be able to cover more ground in her pronghorn form rather than in her human form. Not to mention how good it felt to be in her second skin. It was so freeing.

The snow was falling again, hindering how far she could see and what she was able to smell. All she had to do was either be back before Daerk or find another clan to assist them.

Chapter 8

Daerk and his men strode back into their village. He wanted no one to suspect he had a secret to hide. All they had done was go out for a hunt, and that was all anyone would know.

"Where have you been?" Mira sauntered around the backside of a hut.

"We've brought back some bear meat for the village," Daerk explained, knowing she would most likely report back to Brog. It was no secret Mira liked to get around and win favors with whoever she deemed in charge.

"If you keep hunting like this, we might not have a problem this winter." She tossed him a smile that rounded her cheeks, the freckles on her skin stood out.

"Doubtful." Rir strode up to save him from the woman. "The mammoths have moved further south this winter, and a lot of bigger game are joining them. One lonely bear isn't much hope."

"I thought with the pronghorn clan gone our meat hut would be full again?" Mira grabbed a hold of his arm.

Daerk detangled her fingers from his arm one by one while he tried not to snap her fingers since she was hanging on like a tar pit. "It was wishful thinking at best, Mira. They had nothing to do with the dwindling supply of food. The harsh winter is driving the game further south than we can reach."

She sent him a shocked look. Yes, he disagreed with Brog, it wasn't like it was a secret.

Two words

Daerk strode away before she could talk to him anymore and get himself into any more trouble. She was sure to let Brog know that he still didn't agree with the handling of the pronghorn clan, but how could he?

That situation had been handled all wrong. Killing another clan? Children, women, and elders? It was cruel, nothing more.

He dragged the meat behind him, as he made his way to the meat hut. It was time to stick some more meat in there. Every little bit was better than nothing, and he was going to do his best to make sure his clan made it through the harsh winter.

Pushing through the tent's flaps, he brought the meat into the smoky and warm tent. Looking up he found a clanmate tending a fire, smoking the meat that had already been laid out over wooden poles.

"Where would you like this, Ryion?"

The other man looked up and sent him a broad smile. "Just leave it by the door, and I will take care of it."

Daerk hefted the large amount of meat inside the tent. Then he turned to leave, but Ryion stopped him with a cough.

"Be careful how you tread around Brog. He's been watching you more frequently, and I fear your hunting trips might cause him to lash out."

Daerk scoffed. "Brog can try to scare me, but I'm not going to let him. Someone has to feed this clan, and I'm not going to let him stop me. We've had several additions to the clan only this last spring, and the women and children will need food."

"I just want you to be careful." Ryion shook his head. "Now that he's killed a whole clan, I fear he might just decide to set his eyes on you."

"I thank you for your concern, and I promise to be careful." And he would be.

Ryion was one of the elders in the clan, and Daerk would take his advice into consideration. He knew he was testing Brog's patience, but his clan needed someone to care about their survival.

He headed out of the warm meat tent. Now he needed to find Eron, the clan shaman. Eron was the one who would be able to assist the injured pronghorn woman.

It was unfortunate his mate was a pronghorn shifter because bringing her among his clanmates could be an issue. Yet he knew the moment Brog and his men were gone, his clanmates wouldn't be scared into hatred.

Before Brog had come into power Daerk had always remembered an accepting and loving clan. Once they had the freedom to express their feelings, the clan would open up to outsiders, and he'd be able to bring his mate here.

Daerk made his way through the village until he reached Eron's tent. Pushing aside the tent flap he glanced in to find the tent empty, without even a flicker of light from his fire. He hadn't been here in a long time then.

"Is he here?"

Daerk turned to find Tor right behind him, trying to glance over his shoulder and into the tent.

"No, he isn't. He must be in the caves."

"We should go to him right away." Tor's eyes looked frantic.

"Be calm, my friend." Daerk glanced around to make sure no one was close enough to listen in to his conversation. "The pronghorns don't have mates, which means we will have a long journey ahead of us. Make sure you aren't rushing her into anything."

Tor shook his head. "It might be a journey, but I am pleased with her looks. I only wish she wasn't injured. I would hate to lose my mate moments after I found her. We must get Eron to her before she gets worse." A bit more panic entered his friend's eyes.

Daerk couldn't agree more, but he also hoped bringing Eron would prove to Aiyre that he meant to help her and wasn't involved in the initial attack on her people.

Quickly, the both of them made their way through the village and to the edge of the forest.

"If he isn't at the caves, where else might he be?" Tor asked.

"Let's get to that if we have to, otherwise let us not think about it." Daerk really hoped Eron would be in the caves because there was no time to waste if they wanted to save Ezi.

He glanced over at his longtime friend, Tor, and prayed to all the gods he knew of that his friend wouldn't lose his mate right after finding her. It would be a hard blow for a mate to take.

He'd seen his mother have to deal with the death of his father after a hunting accident, and the only thing that helped her through the ordeal was her children. Tor didn't have children to ground him if he lost his mate.

Thankfully, the caves weren't too far away from the village, and it took them barely anytime to get there.

Two words!

Daerk strode into the pitch-dark cave. He'd grown up traversing the length of these caves, and he was sure of every step he took down the dark path. Tor trailed right behind him.

"What if he is in the middle of a ceremony?" Tor whispered in the dark. "We might anger him... or the gods."

"This involves your mate. Eron will understand if we interrupt him, and I have no doubt the gods will understand as well. Or they wouldn't have given us mates." Daerk did not doubt that Eron would assist them, even if it went against Brog and especially because it involved mates. There was nothing more important than one's mate, except maybe one's offspring.

That thought had him smiling. He could just imagine Aiyre full with his child. He'd waited a long time to find his mate so he could finally begin a family... a huge family. He wanted as many children as Aiyre would provide him.

He couldn't wait to teach his children to hunt and show them all the secrets his father taught him. Daerk stopped mid-step causing Tor to run into his back.

"What is it?"

"Nothing." He continued walking down the corridor, his steps carrying down the stone tunnel.

"It was something." Tor pressed.

"I was thinking what offspring we would have with pronghorn mates."

Tor scoffed. "My first worry is saving my mate's life, then convincing her to be my mate, and finally worrying about our offspring."

Tor was right. Daerk was getting ahead of himself. He needed to worry first about winning over Aiyre, and then about their possible future offspring. He couldn't even worry about offspring if she didn't accept him.

"It doesn't worry you now, though?"

"Why would it? She'd still be my mate, and they'd still be my offspring. I'd treasure them no matter what." Tor's voice held such conviction that it moved Daerk.

"You couldn't take a pronghorn hunting in their animal form," He worried.

"They can still hunt in their human form," Tor replied.

They broke into the main chamber. The ceiling rose high above them with stalactites hanging down like jagged teeth, threatening to fall and smash anyone foolish enough to challenge them.

The cave was well-lit with animal fat torches burning brightly along the edges, and in the middle where Eron sat on a bear fur.

Eron was decked out in his ceremonial outfit, a sabertooth skull over his own, the teeth coming down the sides of his face, giving him a fearsome look in the flickering light, even though he was well past his prime.

"Eron," Daerk called out gently. He was intruding, and he didn't want to be too rude about it.

Eron's eyes opened. "What brings you here to me?"

Tor stepped forward. "I have found my mate, but she is injured to the point of dying. I am afraid she will not make it without your assistance." He rushed.

"Bring her to me then." Eron stood up from the fur.

"Both of our mates are from the pronghorn clan we just attacked," Daerk filled in. "We can't bring them here without Brog losing his mind and killing them both."

Eron stared at the both of them in silence for a few seconds and then shook his head. "Let me grab my herbs, and I will meet you both at the edge of the camp."

To Daerk's relief, it didn't take Eron too long to collect his things. He had to get back to his mate and lay eyes on her again, and he knew Tor felt the same way.

"How far are these mates?" Eron asked. He still looked in tip-top shape, but he'd slowly stopped traveling outside of the village unless it was an emergency. They'd been traveling through the snow for a while now, and Eron was beginning to huff and puff.

"Not too much further, I promise you." Daerk felt horrible dragging him all the way out here into the middle of nowhere, but neither he or Tor knew much about healing. Ask him to hunt down an animal for the clan, and he would be successful. Ask him to heal a broken bone, and he'd be lost.

"I think I can see a light." Tor squinted into the blowing snow.

Daerk glanced over at what Tor was seeing. "It must be the campfire inside the cave."

"Let's get a move on then," Eron grumbled as he pressed forward, the snow whipping his fur cloak around his frame.

Daerk hefted a bag over his shoulder. He'd managed to sneak out some more supplies which he was sure they would need sooner or later.

They trudged up the hill to the shining beacon of light. Shoving through the flap over the entrance of the cave Daerk's eyes eagerly searched for Aiyre, but came up empty.

Tor brushed past him to squat beside Ezi. "Ezi?" His voice took on a panicked tone.

Daerk forgot about Aiyre for a brief second as he turned his attention to the pair in front of him. Ezi looked like she was on death's door.

"You have to save her!" Tor barked at Eron his voice echoing off the rock walls of the cave.

Eron raised an eyebrow in Tor's direction, as he stoked the fire flooding the cave with heat. "Can you take over?" Eron handed Daerk the branch.

Then Eron squatted down next to Ezi as well.

As they examined her leg, Daerk glanced around the inside of the cave. Where was Aiyre? Was she further inside the cave? He couldn't see her leaving Ezi's side, at least not with all the commotion going on over here… unless she'd gone out into the snow for something.

He sniffed the air.

Her scent was still floating thickly through the air. If she had gone, she hadn't been gone for long.

"Who is there?" Ezi's eyes opened, but as she looked around, he could see they were glazed over.

"Is she blind?" Tor looked close to pulling out all of his hair.

Daerk hated seeing his friend like this. He could only hope Eron would save her life.

"She's just coping with the pain from her leg," Eron reassured him. ~lower case~

"Who's there?" ~She~ slurred.

~Sssh~ "Shhh... it's me, Tor, the sabertooth shifter from earlier." He reached out a hand to brush the side of her face, and she flinched away from his touch. Tor withdrew his hand, looking like she'd stabbed a stone dagger into his chest.

"Where is Aiyre?" Ezi asked them.

"I was hoping you could tell me." Daerk rose from beside the fire, unable to keep the irritation out of his voice. He got the feeling he wouldn't enjoy the answer.

"She didn't think you'd return soon enough to save my life, so she went out to search for help."

"How long has she been gone?"

"Since you left."

"Idiot." Daerk strode over to the mouth of the cave, then turned on his heel to glance back at the other two men. "Will either of you need me?"

"Go," Eron commanded as he bent over his pack of herbs.

With a nod, Daerk left the cave and welcomed the frigid air. Why couldn't his mate just sit still? He'd returned within a day of leaving, wasn't that fast enough for her?

Shedding his clothing, he let the shift overtake him. Slowly tan fur spread over his frame, and then his muscles and bones stretched. What seemed to take forever only lasted a mere second before he was able to launch himself into the deep snow.

His powerful legs kicked up snow, as he let his nose guide him. It was hard to pick up her scent with the constant snowfall, but he was determined and unwilling to let anything get in his way.

Chapter 9

Night had fallen, and Aiyre was starting to doubt her sanity. Even her pronghorn form was wishing for the warmth of the cave, but she had to press on. She wasn't about to go back without any help, and there had to be someone out there, someone who wouldn't be a sabertooth shifter.

She could only imagine being mated to such a beast. Those razor-sharp claws and teeth as long as her hand. It would be insane for either of them to think they had a future together. He was a born predator, and she was prey. longer.

She quivered at the very thought of his sabertooth form.

Aiyre hoped Ezi would make it. She was the last clanmate Aiyre had left, and this life was too harsh to go it alone.

A crunching of the snow had her ears perking up. They moved on top of her head, facing forwards, to the side, and then behind her, pinpointing where the noise was coming from. She slowly approached, her long slender legs easily picking their way through the snow.

Millions of flakes flew around her in the dark, but she was able to pick up the scent. It was just of a herd of horses. She relaxed a bit and easily made her way through the herd of horses without causing any alarm.

She was just another prey animal in her pronghorn form. There was no reason for them to care about her presence, and their presence gave her some more confidence.

It was rare for her to go off on her own. She'd always had clanmates to accompany her, so the company of the horses was welcomed.

She left the herd of horses behind, but then a neigh of alarm went up through the horse herd. Aiyre's ears perked back up as fear spread through her. What had the horse herd seen or smelled?

Giving the air around her a quick sniff she tried to pinpoint what it was but came up empty.

The herd bolted, kicking up massive amounts of snow as they fled the scene. All of them were in a panic. Her heart sped up.

Aiyre kicked herself into gear, splitting off from the group, hoping to disappear into the night.

She wasn't going to be that lucky. Her ears picked up something large following right after her. The moment she heard the growl behind her, her blood froze, but she kept moving. Something was coming after her. Her muscles started to burn with her exertions. She could feel her strength waning, so she turned to face her opponent.

A sabertooth cat's shadow could be seen sprinting towards her through the falling snow.

Aiyre readied herself for what might come next.

The sabertooth stopped. Was it a shifter? She still couldn't see it very well through the shifting snow. She sniffed the cold air, but only came up with the overwhelming scent of horses.

When the sabertooth approached her again, she leveled her head at it, brandishing her horns. They weren't much, but she hoped it would be enough to defend herself.

The sabertooth gave a huff of frustration and began to circle her. Quickly, she moved in a circle as well as she didn't want to let the sabertooth get a good attacking angle.

Why hadn't the sabertooth gone after the horses? The odds had been in her favor since the horse herd had been such a large group. Maybe separating from the herd hadn't been such a wise decision after all. Or the gods were just against her.

The sabertooth growled at her again and took a swipe at her with its massive claws. Shifter or not it looked ready to kill her, and she wasn't planning on being its next meal. — A pronghorn is far too small to fight a sabretooth in any way.

Raising up on her hind legs she tried to knock the sabertooth in the head with her hooves, but it quickly dodged her attempts and came back in to swipe a claw at her. It barely missed her thigh.

Aiyre jumped back into a sprint, hoping to gain some distance with her surprise leap into action, but the sabertooth was quick to jump in front of her path and stop her.

She was going to die out here, and Ezi was probably going to die as well. There went the last of their clan.

The sabertooth launched itself at her, claws extended. She turned to dodge, but one of the claws latched onto her thigh, yanking free a piece of skin. She let out a yelp of pain, almost shifting back into her human form with the force of the pain shooting through her.

Dislodging herself from its claw, she faced it as it made another lunge at her. She put her head down, hoping to at least do it a little harm before it claimed her as its next snack.

Another sabertooth flew out of nowhere and began attacking the first with a fury.

It stopped her short for a couple of seconds, and then she got her butt moving. She needed to now find some shelter so she could tend to the wound on her thigh. She also needed to get as far as she could from these two sabertooths who were fighting over her. She wasn't ready to be either of their snacks.

Limping away from the fight she tried in vain to find somewhere to hide herself away. She wasn't about to stick around and see which one won the rights to eat her.

Daerk had heard the scream of an animal and raced over to make sure it wasn't Aiyre, but it had been. He was just glad she was still alive when he got on the scene. His heart had nearly stopped when he'd scented her in a fight with a wild sabertooth.

Foreleg

The wild sabertooth took a swing at his head with a massive paw of razor-sharp claws, and he dodged before hooking his own claws into the wild sabertooth. He tore some flesh from the sabertooth's forearm, and then it bolted into the snowflakes, not wanting to risk death.

It was for the best. It may have tried to eat his mate, but it was only a wild animal trying to survive. He didn't want to kill the sabertooth, since his clan respected them.

Turning around he looked around the area and found Aiyre gone. He understood her being scared and fleeing, but now he was going to have to find her all over again. He shook his head as he growled.

The gods had given him a frustrating mate. She was independent and willing to do anything for her clanmate, even if it might put her in danger. Despite her frustrating traits, he had to admire her for her tenacity.

Sticking his black nose in the air, he sniffed the air. In no time, he picked up on her scent... and blood. His stomach rolled. He had no idea how injured she was before she ran off. Maybe she was bleeding to death right now.

Snow flew behind him as he charged into the dark, letting his nose lead him.

Then he spotted her as the snow died down a little bit. She was laying on the ground in her human form. This was bad. Shifting into his human form, he dealt with the cold shoving it from his mind. Nothing was more important than seeing to his mate.

"Aiyre?"

Her eyes flew open. "You found me."

"Of course." He bent down next to her to examine her thigh.

"I wasn't sure you'd return in time to save Ezi, so I left to find help." She explained as she brought her arms up to hug herself in the cold.

"I know." Her wound was bleeding a fair bit. It wasn't large, but it still worried him. "If I shift, will you be able to wrap your arms around my neck?"

She nodded stiffly. "My arms are working just fine."

Now he would just have to get her back to the cave before she froze to death.

Daerk shifted back into his sabertooth form and laid down next to her so that she could wrap her arms around his neck. Once she was in place, holding onto his fur with a solid grip, he tore off through the night. He was getting them back to the cave.

"You're so warm." Aiyre murmured as she snuggled her face against the fur around his neck.

He chuffed in amusement wishing he could say more, but unable to in this form. He also wished she was in a more sound mind, rather than freezing, so he could get her used to his sabertooth form. After the attack on her people, he wanted to make sure she didn't fear his other form, because his sabertooth would do anything to keep her safe.

※ ※ ※

Aiyre was freezing. Her front was pressed against his warm fur, but her backside was almost painful with the cold night air rushing past them. She wasn't sure how much longer she would be able to hold onto his fur.

Slowly, she felt her fingers start to slip, and she knew they were nowhere close to the cave. She tried to tighten her hold on his fur, but her fingers were too frozen for her to move them.

Her fingers slipped all the way, and she flew off his backside.

Daerk rounded, and she got a good visual of his sabertooth form. He was definitely intimidating in this form. Those long canines of his draped well below his jawline.

It brought back memories of the night when her people were attacked, and she'd been faced with killing sabertooths or dying.

He shifted into his human form and bent down next to her. "How are you?" His eyes skimmed over her, and she could read the worry in those depths.

"Cold." Her body shivered uncontrollably, and she couldn't get her pronghorn to shift. The thing was being stubborn, refusing to show up.

He glanced around, and then picked her up in his arms and carried her through the snow.

"Aren't you freezing?" She asked, her teeth going a mile a minute with the cold that was racking her body.

"I am."

"You should just leave me and see to yourself. It was my fault coming out here. I should've believed you would return as quickly as you could."

"I'm your mate." His gold eyes glanced down at her, their depths full of intensity. "Leaving you to fend for yourself in the cold was never going to happen." He sent her a wink. "Even if you did something stupid."

"Thank you." She nuzzled her face against his warm chest.

She was too cold right now to have boundaries, and the blood loss wasn't helping, but at least she could feel it scabbing over… more like freezing over. Hopefully, she wouldn't lose any more blood now.

He took them into a nearby forest, placed her on the snow, and then went about clearing an area of snow. Once he reached the ground, he picked her back up and placed her on the ground.

Daerk gathered as much wood as would fit in his arms. She watched on as he got a fire going, the flames reaching sky high as he continued to build up the fire into a bonfire. The nearby snow started to melt, and she was able to feel the heat from the fire reaching out to defend them from the winter.

He walked over to her and laid down against her back as her front was warmed from the fire.

"Won't you be cold back there?" She asked, her teeth had finally stopped chattering, but she was still freezing.

"Yes, but would you be comfortable with me enough to let me shift back into my sabertooth form?" His voice held a hopefulness that choked her a bit. He was being so attentive and sweet to her.

"I will be fine with it." Mainly, because she would be warmer with him in his sabertooth form.

"It would be best if you could change back into your pronghorn form as well." He advised as he moved away from her.

"I'll give it a try." She just hoped her pronghorn side would shift willingly. Aiyre focused in on her pronghorn side, and with a little effort, she let the shift come over her until her skin was covered by a protective layer of soft brown fur.

She heard nothing from behind her until something large and furry curved around her backside.

Aiyre was tempted to look behind her and examine his sabertooth form, but at the same time, she was too scared. Her heart pounded away in her chest, and she had no doubt he could hear it. Her pronghorn was not happy about this. It continued to protest cuddling with a sabertooth, no matter how much she told it to be quiet.

Daerk might be her mate, but that didn't mean he couldn't still be intimidating. Her pronghorn knew what he could do, even if she kept trying to tell it there was nothing to fear. If he'd wanted to kill her, he'd had plenty of chances.

She snuggled her back against him anyway, because he was warm and he was saving her life. With both him and the fire she had no trouble warming back up.

After less than an hour, he moved behind her, and then came around, signaling that she should get back on top of him.

Aiyre shifted back into her human form, goosebumps spreading over her skin instantly. "Already?" She was so warm and cozy where she was.

He chuffed through his nose.

"Fine." Aiyre climbed back on top of him and wrapped her arms around his neck. Her fingers were warm and nimble, and she was able to get a good hold on his fur.

Then he shot off, the cold air once more chilling her bare skin. She couldn't wait to get back to the cave and get some fur clothing back over her bare skin.

Thankfully, it didn't take them much longer to reach the cave, but it was long enough for Aiyre to regret her decision to leave the cave. Her nose was completely frozen, and she could feel icicles forming on her braid and eyelashes. She needed the warmth of a fire again.

Once they arrived at the mouth of the cave, she slipped off his back, her muscles frozen from the cold, and she walked stiffly inside the cave. She went straight for her fur clothing, which she quickly slipped on before rushing over to the fire to enjoy the warmth pouring off of it.

Daerk followed her in and grabbed his own clothing, but not before she got an eyeful of pure muscle and a nice-sized member dangling between his thighs. She found it a bit difficult to swallow, her gaze completely glued to the sight before her.

He sent her a smirk when he caught her staring at him, before he covered up. She found herself wishing for more time to take in the view his body had given her. Her lips tingled in delight as she thought about him demanding her surrender as he pushed her up against a cave wall.

"Aiyre?" Ezi's weak voice broke through to her shaking her out of her erotic thoughts.

"Yes?" Aiyre looked over at her longtime friend. Ezi's eyes finally looked clear, and her leg even looked a bit better with less of a purple tinge and back to looking like healthy pink skin.

"Are you alright?"

"Am I alright?" Aiyre shook her head confused by the question. "You should be more concerned about yourself."

"But your leg." Ezi pointed at her. "I saw it when you came rushing in." Ezi reminded her of her own injury.

"Oh." Aiyre looked down at her thigh where a red mark was slowly growing across her leather pants. Then the pain started to come back as she stared at the wound.

Daerk grabbed a fur blanket and held it up in front of her.

"What are you doing?" She asked as she frowned up at him.

"Making sure you can take your pants back off without an audience, and so Eron can take a look at the claw mark on your thigh."

She raised an eyebrow. "We're shifters. We're used to being naked."

His gold eyes just stared down at her.

Quickly, Aiyre shed the pants, and then took the fur blanket from him, so she could sit back down and keep everything covered except for her injured thigh. She got the feeling he was being stingy about nakedness just because they were mates. Which would have to change, because being a shifter meant a lot of running around in the nude.

The man named Eron made his way over to her with a pack of supplies, pushing past Daerk. Daerk moved around her so he could get a better visual while Eron had room to work on her leg.

"Your shaman?" She asked as she looked up at him.

"Yes." He folded his arms in front of his chest, his eyes never leaving the mark on her thigh.

Eron looked up at her. His eyes were a striking blue, and he had a shock of blonde hair that was going grey on his head. He had a kind face, aged by time, but still keeping features of a once-dashing man.

"How is it?" Daerk asked on her behalf sounding more concerned than she felt.

"It's fine." She remarked. It was little more than a scratch. It had just shocked her system. She'd thought she was going to die and her pronghorn side hadn't been sure which form would save her best.

"You aren't a healer." Daerk shushed her.

"She is right. It will be fine with time to heal. It looks like it was just the upper layer of skin. I will still wrap it to make sure infection stays away." Eron began mashing some herbs together.

"Good."

She glanced up to see relief wash over Daerk's face. Her heart pinched in her chest. He'd been worried about her, and for some reason, it caused her heart to putter in an arrhythmic beat. Despite what he might be, she found herself feeling special with all the worry and attention he sent her way.

"What happened out there?" Tor surged onto his feet and rushed over to take a look at her wound.

"A wild sabertooth got a claw into her thigh," Daerk growled, both at her and the fact that he hadn't prevented the injury. His hands moved to his hips as he glared down at her.

"I'm guessing you saved her?" Tor glanced between them.

"Yes! He saved me!" Aiyre vented. "I wasn't the one who defeated the sabertooth."

"Feel better?" Daerk asked as he folded his arms in front of his chest and raised an eyebrow in response to her temper tantrum.

"I do." She glared up at all of them.

"You could have given me some time," Daerk grumbled. "I told you I'd be back with help."

"I was afraid she wouldn't live long enough. You said it might take two days, and I didn't think she had two days." Her nose wrinkled as she smelled the mash of herbs Eron was placing over her wound. It smelled like rotting flesh.

Then he wrapped up her thigh in a strip of leather.

"That should stave off any infection, but let me know if you feel any pain or see anything change, like color or odor," Eron informed her. Then his eyes landed on the old wound on her arm, but after a quick inspection, he didn't deem it necessary to worry about it. Eron rose and went back over to Ezi to check her bandaging.

"I don't think I'll be able to smell an odor change with that paste." Aiyre scrunched up her nose some more as she leaned away from the herb mash on her leg.

Eron glanced over his shoulder as he rolled his eyes. "Breath normally, and you will get used to the smell." Then he turned back to Ezi.

Breathe

"Will she be able to use that leg again?" Aiyre asked as Daerk held up the fur blanket so she could get her pants back on with privacy.

She rolled her eyes. He was going to have to get over hiding her body.

"We will have to see," Eron said, making no promises. "It appears to just be a twisted ankle, and the wound is healing, so everything should be fine."

Ezi smiled. "It will all be fine."

Aiyre wasn't so sure about that. Not being able to move around without help would irritate her past insanity, and she feared Ezi would be no different.

Daerk didn't seem able to keep his eyes off of her, and it made her feel uncomfortable, more because she was finding it hard to keep her eyes off of him as well. The damn sabertooth was too good-looking for his own good.

"Are you hungry?" He squatted beside her, and she breathed in his masculine scent eagerly as it flowed around her, weaving a spell over her.

He was definitely someone to fear because she could feel an attraction pulling her closer despite her best intentions to keep away. And that scared her witless. He may have been one of the sabertooths involved in murdering her clanmates... although she was beginning to wonder if that was just something she was telling herself falsely.

He'd still given her no reason to believe he was a man who would be involved in such a cruel attack.

"Yes. I need something to eat."

Daerk pushed himself back up to his feet and made his way out of the cave, and then came back inside with some frozen pieces of bear meat. He stuck them on a branch and placed them over the fire. Then he came back to sit down next to her.

A little too close. Aiyre scooted away.

"What you did may have been foolish, but it was brave as well," Daerk murmured.

"Was it?" She figured it had been a bit harebrained.

"It was." He turned his head so his golden eyes could run over her. "You wanted to save her life. I respect you for being so kind and loving to a clanmate. Such dedication is a good trait for a mate."

Aiyre's nose crinkled. "I don't know how you plan on this working. Your clan won't accept us." She pointed between them.

"You don't know my clan." He shook his head, as his golden eyes bored into her. "Our current leader has led them astray, made them afraid, and fed them lies about yours. What they need is to see the truth and have the peace of mind that their leader won't kill them for speaking their mind." ~~minds~~

She cocked her head to the side as she fiddled with her braid. "And how do you plan on making such an environment safe for us? We would never be able to defend ourselves against a clan of sabertooths, if they decided they didn't want us among them."

Daerk leaned towards the fire and tested the meat with a finger, and then put the branch holding the meat back over the flames. "I agree that it would be hard to bring you into the clan, but staying out here and starting our own clan would be a lot harder and dangerous."

"Or Ezi and I could leave and find another pronghorn clan to join." Aiyre tossed out the other option. No-one had short hair during the Ice Age!

"And Tor and I should be happy with such an idea?" Daerk snorted as he shook his head of short brown hair. "To let our mates out of our sight and hope life goes well for you? To miss our opportunity to have offspring with our mates?" She watched the muscles in his neck tense at the very idea.

Ezi had been right then. She was Daerk's mate, and Ezi was Tor's mate. The gods must be insane. Then again, she'd always been taught she should have faith and believe their gods would do what needed to be done. But a sabertooth mate? She wasn't sure they were right about that.

"You could have another woman," Aiyre argued.

"Could I?" He arched an eyebrow. "Your people have no mates, yet you assume you know how it feels." He leaned in close, their noses almost touching. "Having a mate is like having a piece of you outside of your chest, a part you now need to keep safe, a drive inside of you pushing you to claim your mate, to keep her in your arms, and to fill her with offspring. I will never just let you go."

Aiyre gulped. His voice was full of passion, and she believed every word he uttered. This had clearly been something he had been striving for his entire life. And it made her worry he wasn't about to let her go. Not that she had anywhere to go now that she was clanless.

Daerk backed off and examined the meat again. Determining it was ready, he took off a piece and held it out to her. She tried to take it with a hand, but he withdrew the meat and shook his head.

He held it back out and brought it up to her lips, a wicked gleam entering his eyes. She opened her mouth and let him place the piece inside her mouth. Her lips closed around his fingers as she took the meat from him.

Daerk sent her a heated glance, a fire burning deep in his golden eyes.

She felt her stomach flitter around in excitement, and she turned her gaze over to where Ezi was sitting against a cave wall. Ezi was staring directly at them and raised an eyebrow in Aiyre's direction.

Aiyre had no idea what was going on, so she shrugged her shoulders in response. She got the feeling it would be only a matter of time before things between them heated up. His eyes didn't just watch her. They caressed her with every glance.

He fed her a couple more pieces of the bear meat, seeming to get some joy out of the action, and she was hungry enough not to care that he was hand-feeding her. He held out another piece, and she slipped her lips around his fingers before taking the meat with her teeth. As she pulled away, she bit her lip and watched as his eyes flickered down to the small movement.

"Would you like more?" He asked.

Aiyre shook her head. "I think I just need some rest after such an exciting day." More like thrilling. She was tired, and the heated looks he sent her way were going straight to her head, confusing her. She needed to remember he was a sabertooth and from a clan that had murdered hers.

He inclined his head, but his eyes never left the sight of her.

She settled down for sleep near the fire, as everyone else settled down for the night. It was peaceful, and she found herself relaxing for the first time in days. Here she thought she might spend the rest of winter alone.

Daerk settled near her, but she found it surprisingly comforting to have him not far away. Even her pronghorn was warming up to him after his recent save of her life.

Chapter 10

Aiyre woke slowly as she felt movement near her. Looking over her shoulder, she watched as Daerk rose and made his way further into the darkness of the cave. He disappeared into the murky darkness where the firelight didn't reach.

She wanted to roll over and ignore him, but... she was intrigued and had to know what he was doing. She sat up on an elbow and watched his shadow disappear around a corner in the dark recesses of the cave. She rolled her eyes. Why did sabertooths have to be so strange?

She laid her head back down on her fur and tried to get back to sleep, but she couldn't. She had to find out what he was up to back there.

Curiosity pulled her off her fur. She quietly padded her way to the back of the cave and peered around the corner, and there he was, just standing, looking at her with those eyes that sent shivers racing over every inch of her skin.

"Hello," His deep voice greeted her, almost seeming to purr at the end.

She found her feet pulling her further around the corner. "What are you doing back here?"

"Wishing to the gods you would join me and glad my wish came true." His heated eyes washed over her.

Aiyre found herself smiling. "Why?" She had some ideas, but she wanted to hear it come out of his mouth.

"To see if my mate would accept me." His hands reached out, and he lightly grabbed onto her shirt, pulling her further into the dark.

His head dipped, and he placed a kiss against her lips. Aiyre wasn't too sure what to do with herself. He pulled away, and then came back for another kiss when she didn't protest his attentions.

She was curious, and maybe it was because she had sleep still fogging her mind, but she wanted to explore more of this. Recently, she'd been faced with death, escaped that barely both times, and now she was facing a possible life of loneliness unless she accepted this matehood.

Right now, all she wanted was to feel loved and enjoy the presence of another. After all the death in her life, she was ready to enjoy life, even if he was a sabertooth. She was desperate for a connection, any connection.

Their lips melded together, and she felt her toes curl in excitement as his hot lips coaxed hers to open her mouth. It was something new, something she wanted more of, and she could care less that it was a sabertooth causing her to feel this way.

One of his hands weaved its way into her hair and massaged the back of her scalp. He growled when his hand encountered the braid, "We need to set your hair loose."

"Mmm-hmmm," She agreed, her mind going hazy with lust. She'd probably agree with anything he said at this moment.

"You taste so sweet," Daerk murmured against her lips. His tongue flickered against the crease of her mouth, and she opened her mouth, allowing him access.

His tongue darted in and played with hers before retreating back to his own mouth. Playing with her and teasing her.

As they kissed, his hands worked their way through her braid until her hair was set loose around her shoulders, and he was able to run his hands through the strands. "Much better," He growled.

Then his hands moved down to the hem of her shirt and pulled the fur shirt up and over her head. He let it drop to the floor of the cave.

Cold air rushed up and brushed over her nipples, puckering them. She sucked in a sharp breath at the sensation rolling over her. She'd been naked in front of men before, but not in front of a man who was staring at her like he'd never seen anything prettier.

His hand came up and played with her hot flesh. "You are so toned, yet you have such soft areas on your body," He growled. The enjoyment in his voice pleased her all the way to her toes.

* * *

Daerk couldn't believe it. He was finally about to enjoy his mate for the first time, and he was having a hard time containing his absolute delight. Images of her naked body flashed in his mind's eye. He couldn't wait to have her panting underneath his body as he drove his hard shaft into her wet and welcoming sheath.

The moment her shirt was off of her body, his hands had a mind of their own. They molded and cupped her full breasts. His thumbs rubbed over the hard nipples, causing Aiyre's mouth to pop wide.

Daerk smiled. This was better than any fantasy he could have ever imagined. Soon his tent would be filled to the brim with children, and he wouldn't have to spend another night alone. But maybe he was getting ahead of himself. Just because she spent a night with him didn't mean he'd won her heart.

His cock had gone hard a long while ago. Now all he could think about was seeking his release, but he also wanted to explore his mate. This would be their first joining, and he didn't want to rush it and have it be their last. This was his opportunity to sway her mind and heart into trusting him.

All he sought was her pleasure and happiness.

His hands stroked down to her waist, and then stroked their way to her butt, which he gave a light squeeze. He'd been telling the truth when he said her softer curves had pleased him. She was toned from a life of living in their harsh world, but she still had a layer of pleasing flesh.

Daerk quickly made short work of her pants, dropping them to the cave floor and leaving her naked in front of him.

"Undress me." He commanded her.

Aiyre stepped forward and put her hands at the hem of his fur shirt. She paused, and for a second he thought she might back out of what they were doing, but then she pulled the shirt up. He bowed his back so she could get the fabric off his tall frame without struggling on her tiptoes.

She flung it across the cave, and he smirked. "Eager?"

Her tongue darted out to lick her lips. "How can I be eager when I have no idea what I am getting into?"

"You have yet to be with a man?" He found it surprising, to say the least. "As part of an unmated species, I would have expected you to have several partners by now." Not that he wasn't pleased to find it was the opposite.

She shrugged her shoulders. "I was too focused on other things, like proving myself to my clanmates."

"Why?" He wanted her, but he needed to know her as well. They were about to spend a lifetime together, but he wanted to know everything about her as quickly as he could.

"They took me in when I was a child. She admitted. "When they could have just let nature take its course."

His heart went out to her. Not only had she lost one family, but then his people had killed her second family, but if she were willing he would eagerly make her feel loved and welcomed. All she had to do was accept him.

"Come, let me take your mind off such troubling problems." He reached out a hand coaxing her towards him.

She stepped closer, and he directed her hands to his pants. Soon they would both be naked, and then he would be able to show her exactly what he could offer her between the furs.

Aiyre untied the leather strap and sank to her knees as she pulled his pants down his legs. He stepped out of them and kicked the pants across the cave floor.

Her eyes focused in on his cock, and he felt it jump eagerly in front of her gaze. "Like what you see?" He held his breath.

"Yes." She sighed, her soft brown eyes just staring at his rigid length.

"Suck on it." He commanded her again. The image kept flashing through his mind, and he hoped she would. After she'd sucked on his fingers as he'd hand-fed her earlier in the night, all he could think about was her doing the same to his cock.

Her head dipped closer, then her hand took hold of his hard length, and she guided it in between her soft lips.

night-time

Daerk groaned but tried not to make too much noise. He knew she wouldn't want them advertising their nighttime encounter to the sleeping occupants of the cave further down the corridor. And he definitely didn't want her to cut this short because she was afraid the others would find out what they'd shared.

The tip of his cock entered her wet hot mouth, and he nearly came right there. It was pure bliss. His teeth gritted against each other, as her sweet little tongue swirled around the tip of his shaft.

For a woman who hadn't been with a man, she had a natural talent of pleasing him. Her mouth went up and down on his cock as her hand followed close behind.

Placing his hands on her shoulders, he pushed her away.

Lower case

"Did you enjoy it?" She asked, her brown eyes tipping up as the tip of her tongue licked her lips delicately.

"Too much." He smiled down at her. "Lie down." He directed her. Just a few seconds of her sucking on his cock and he felt ready to burst.

She obeyed him, laying down on her back on some of their discarded clothing, her brown eyes filled to the brim with expectation and desire. She was as ready as he was, and it sent his sabertooth purring with pleasure.

He bent down next to her, his cock still straining for release. Her mouth had given him a taste of the pleasure he would enjoy inside her hot sheath. His finger ventured to the junction of her thighs, dipping between her plump lips and feeling the moisture that had collected between them.

"So hot," Daerk whispered his voice taking on an animalistic growl. His inner sabertooth purred with satisfaction demanding to be heard by their mate.

His finger slid up and down her lips spreading her wetness about, and then he found the nub at the top of her lips. When he circled it with a fingertip, she sucked in a harsh breath and then arched her back against his hand as pleasure shot through her.

He could smell her desire rising. His sabertooth purred some more.

Daerk continued to rub the pad of his finger against her nub, wringing out moan after moan from her lips. Bending over her he captured her mouth with his before she woke the people down the corridor with the pleasure that was building inside her sweet little body.

Aiyre trembled below him, as he felt her thighs clench around his hand. She came quickly, quivering around his hand, as she moaned into his mouth. His sabertooth reveled in her sounds of bliss.

Once she finished, he pulled away, a smile dancing across his lips. "You are an amazing mate."

Aiyre blushed under his praise. "And you?" She asked. She was eager to do more, before she backed out… not that she thought she would. She was so hot and bothered. She'd come, but now she wanted to bring him to climax as well.

"Are you ready for me?" His fingers brushed over her slickness, causing her back to arch again as he lightly touched her sensitive nub. "You feel ready." He purred, his golden eyes gone a shade darker, and she could swear she saw the sabertooth inside him ready to pounce. Her inner pronghorn quivered.

"I'm ready." Her mind had gone nearly blank with the pleasure he'd been basking her in, and she wanted to feel him fill her.

Daerk moved over her, placing himself between the juncture of her thighs. "I've dreamt of this moment for most of my life, and I could never have imagined a more perfect mate."

Aiyre blushed at the emotion in his voice. She hoped she wasn't leading him on by sharing this night with him. She was in need and wanted him, but she still wasn't sure what life a sabertooth and a pronghorn could share together.

She'd just take it one step at a time and see where it led.

"Please." She begged him. She was tired of talking, and just wanted more of what he could offer her.

His head dipped down, and he captured a nipple with his mouth, sucking it deep into his mouth and gave it a slight nip with his teeth. Then he let go of it with a wet pop.

Aiyre wanted him to capture more than just her nipple. She wanted him to claim her, to mark her as his own. She may have already come once, but her body was ready for a second time. She could have never imagined it was so amazing to lay with a man. She'd been too focused on proving herself as a hunter to her clan.

Kissing his way down from her breast, she felt her skin tremble under his administrations.

"I need you." He mumbled against her hot flesh.

"Yes." She panted.

Aiyre felt the tip of his member prod her hot entrance. She trembled below him from excitement, but also a little apprehension. Sucking in a calming breath, she prepared herself. There was no going back, once he entered her.

Slowly, Daerk eased into her entrance. Her mouth popped open as he stretched her entrance wide, and then her jaw clenched as he pressed against a barrier inside her sheath.

"Slow or fast?" He asked, sounding like he was on the brink of losing control. His words almost seemed more animalistic with the building tension inside of him. She got the feeling his sabertooth was right there with him.

"Fast." She decided, not exactly sure what he was speaking of and unsure what she should say.

Daerk's hands wrapped around her waist, and then he plunged into her entrance with one swift stroke. His lips captured her scream of brief pain, but he continued to plunge in and out of her, easing the pain away until pleasure once more soared through her body.

"You feel amazing." He groaned, as he continued to move inside her. The head of his cock stroking the ridges inside her.

Her head fell to the side, as pleasure washed over her mind. He drove his member to the hilt, their hips touching with every thrust inside her. Wave after wave of pleasure soared through her. Her hips moved with his thrusts, matching him with the same eagerness. She wanted nothing more than to come again.

Her hands came up to his shoulders, and she lightly scraped her nails down his back until she reached his well-toned buttocks. She squeezed them, spurring him on a little faster.

Suddenly, the pressure built until she couldn't take it anymore, and she felt her body shatter into a million pieces as her body closed down around his member.

He let out a groan, as he burst inside her. His hips kept thrusting into her, and she felt him shoot his seed deep into her. Her contractions milked every drop from him as he shattered around her.

Leaning down he pressed a soul-searing kiss to her lips. "I don't wish to withdraw." He laughed, and she could see the twinkle in his golden eyes despite the dark. "I've waited so long to be joined with my mate."

Aiyre laughed and pushed lightly on his shoulder. He rolled off of her, his member leaving her entrance. The moment it had gone, she felt as though she was missing something. But he didn't give her long to dwell on it, his arms wrapped around her, drawing her into his embrace.

"You laugh at me?" He asked as he nipped her earlobe with his teeth.

She swatted him with one of her hands. "We've only just met."

"You can't deny there is something here," he motioned between their still-hot bodies, "even though you pronghorns don't have mates."

He waited for her to deny it, but she couldn't! There was something between them, and it was the very reason why she'd slept with him. Something beyond their power was driving them together, and she cursed it. She wanted to hate him for what his clan had done, but it seemed impossible.

She snuggled her back against his chest, enjoying the warmth from his body which wrapped around her like the caress of a blanket. Turning around, she buried her face against his chest, his scent entering her eager nose. Her hands wandered over his chest, twisting lightly in the fine hairs that dotted his chest.

She could have stayed like that for years and never wanted for anything. Sadly, reality slowly came back to her as the high from what they shared wore off.

As much as she wanted to stay there in his arms, she knew she had to get dressed and go back to her place by the fire. If she fell asleep here, she might not wake before the others, and then what they did would be evident to the rest of the group.

Right now the only people who knew what they'd shared was just them, and she wanted it to stay that way for now.

Aiyre pulled away from his grasp.

"Where are you going?" He mumbled from where he was still laying sounding like he had almost fallen asleep.

"To go sleep beside the fire. Where it is warm."

"I can easily keep you warm right here." Daerk's arms opened as he welcomed her right back.

It was tempting to roll back up in his arms, but she had to keep her distance for now. The future was still unknown, and she wanted to keep her options open. Sharing his furs was one thing, but giving him hope of a future she couldn't promise was a whole other thing.

Aiyre rose and gathered her clothing from the cave floor.

Daerk groaned as he rolled over and rose to his feet as well. "My mate is shy and doesn't want the others to know." He surmised.

She glanced over her shoulder to see him sending her a smirk through the darkness.

"I'm not shy." She argued.

"No?" He slipped on his pants. "Why not stay in my arms then?"

"It's not because I'm shy… it's because I just slept with a sabertooth shifter." Aiyre slipped on her last piece of clothing and fled the area. Quickly, she made her way back to the front of the cave.

She glanced around, and everyone still appeared to be fast asleep. Tor was still near Ezi, but not too close to cause concern. She'd keep an eye on him though. She didn't need him unnerving her friend when she was injured both physically and emotionally.

Settling down she watched as Daerk made his way back to his spot next to the fire. He threw a couple more logs onto the dwindling flames, stoking it up a bit and spreading a wave of heat throughout the cave.

Aiyre put her head down on her fur and closed her eyes. Flashbacks of what they had done wouldn't leave her alone. They plagued her like a bad dream. She hadn't thought she would enjoy such a personal encounter with a sabertooth shifter, but she had.

Chapter 11

"My leg feels a lot better." Ezi sat up against the rock wall of the cave. Her feet kicked out towards the flames.

"I'm glad." Aiyre tossed her a smile.

Eron was again checking on Ezi's leg, which he had set. Her leg was now a normal color, and Aiyre hoped that was a good sign. The gods owed them some good luck after everything that had happened.

She took a bite of some meat and watched Daerk out of the corner of her eye. The blush that formed on her cheeks just wouldn't stay away. All she wanted to do was go back into the dark of the cave and strip naked with him again.

He caught her staring at him, and he sent her a wink.

She frowned.

"I was hoping Eron wouldn't mind coming back to my village to perform a death ceremony over my people. He may not be our shaman, but it would be better than nothing." Aiyre looked between Eron and Daerk.

Daerk looked over at Eron. "Would you mind?"

Eron shook his head. "I have everything I need to speak over their bodies." He patted the bag beside himself.

"Thank you." Aiyre was glad something would be done. Hopefully, no predators had found them by now, but there was little she could do about that. It was winter, and the ground was frozen solid, which wouldn't allow her the chance to give them a proper burial.

"I wish there was more we could do." Daerk handed her another chunk of cooked meat.

Aiyre shrugged. "What you are doing will help them with their journey to the Eternal Hunting Grounds." She looked around the cave. "I will want to visit our sacred cave to send them on their way though." To be truthful, visiting the sacred cave would be more for her than for her clan. It would be one more way for her to say a final goodbye.

He nodded. "When Eron is ready we can head out."

"I'm ready." Eron stood and looked at them.

"Are you ready?" Daerk turned to her, but she was already on her feet. "I don't want you to irritate your leg."

"It was barely a scratch." She waved it away unconcerned.

"It was more than that."

She frowned at him. "I can walk." Aiyre wanted to get this over with. Going back to her village would only bring that horrible night back into her mind. She didn't look forward to it, but she had to see Eron speak over their bodies. She hadn't been able to save them that night, but she could at least help them on their way to the afterlife.

Daerk grabbed a couple of packs.

"What are those?" She asked as she glanced over at the full packs.

"Tents and other supplies, just in case we don't make it there within the day." He looked down at her leg. "We have no idea how tired you might get with your injury."

She wanted to take offense at his comment, but at the same time, she wasn't sure as well. Her leg was still a bit sore, even if she wanted to play it off as feeling normal. There was always the chance she could cause it to begin bleeding again.

"What about Ezi? She can't come with us." Aiyre turned worried eyes over to her friend.

"I will stay here with her." Tor volunteered, looking a little too eager for Aiyre's taste.

Aiyre hesitated. "Are you alright with that?" Aiyre looked down at Ezi.

"I'll be fine." Ezi rolled her eyes.

Aiyre wasn't sure she wanted to leave Ezi alone with Tor. She didn't know this man very well, and she wasn't keen on him pressing any advances when Ezi had just lost her partner.

Grabbing her spear, she leveled it at Tor. "Anything happens to her, and I will hold you responsible." She wasn't entirely sure if she could beat him in a fight, but she'd do her best if he did something to Ezi.

He held his hands up in the air. "I will keep her safe. Eron has shown me how to tend to her leg."

"It is fine," Ezi reassured her.

Aiyre relented. "Let us go then." She wanted to get out of there so they could get back sooner.

She made her way out of the cave, pushing past the fur only to have the blowing snow greet her. Pulling up her hood, she tied the leather straps under her chin. She slid on her fur gloves and hefted her spear as she made her way down from the cave.

"Will you know the way from here?" Daerk slid down the hill until he was next to her.

"I've lived in this area for as long as I can remember, so I sure hope so." She wasn't familiar with this area specifically, but she knew in which direction she needed to head to get back to her village. Then she'd be able to spot landmarks that would help her back to her village.

"What happened to your parents?" Daerk insisted on walking right next to her.

How close did she want to get to him when it came to the information of her life? Nothing was secret. She just worried about them getting to know each other.

She glanced over at him. If he behaved like the sabertooths who'd attacked her village this would've been easier, but he was kind and watchful. He wasn't like any sabertooth she knew, and neither were any of the others he'd introduced her to so far. All of them had been too relatable to people in her life.

"I'm not quite sure on all the details." Aiyre tried to think back to when Naru had spoken to her about it. "I was too young to get the whole story. All I know was that my parents were killed by a bear, and my clan took me in and never made me feel unwelcome. Bhirk made sure everyone knew I was his daughter from then on, and that was all they needed to know."

His eyebrows raised slightly.

She smiled. "I know. Usually, a clan leader wouldn't welcome a child that wasn't of his own blood into his hut, but Naru, his wife, wouldn't let me go. They'd never been able to have any of their own children."

Images of Naru and Bhirk flashed through her mind, and she couldn't help the small hitch in her chest. She'd never see them again, and she still found it hard to believe. They'd always been there for her, since her very first memories.

"I can see how much they meant to you when you speak of them, and I'm sorry I can only apologize for what happened to your clanmates." She could hear the remorse in his voice.

She nodded, feeling a bit too choked up for words. Images of Naru and Bhirk kept flashing through her mind unrelenting and torturous. Naru hadn't deserved to die in such a brutal attack. Naru had been like a mother to her. She'd always been there and had always made Aiyre feel welcomed in their tent.

"I suppose I just wish I could have done more."

"Against an attacking clan of sabertooths?" Daerk shook his head. "If they loved you like their own, then they wouldn't have wanted you to try and do more. They would've just wanted you to live."

She knew his words held a lot of truth to them, but it still didn't make her feel any better about their deaths. "I hear what you're saying."

He moved slightly closer. "I too lost a parent."

Aiyre glanced over at him. "How?"

"A hunting accident."

"I'm so sorry." It wasn't like it was uncommon to lose a family member, but it didn't make it any easier. Sadly, death was always nipping at their heels in this harsh world they lived in.

He shrugged. "It's been years, and I've had time to recover from it. It will take time, but you will recover as well."

She nodded. All it would take was time. She knew it, but it didn't make the loss any easier.

The snow was higher than ever, making their journey a hard one, and the snow just kept coming. There didn't seem to be an end in sight. It was definitely winter. The snow billowed around them like it was trying to hinder their progress, but they refused to let it defeat them.

Aiyre used the butt of her spear to help her through the snow, as they kept going for several more hours. The snow was building up, and she dropped back to follow in Daerk's steps, so it took her less effort.

But the journey was taking its toll on her leg, and soon she was limping, using her spear as a cane rather than a walking stick.

"Let me carry you." Daerk stopped in his tracks and waited for her to catch up.

"I'm fine." She waved him off. "I can walk on my own."

"You're going to cause your leg to get worse." He glowered at her.

They both looked over at Eron.

"Perhaps we could stay the night here? The snow is falling too thickly to see, and my old bones need a rest."

Aiyre smiled. Eron was a good man, not wanting to take either side, so he created a whole new reason for them to make camp. One where neither of them would be able to deny him.

"Then we make camp and head back out in the morning." She agreed and looked over her shoulder at Daerk.

"Agreed."

He shouldered off the pack and took out a couple of tents. Eron and Daerk each took one and set up camp.

"We won't be able to set up a fire with this wind, and not being able to see any wood in this thick snowfall." Daerk finished putting up the tent and held open the flap.

Aiyre walked in, ready to lie down and let her leg rest.

"Should you take a look at her leg?" Daerk worried from the tent entrance, as Aiyre sat down.

"She can let me know if she experiences any pain or discoloration." Eron gave her a nod, and she returned it. "Until then it will just need to heal. It wasn't a deep wound, and it looks much worse than it really is."

"I'll be sure to let you both know if the condition of my leg changes." She reassured both of them. She understood why Daerk was so protective, but she wasn't a child. She would speak up if she needed Eron's healing hand.

Daerk stared at her with those intense golden eyes of his, looking like he might try to disagree with them.

"I'm fine right now, and you're letting the cold air in." She pulled her hood closer around her face.

Daerk strode inside her tent and closed the flap behind him securing the flap with a leather strap so that the wind wouldn't rip it open.

"Won't you stay with Eron?" Aiyre scooted over in the small tent.

"He will stay in his own tent. You are my mate, and we will share a tent." His gold eyes were fixated on her.

"He might get cold."

"Doubtful." Daerk rolled his eyes. "He will change into his sabertooth form and be plenty warm."

Aiyre couldn't come up with any more reasons to kick him out of her tent. He wanted to be in here, and she figured she'd have a difficult time convincing him to leave.

"Don't you want me in here?" He asked with a purr curling his words.

"Not really. I barely know you." She glared at him.

"Then let's change that." He prowled closer. "What would you like to know about me?"

Aiyre thought on the question even though he was making it difficult for her mind to think with him staring so intently at her. As she put her head down and looked at the thin branches that held up the roof of the tent, she continued to think what she would want to know.

"Do you have any family?" She knew about his father, but she wanted to know if he had anyone else still alive.

"I do." Even though she couldn't see him too clearly in the dark tent, she could hear the smile on his lips. "I have a mother and a sister living in the women's tents."

"Women's tents?" She looked across the tent at him.

"Where the unmated women live until a man takes them into his tent." He explained.

"I thought your people got involved before they found their mate."

Daerk let out a growl. "They would only welcome their mate into their tent, except for any man who has no respect for their mate, like our current leader. There might be those who might spend a few nights together to ease an itch, but it wouldn't be anything more."

"This leader you speak of is the dangerous one you spoke of earlier." It would probably be best that she learned about his world, in case Ezi and herself found themselves with no choice but to stay with the sabertooths.

"He is, and he has taken several women into his tent," Daerk growled, displeased with such an act.

"Along with his mate?"

"He is unmated." Daerk snorted. "Just wait until he finds his mate and has to explain all the women and children in his hut." A small smile spread across his face. "She'd turn tail and never look back."

"Unless she's like me," Aiyre pointed out.

"True," Daerk conceded. "If she is a shifter who doesn't have mates or is human, she might not mind and understand the number of women in his tent. If she's a sabertooth, though, she will never understand why he didn't wait."

Aiyre nodded as she took in the information. "How do you plan to bring us among your clan when your leader doesn't tolerate our people from even a distance?"

He stayed quiet.

"You don't have a plan then?" She quirked an eyebrow.

"I never thought my mate would turn out to be a pronghorn shifter. It wasn't like I had a plan for this." Daerk scrubbed a hand down his face, drawing her attention to the stubble that was slowly starting to pop up on his jawline. It was unfair that men could grow beards to protect their faces from the cold, while women were unable.

"Disappointed?" Aiyre asked, wondering if he would have preferred a sabertooth over her.

"Not at all!" He declared looking startled by her question. "I may not have expected it, but it isn't a disappointment to have you by my side."

The dark slowly chased away any remaining light from inside their tent as the night crept upon them. Howling could be heard far in the distance from direwolves, and she shivered.

"Come here."

She raised an eyebrow but did scoot closer to him as he laid down on a fur. She was an injured pronghorn. Like it or not he was her best hope now that deep winter was determined to set in a little earlier than expected. And the howling of distant direwolves scared her pronghorn side more than a sabertooth claiming to be her mate.

Daerk gathered her into his arms and drew her against himself. He pulled a couple of furs out from the pack and laid them over them as they settled down.

His hand caressed her hip and then dipped under her shirt. His breath tickled her ear from where he laid behind her, and she could feel his hard member pressing into her back even through all the thick layers of their fur clothing.

Her breath hitched in her chest. "What are you doing?"

His hand made its way up her trembling stomach.

"I want to please my mate again. All I can think about is you moaning in my arms." He growled in a low voice.

"Isn't it a bit cold out?" Aiyre wasn't keen on getting undressed in this kind of weather. The tent was just as cold as the outside snowstorm.

"I'm just looking to hear you moan my name. We'll take care of me at a warmer time."

His hand dipped below the waist of her pants and made its way down to the lips of her entrance. One fingertip rubbed against her nub, and pleasure soared through her. Then his finger slid between her lips.

"You're not yet wet for me, but you will be." He promised in her ear his voice as smooth as the most exquisite fur.

His finger entered her entrance, and she sucked in a harsh breath as her body responded eagerly to the sweet pressure. Slowly, his finger stroked her. He flipped her onto her back so he could capture her lips with his mouth as he continued to stroke in and out of her entrance. The stubble on his face tickled the smooth skin of her face.

Aiyre let out a moan, as she felt her thighs grow slick with her pleasure. His finger left her entrance to spread the wetness around. Then he circled her nub with his fingertip again. It was nearly enough to send her over the edge with the immense pleasure stampeding through her.

His fingers abandoned her nub to enter her once more, and her body shattered with her release. She bit down on her lip to prevent herself from yelling out with her pleasure.

Slowly, the contractions stopped, and his fingers left her center.

"Did you enjoy it?" He asked with his silky voice.

Aiyre chuckled as she looked up into his eyes. "Of course." She looked over at him. "Do you…?"

"Need something?" He grinned. "I will always want you, but it is a lot harder to please me with our clothing on." He pulled her back into his chest, and Aiyre allowed it. It did feel nice to be in his arms. "Pleasing you is enough for me… at least for now." His voice promised more to come later.

"Why are you doing this?"

"What?" Daerk asked, sounding like he was already falling asleep behind her.

"Why bring your shaman out here to say something over my dead clanmates?"

"I am determined to show you that I wasn't involved, and I have nothing but your happiness in mind. I will take as much time and effort as is needed." One of his hands skimmed over her covered arm in a caress.

Her heart thudded in her chest at his declaration. It felt nice, but she still wasn't sure how she felt about it, and she had no idea what Ezi was thinking. If Ezi wanted to leave, then Aiyre would want to go with her. Ezi was her last connection to a life she had enjoyed more than she could say.

She would just have to take everything one step at a time and see where it took her. So far, life had been unpredictable, and she wasn't sure whether or not the gods would throw more at her.

The next day they'd risen at the break of dawn to find the sun shining with barely a cloud in the sky. All the fresh snow sparkled under the rays, reflecting back the light blinding them until their eyes could adjust. Then they'd set off the moment they were packed.

Space not needed

They'd been walking for another few hours before they finally crested a hill and spotted her snow-covered village below. The soft pillowy fluff had covered everything, but the outlines of the tents could still be seen.

It angered her that the village appeared to have just disappeared. All those bodies and it was just wiped from memory and existence by some persistent snow. At least, predators hadn't yet stumbled onto the village, but she knew they would. It was only a matter of time. Not needed

"Will you be alright?" Daerk placed a gloved hand against her back, rubbing her slightly.

Aiyre nodded. "I never thought I would keep coming back, but I'm glad for the reason. They deserve to be sent on their way to the Eternal Hunting Grounds. They've been laying down there for long enough." She and Ezi had done what they could, but a shaman would be able to do so much more for her people.

Daerk rubbed his hand over her back, and then squeezed her shoulder. "He will do everything he can for them."

She slid her way down the hill, the two men following after her. Once they made it to the bottom of the hill, they walked into the snow-covered village, careful of where they walked lest they step on the body of one of her clanmates.

Eron picked a spot and laid out a fur, which he knelt down on before pulling different dried herbs out of his pack. Taking a still-hot coal out of a small container, he used it to light the dried herbs.

Then he proceeded to chant, and Aiyre closed her eyes. She hoped with all her heart that this would give her dead clanmates some assistance with their passing into the afterlife.

"Do you need anything?" Daerk whispered as Eron continued to chant, waving the burning herbs in the air.

Aiyre shook her head.

"I can promise you that we will come back in the spring when the ground is softer and give them a proper burial."

He was definitely making it difficult for her to hate him when he was so kind to her and her dead clanmates. This sabertooth was too sweet for his own good, and she worried he might actually capture her heart.

As Eron chanted and the scent of the herbs washed over her, she felt like Naru was calling her name and spurring her on to live life. Her chest tightened as she saw Naru's face flash behind her eyelids. She missed her family and friends more than words could describe, and it'd only been days since their demise.

Eron stopped chanting, and she opened her eyes as he rose and packed up his supplies. He walked over to them. "This is as much as I can do for them right now. I can assure you their spirits will go to the Eternal Hunting Grounds. Unfortunately, there's nothing we can do for their bodies until spring."

"It's better than nothing." Aiyre smiled at him. It really was better than nothing. Now she wouldn't have to worry about their spirits roaming the land, lost and bewildered. "There's nothing more we can do for them right now, and I'd like to get back to Ezi as soon as possible."

Daerk nodded. "Your dedication to her is admirable."

"She's the last clanmate I have alive. If she dies, I'll be alone." More alone than she already was.

The light in his eyes dulled a bit. "You won't be alone."

Eron coughed and walked away, giving them some privacy.

"I understand what this matehood means to you, but I'm still dealing with this." Aiyre pointed to the village that had been brutally turned into a burial ground. "You come from a clan that destroyed our lives. It won't be easy." She wasn't entirely sure she could forgive the sabertooth clan.

"Not all of us were responsible for what happened here." She could see his jaw clench.

"You've said, but should I just take your word?"

"No. You should look at my actions and into my eyes. You'll find an honest man." He said it with such passion, and he was right. His actions had so far spoken volumes about the high esteem he held her in.

"I just need more time."

Amazingly enough, Daerk inclined his head and started to make his way away from the village. She quickly followed after.

"I'd like to make a stop at our sacred cave," she told him quickly.

"I will join you."

Aiyre shook her head. "It isn't far, and I'd prefer to go by myself." Daerk looked ready to stop her, but she wasn't having it. "I may be your mate, but I still have some things I need to do on my own."

He relented with a sigh. "Don't take too long. Or I will come in search of you."

"I won't take longer than needed," she promised.

Then she dashed off before he could change his mind. She wanted to visit their sacred cave, not only to say goodbye once and for all to everything she knew but to see if any of her clanmates might have gone to the cave for shelter.

It didn't take her long to reach the cave system. Aiyre strode into the dark entrance and immediately felt all their ancestors rush to the entrance to greet her. Anyone who had ever lived in their pronghorn clan had passed through these caves at some point, whether it was to seek the guidance of the gods or for a ceremony.

She wandered deeper into the cave until she reached the innermost chamber. The same chamber they'd celebrated Ezi's joining. She just stood there breathing in and out, looking for Naru and Bhirk to brush past her.

It never came though. The cave was empty except for herself. It made her hopeful Eron's chanting had helped her clan to the Eternal Hunting Grounds. Opening her eyes, she began to walk around the outside of the cave walls. She quickly stripped off one of her fur gloves and ran her fingertips across the rocky wall. Every once in a while, she would come across something painted on the wall, and she would trace the outline with a finger, using the light from the smoke vent at the top of the cave.

This would be the last time anyone from her clan would visit the cave. No more depictions of animals would be painted here, at least, not by any of her clanmates. Her heart hitched in her chest.

"Goodbye." She whispered as she strode back through the corridor and then back out into the winter world that she called home.

It was time for her to get back to Daerk before he worried himself into a puddle. Or came rushing to her aid.

When she got back to the village, she found Eron and Daerk speaking amongst each other.

"I'm back." She smiled over at him. "We can get moving again."

Daerk shook his head. "We should rest for a while and have Eron check your leg again before we leave."

"It feels fine, and it isn't too far from here." It'd only take them a couple of days at most.

Daerk rounded on her, his face getting close to hers. "You might not trust me, but you will listen to me on this matter. We will rest and have Eron check your leg. Then we will head to the cave."

She opened her mouth, but he shook his head. "Ezi will be fine with Tor looking out for her safety. I trust him." *Lower case*

"I'm more afraid of what Tor will do with Ezi while we're gone." She confessed.

comma He looked like he wished he could just shake her. "Do you not have a positive thought in that head?"

"My clan was killed in front of my eyes. How much more positive can I get?" Her eyes narrowed at him.

He let out a growl and stomped away from her through the snow. He grabbed his pack and walked away. "You can stay with us to rest, or you can start walking back on your own and without your supplies."

Was he being serious with her?

"I don't need you to get back there." Aiyre walked off. She'd been living out here for years. It would be hard without supplies, but she could always turn to her pronghorn form for assistance with the cold and with making progress through the snow.

Predators would be a concern, but if she played it safe and kept her nose sniffing, she might just be able to avoid them all.

She passed by the area Eron and Daerk were making camp at and kept on walking. He didn't know her as well as he thought. When she was determined to do something, nothing but force would hold her back.

Ezi had to be worried about being left alone with a sabertooth shifter. She just had to be, and Aiyre knew she had to get back to her as soon as she could. Her friend was in a delicate state… or maybe she was only saying that because she was the one in a delicate state.

Hefting her spear with one hand, she made her way through the snow. A few minutes passed with no incident. The small camp Daerk and Eron had set up was now in the distance.

Maybe he wouldn't stop her after all, and she was glad of that. Ezi was traumatized enough, and she didn't need a sabertooth sniffing around her injured friend.

Then Aiyre heard a roar tear through the air from behind her.

Turning on her fur-booted heel, she took a glance back at where the small camp had been set up and found a sabertooth cat barreling right for her. Even though she knew it was Daerk coming after her, it still sent her heart into a flutter of panic, and the blood flushed through her system.

Her pronghorn begged to be released so they could bound through the snow and run, but she refused, knowing it would get them nowhere quick.

His muscled legs rippled with the power of his cat's form, and he quickly ate up the distance between them.

Aiyre leveled the spear at him. She had no intention of killing him, but she couldn't help the defensive posture when she saw a sabertooth heading straight for her. To say it was intimidating would be an understatement. _Lower case_

"I'm not going back!" She hollered at him. Ezi needed her when she was in such a delicate state.

Daerk sprinted right up to her and rolled to the side as he dodged a stab of the spear she sent in his direction.

He let out a growl that shook the very ground she stood on, before lunging at her and knocking the spear out of her hands as he landed on top of her. His massive paws held her arms down by her head, and the rest of his body straddled her legs.

"I'm not going back with you," she growled up at him.

He shifted above her, back into his human form. "Good thing you won't have a choice in coming back with me."

He rolled off of her and jumped back onto his feet. Aiyre tried to scramble away, but one of his hands latched onto her ankle and pulled her back across the snow. She felt some of the icy crystals work their way into the crevices of her clothing. She shivered as the snow met her skin.

"It won't be that easy," he growled.

"There's no reason for us to make camp," Aiyre grumped.

"We should have your leg checked by Eron. I don't want it getting infected and having you die. I've waited all my life for my mate, and I'm not about to lose her to her stupidity and stubbornness."

"I thought the other night you were proud of my stupidity and stubbornness?" she shot back.

"I can only take so much stupidity and stubbornness."

"We should get back to Ezi." Aiyre reached out her gloved hands but couldn't get a grip on the snow as he pulled on her leg.

"How many times do I need to tell you that Tor will take care of her?" He looked completely exasperated with her. "You need to trust me, and that means trusting my judgment. I've known Tor all my life, and he would never do anything to Ezi. At least, not without her permission." He winked at her.

She rolled her eyes. "And that's what I am worried about. None of you know what she's been through, and what she lost in the attack on our people. If Tor pursues her now… he'll just push her away." She sent him a stern glance. "I'm helping you as much as you're helping me. Ezi isn't ready for another partner."

Daerk paused and seemed to take in the information but shook his head. "Tor will know how and what to do with his own mate. His instinct will guide him true."

Aiyre gritted her teeth together. He was so thick-headed that he believed this matehood would guide them true. She could only imagine Tor's anger when Ezi inevitably refused his attentions.

Daerk pulled her over the snow and towards him, causing more frozen crystals to bunch up inside her furs.

Lashing out with a foot, satisfaction soared through her as she heard her foot connect with his jaw, snapping his mouth shut. It stunned him for a brief second, and she used the opportunity to dash away from him.

What was she thinking? She had no idea. She wasn't used to being bossed around, and she wasn't enjoying the experience, so she'd decided to fight him back. It was also kind of… thrilling. She wanted him to growl at her, and she had no idea why.

scooped. Swooped makes no sense.

Daerk swooped her up in his arms, pressing her firmly against his chest, trapping her arms by each of her sides.

"Let me go! What is your problem?"

"You are my problem," He growled in her face.

comma

"Then let me go!"

"As much as you frustrate me, you still make my balls ache with need. And the more you squirm, the more you turn me on." He leaned in towards her.

Aiyre froze in his grasp within a split second.

Looking up she found him smiling like an idiot. If only she had her spear, so she could mar that ridiculously handsome face of his. He frustrated her as well… and turned her on in return.

He marched through the snow, not even flinching from the cold that had to be bombarding his feet and bare skin.

Eron watched them with a smirk on his face as they marched past, probably remembering memories of when he was young.

"Come take a look at her leg. We don't need her falling down with illness and infection," Daerk instructed Eron.

comma

"I'm right behind you."

Daerk plopped her on the ground of the tent, and then stormed out, allowing Eron inside. The tent was really only big enough for maybe two people, and she was glad for that.

Eron kneeled beside her, and Aiyre watched the tent flap fall shut behind him.

"Does he have to behave like an animal?" Aiyre asked, glaring at the tent flap.

Eron shrugged, as his hands unwrapped the leather from around her leg. "We sabertooths are driven to find our mates, and once we find them, we then have the drive to keep them safe and fill our tents with offspring."

With the passion with which Eron said those words, it had her heart nearly breaking in half. There was a deep sadness in there that she could only wonder about.

"Have you found your mate, then?"

Eron heaved a sigh, as he wiped the older mixture of herbs off her wound. "I have waited my entire life to find her, but she has eluded my grasp for all these years." He met her eyes. "I fear I will never be lucky enough to find her."

Aiyre was shocked to the core. "Some don't find their mates?"

"It's one reason why Daerk will never let you out of his sight if he can help it." Eron nodded his head. "If I ever found my mate, I wouldn't let her leave my side lest she disappear and leave me to finish my life alone."

Aiyre grimaced.

"You don't want Daerk?" Eron asked, a little surprised she wouldn't want him.

"It's not that. Tor and Ezi shouldn't be left alone. He won't understand what she has gone through and pursuing her will only push her out of his grasp." Not that she was worried about that. She was just worried about the stress his attentions might put on Ezi's mind.

"Why?"

Aiyre shook her head. It wasn't her place to spread Ezi's life out for others. "You'd have to ask Ezi about her past. It's not my place. I just need Tor to understand she lost a lot more than a clan the day we were attacked."

He nodded as though he understood. At least someone understood why she wouldn't want to share anymore. Two words

"Give Daerk a chance. Comma" Eron urged her.

"Your clan killed my friends and family. I need time to learn to trust a sabertooth."

"Have you explained to Daerk?"

"I've tried, but he is too thick-headed to understand." Aiyre sighed as she leaned back on her hands. "He thinks Tor's instinct will lead him correctly, but a frightened, injured woman won't want the attentions of a sabertooth."

Eron put some new herb mash onto her wound, which was looking much better. Then he wrapped the leather strip around her thigh and tied it off. "Give them both some time. Persuading a sabertooth to not win over his mate would take more energy than you have."

She watched him pack up and leave the tent. She'd do her best, but Daerk was so frustrating with his matter-of-fact way and his mate-claiming. Aiyre sighed once more. She supposed she'd leave it to Tor, but it wasn't like anyone could say she didn't warn them when Ezi refused Tor. It was only a matter of time, not an if, but a when.

"How's her leg?" Daerk turned as soon as he heard the tent flap shuffle behind him. While Eron had been tending to his mate, he'd slipped his clothing back on to guard himself against the cold.

Eron walked up to him, placed a hand on his shoulder, and guided him a little further away from the tent. "Perhaps you should be more patient with your mate."

"Because you are an expert?" It came out before he could think about it. Eron's face flinched a bit but held firm. "I didn't mean that, Eron."

Eron sent him a sad smile. "I know you didn't mean anything by it and perhaps I don't know what I'm talking about, but she doesn't have the same instinct screaming inside of her. You say rash things sometimes, and she needs to see the side I know. She is also anxious about her clanmate." Eron shrugged. "I'm finding myself agreeing with her. Ezi is young and injured, and I can see Tor's interest scaring her away."

"I know this" Daerk relented. "It's part of the reason I want her by my side. Finding someone that loyal to their clanmates can be hard to find."

"Then maybe you should help her, instead of standing against her." Eron quirked an eyebrow.

"Tor will know how to behave with his mate." Daerk was starting to doubt it though. Maybe his friend would come on too strong and scare his mate away. It wasn't like they were dealing with another sabertooth. They were dealing with pronghorns who'd lost everything in one night.

Eron scowled. "Are you sure of that when even you are having trouble with your own mate?"

Then he left Daerk alone to think about that. Eron might be an older man, but he knew how to make his words just as sharp as a spear. But he could be right. Daerk might be pushing his own mate away. Giving in to her needs might make her more receptive to his own advances.

He was reluctant to give in and admit defeat… but if it helped him win her over, then so be it.

Crunching through the thick snowfall, he opened the tent flap. "You want to get back to Ezi?"

Her head perked up, and her soft brown eyes zeroed in on him. "Yes." Her face was guarded, as though she expected him to be tricking her.

"Then get up and help me get everything packed." He moved out of the way of the entrance.

Aiyre rose and walked out of the tent. She looked adorable in her fluffy fur clothing. The only visible part was her round face, which was framed by the fluffy fur of the cloak hood.

"Are we taking this down?" She asked, jarring him back to reality.

He could daydream about her at another time. First, he had to get her back to her friend and prove himself to her. They were on the same side when it came to doing what was best for Ezi and Tor. He just hoped he was right about instinct guiding Tor correctly.

"We are." Daerk stepped forward to help her with the folding of the tent's wood structure. After he tied it up, he placed it on top of his pack and slipped his gloves on over his hands. The only skin left to the harsh winter air was his face.

Eron already had his tent down and packed the moment he realized they were leaving the temporary camp.

"Thank you," Aiyre whispered over at him. It was barely audible, but his ears were able to pick up on it.

Maybe Eron had been right about making sure Aiyre knew he was on her side. Eron might be mateless, but he had good advice after watching everyone around him make mistakes and good choices. He'd make a woman a good mate if only he could find her. He might be older, but he deserved to find happiness. It was never too late.

They made their way through the snowy environment, and as they passed the area where he tackled her, she picked up her spear which had been laying on the ground.

"This saved my life when your clan attacked." She stated simply.

Daerk's heart lurched in his chest at the thought that she'd been so close to being taken away from him. One of his clanmates could have taken his mate away, and that alarmed him to the core. Brog could have taken away his one chance at a lifetime of happiness.

His people were good, he knew it. It was just Brog that was leading them wrong as he created a village full of fear. Brog had to be taken care of, but Daerk wasn't ready to challenge his leader.

Daerk wasn't sure he would be able to lead his people any better than Brog. He'd hate to take control only to lead them to their deaths this winter. Brog hadn't prepared them correctly for winter, and now it was up to them to survive by the skin of their teeth.

He glanced over at Aiyre. "I'm glad you made it out alive."

"Barely," She supplied. "It was pure luck. Your clanmate had been hunting me in his sabertooth form." He watched her shiver. "It was close, but I somehow got the upper hand in the fight."

Daerk couldn't help the growl that rumbled up and out of his mouth as his sabertooth threatened to shift. He shoved the beast down. His mate wasn't in danger right now and shifting would do nothing.

Her eyes went wide, and she gave him a wary look as she caught the growl and the lengthening of his canines.

"I was so close to losing you, and I wouldn't have ever known." The words were hard to say without his sabertooth adding a growl of frustration. He could have lived his life without ever seeing her or knowing she existed. It made him want to throw up.

"Where were you if you hadn't been involved in the attack?"

Though he was sure he'd told her before, he was happy to tell her again. He hoped this would be an important moment for them when it really sunk in that he had nothing to do with the attack. That there really had been no way for him to get involved.

"I was out hunting to restock my clan's meat tent before winter came full force." He told her honestly. "Tor and Rir came to find me the moment my clan leader led the attack. There was no way for me to get back in enough time to interfere with the plan."

"And you would have interfered?" She turned to look at him.

He had to think about the question for a few footsteps before he could answer with complete honesty. "If I hadn't known you, my mate, was down there, most likely not. Brog would've killed me, and then still killed your clan. If I had known you were down there?" He shrugged his shoulders. "I'm not sure. I would've at least seen to your safety, if not challenged Brog right there and then."

She studied his face for a moment, and he hoped she saw what she needed to see. He had to prove to her that he'd meant her people no harm. He just hoped his words wouldn't put more distance between them, but he wasn't about to lie to her.

They continued to walk in silence for most of the day until he noticed Eron beginning to drop behind them slowly.

He knew she wouldn't like the words he was about to say, but there was no choice. "We might have to make camp tonight. I don't want to push Eron through the night. He might act young, but he hasn't traveled outside of the village for a few years now." It looked like she wanted to argue with him when he noticed her mouth opening. "I'm truly saying it for Eron's health."

Aiyre pursed her lips, but then she gave a nod from under her thick fur hood. "We can stop for the night then."

"Ezi will be fine for one more night, and then you can be reunited with her." He reassured his mate, who he knew was eager to get back no matter what.

As he looked over at her, he couldn't help but be sucked in by how lovely she was. She had a cute nose poking out past all the long fur along her hood that had him wanting to place a kiss on the tip. She wasn't just pretty though.

Her confidence with her spear had him wondering about her ability to hunt. She might be a great asset to their clan, and a fantastic partner for him. If he did take over the clan… she might just make a great leader by his side. Their clan needed strong leaders and good hunters. She could be someone he'd feel proud to have by his side and help him lead his clan through the harsh winter.

It was something he would have to think about. If he took over the clan, he could assure Aiyre of her safety. Brog was a loose arrow. He and his men would be sure to kill his mate and Tor's mate as well. There was no way he could bring either of the pronghorns into the clan with Brog around.

There might still be problems bring Ezi and Aiyre into the clan, but Brog was the biggest threat to their lives.

Brog's mission in life was to make Daerk's life hell, and anyone who liked him would feel the full force of Brog's animosity. Brog thought of him as a threat, but before now, Daerk hadn't anything so precious to protect. Now, though… now he had a mate, and he would do anything to see her safe. Even challenge Brog, despite his uncertainties of leading a clan.

Chapter 12

Night fell quicker than Aiyre had hoped for, and they were still some ways away. She wished she could get back to the cave and check in on Ezi, but it wasn't going to happen tonight. Daerk wanted to make sure they wouldn't push Eron too far, and she understood his concern.

Eron might not look especially old, but he was slowly falling behind them the longer they walked. [*Two words*]

"Time to set up camp before the direwolves and bears come out hunting," Daerk said as he pulled the tent out of his pack. "And before Eron collapses on us." He added quietly. [*comma*]

Aiyre couldn't help the snort that flew out of her nose. "With the area smelling of two sabertooths, I think we're safe from bears and sabertooths." [*direwolves, surely?*]

He sent her a smirk. "Believe in the ability of your mate to protect you and keep you safe?"

"I believe a fellow predator would respect your space and not risk a fight. I believe in your scent, not you." She crinkled her nose for added effect.

"If you're saying I smell, I would have to disagree with you." He lifted an arm and gave it a loud sniff before sending her a smile.

"Whatever makes you happy." She stabbed the butt of her spear into the snow and took the tent off the pack he'd placed on the ground. She started to unfold it, so they could get it set up.

Daerk walked over and helped her with getting the tent set up. Once their tent was up, he went over to assist Eron, and she took the moment to take him in.

He was a tall man and a formidable warrior in either form. If she was going to be forced to be stuck with a man, he wasn't the worst choice. Maybe a little thick-headed and demanding... but he seemed to be honest and true. More importantly, she was starting to think he really hadn't been involved in the attack on her clan and was slowly winning her over.

Aiyre just wished he was naked again, instead of being hidden inside all those thick furs which were hiding his body from her eager eyes. She wanted to share another night with him as they'd done back in the cave.

He didn't smell foul like she'd told him, he actually smelled like safety and warmth. It stirred her inside and drew her in, especially after all the horrible things that had happened recently in her life.

He turned around and raised an eyebrow when he caught her just staring at him. Blushing, she turned away, trying to pretend like he hadn't been the sole focus of her thoughts.

"You need me?" Daerk's voice spoke right behind her.

She let out a gasp and spun around. "I didn't even hear you make a sound."

His hands made their way to her hips, and he drew her into his body and his warmth. "I wouldn't be much of a hunter if I always made noise."

"You made noise the last time you chased me down."

"Because I wanted you to know I was coming for you," He growled in her ear, sending shivers up and down her spine.

His lips captured hers and demanded her surrender. She melted against him. She might have some reservations about his clan, but she couldn't deny the fact that she was attracted to him. There was a pull forming between them that she found hard to resist.

Daerk was a man who would be able to take care of a woman and his offspring. And she was his mate. Just thinking about being his mate sent her heart a-fluttering. It definitely appealed to her. More than when Girk had asked to join with her.

His hand made its way to her breast, but she slapped it away. Daerk backed up slightly, his eyes wide with shock.

"Inside the tent." Aiyre grabbed a hold of his hand and led them over to the tent entrance and walked in, Daerk hot on her heels.

"No need for privacy, dear. I'm going to make you scream my name tonight, and Eron will know exactly what we're doing." Daerk promised.

She wasn't even allowed a chance to blush before he tackled her to the ground. "Won't it be cold?" She asked.

"We'll have it toasty warm in here in no time." He promised her as he shed her fur cloak, and then tugged her fur shirt up and over her head. "Resisting you is impossible. The cave might be warmer, but I need you, now."

Her nipples puckered in the brisk air, but he didn't leave them much time to freeze. He captured one of the rosy buds with his mouth and cupped the other breast with his hot hand.

His tongue swirled around her nipple, drawing a sigh of desire out of her mouth. His fingers pinched her other nipple lightly, and she felt her cheeks flush as heat pumped through her body. Lightly, he nipped her nipple between his teeth and sucked the brief shock of pain away.

"Daerk," Aiyre groaned, as desire built within her.

He abandoned her nipple and spread searing kisses across her chest and up her throat. She turned her head to give him better access, and then he planted a hungry kiss on her lips. The world around them melted away, as he became her sole focus.

Her hands rose to his head, and she dug her fingers into his hair. Her fingernails scraped across his scalp, and he purred into her mouth.

Slowly, his lips coaxed hers open until he was able to slip his tongue between her lips. She sighed in pleasure, as their tongues fought for control over the other. Then he broke away and planted one last kiss on her lips before sliding down her body and quickly undid the leather straps at her waist.

"Lift your hips," He commanded her.

She obeyed, and he whipped her pants off of her. Then he tore off his shirt, and she took a moment to appreciate the sight before her. He was well-built, ready to take on the harsh world they lived in with the many dangers that lurked behind every tree.

Daerk grinned ear to ear. "Like what you see?" He scrubbed a hand across his chest, and then down towards his pants, and her eyes followed eagerly.

"I do, but I'd like to see more." Aiyre smiled back at him as she licked her lips and waited impatiently for him to undo and strip off his pants.

Daerk did quick work of his pants. Once they were finally stripped off his form, she had the view she wanted. Lusted for.

His cock stood proudly above the dark hair lining his legs. A bead of cum glistened on the tip, and her body responded immediately. He wasn't the only one eager to join together and experience the bliss that could be between them.

"Spread your legs."

She did and watched as his eyes darkened with the passion that rushed over him at the sight of her.

Space not needed

The moment she spread her legs before him, Daerk felt his cock twitch in excitement. He couldn't wait to be back inside her, enjoying the bliss they could create together.

He let his gaze linger on her glistening lips. She was already aroused. His sabertooth purred its approval. His mate was just as eager as he was and it pleased both of them.

comma "I will attempt to do my best to be gentle with you." He promised. "Our last joining was rushed, but this time it will be different."

Aiyre spread her legs wider and shook her head. "I don't want you to be gentle. I want you to claim me." Her eyes widened as she realized what she'd just said, but a grin spread across his face.

"You want me to claim you?"

A wary gleam entered her brown eyes, and he wasn't having it. He leaned over her, his chest brushing over her pert nipples. His lips landed on hers, as one of his hands worked its way between her thighs until it found her wet center. With ease, he found her nub and circled it with a couple of his fingers.

Daerk pulled away from her lips, never letting his fingers stop their work. "You want me to claim you?" He asked again, eager to hear what she'd say. *Lower case*

"Yes!" She moaned, as her hips bucked a bit under him.

He growled at her and felt his canines grow a bit. His sabertooth was pleased with her declaration. Their first joining had been a bit rushed, and he hadn't had enough time to think about claiming her.

A bite-mark… on his mate. His sabertooth purred.

His hand abandoned her nub before she plunged over the cliff of pleasure.

She surprised him when she wrapped her legs around his waist, and her hands worked their way into his hair and drew him down until his body was pressed against her. "I'm ready."

Daerk shifted his hips until the head of his cock was pressed against the entrance of her pussy. He groaned as he felt her slickness welcome him. He thrust his cock forward and felt her stretch to accommodate his width.

"So wet." He groaned as his eyes slid shut. She felt so good around him, gripping him and pulling him deeper inside of her. Once he entered her fully, his hands gripped her hips, he pulled out and thrust back into her.

Her hips jumped in excitement as she met him thrust for thrust. "Hmm." She purred as her teeth gripped her pink bottom lip.

"As much as I enjoy seeing the pleasure sweep over you, I want to hear you." He growled down at her.

She let go of her bottom lip right before a moan ripped out of her throat filling the tent with the sound of her pleasure.

Daerk drove into her wet sheath with force until he sent her ample breasts bouncing. "Oh, gods!" His eyes watched her breasts bouncing, those pink nipples teasing him.

With a growl, he bent down and captured one in his mouth while he continued to drive into her.

"Daerk!" She cried out as her head fell to the side baring her neck to him.

His sabertooth demanded he brand her as his. He let go of her nipple with a smack of his lips. His canines enlarged, and he dove straight for her neck.

His teeth entered her flesh, and she cried out, but not in pain. In pleasure.

Her hips bucked wildly underneath him, as she began to collapse around him, her sheath pulling him in eagerly. He groaned as he held on tight to her neck. Then she broke, and he felt her begin to milk his cock.

Daerk's eyes shuttered, as he came in her tight sheath. He felt Aiyre's nails dig into the flesh of his back until she relaxed in bliss. He slumped against her and then broke his hold on her neck.

Reluctantly, he left her warm sheath. He rolled over and drew her into his arms before pulling a couple of pieces of their fur clothing over them to keep them warm.

"You're making it hard to hate you, sabertooth." She grumped as she tucked her head into his chest.

"That's the point." He chuckled. He was winning her over slowly, bit by bit. She might resist him, but he was confident he could win her over in no time. The gods wouldn't give him a mate he couldn't win over. He was sure of that.

The next morning, Aiyre found it difficult to make eye contact with Eron. Daerk had indeed made her scream his name at the top of her lungs, and she couldn't believe it.

Her gloved hands did short work with tying up the tent. She was ready to get back to the cave and see Ezi again. She wanted Eron to check up on Ezi's leg. It would be a shame if Ezi lost the use of one of her legs. It would be one more thing they'd have to deal with, but they'd get through it because she would stay by Ezi's side and help her handle it.

But maybe she was getting ahead of herself, since Ezi's leg was healing very well due to the care Eron was putting into it. Without the help of these sabertooths, they might already be dead.

She watched Daerk as he assisted Eron. What she'd said last night had been true. He was making it difficult for her to hate him. She still hadn't forgiven his clan or accepted this matehood, but she wasn't sure she hated him.

They finished packing and got on their way. She felt her heart sore in her chest. All she wanted to do was get back to the cave and scare away Tor. Daerk wanted her to believe that Tor's instincts would guide him correctly, but she wasn't so sure about it, and she couldn't help but worry.

Thankfully, it took them very little time to trek their way from the campsite back to the cave. The moment it came into view she rushed ahead of her small group. She needed to get in there and make sure Ezi's leg hadn't relapsed.

She pushed through the flap at the entrance to spot Ezi sitting by the fire. Tor was standing at the other side of the fire, glaring at Ezi. A strange twist. Aiyre eyed Tor warily, wondering why he would be glaring when just a couple of days ago he couldn't get enough of Ezi.

"Are you alright?" Aiyre turned her attention back to Ezi.

"Yes." Ezi sent her a smile. "Look, I can even stand." Ezi used the wall to help her stand up, but then her leg collapsed beneath her, sending her plunging towards the fire pit in the cave.

Both herself and Tor darted forward to catch her, but she was closer and caught Ezi first.

Aiyre pushed her back towards the cave wall. "Maybe we should wait on showing off until you have more time to heal."

Ezi nodded. "Just a little excited to get my feet back under me."

"I can understand." She helped Ezi back down into a sitting position. "Just remember not to get ahead of yourself and make it worse."

"She's been trying to stand since you all left," Tor said, his voice dripping in disapproval.

Daerk and Eron finally made their way into the cave, and Aiyre placed her spear against a cave wall before taking a seat next to Ezi.

"She's just excited." Aiyre felt the need to defend Ezi.

"She'll make it worse," Tor growled, his eyes never leaving Ezi.

"Movement might not be the worst thing, but putting weight on it might make it worse." Eron came to stand on the other side of Ezi and then squatted down to take a look at Ezi's leg. "It really is healing quite nicely. Better than I would've ever thought."

"Thanks to you." Aiyre smiled over at him. She looked over her shoulder. "And to you." She said to Daerk because without him Eron would never have seen to Ezi's leg.

He inclined his head. "We did nothing but bring him here to you." Daerk motioned to Tor.

Aiyre wasn't ready to be friends with Tor though. What she needed was some quiet and some time alone to speak with Ezi.

"We could use some more water." Aiyre motioned to the sacks made from the stomachs of animals. They really were getting a little low on water.

"I'll grab some snow to melt then." Tor grabbed the sacks and left the cave.

She eyed Daerk, motioning with her head that he should leave. He took the hint.

"Would you like to join me for a walk?" Daerk asked Eron.

Eron looked between them all and then let out a sigh. "If I must."

She felt bad to make Eron go back into that horrible weather, but she needed some space to talk openly with Ezi.

Once all the men left she jumped to her feet and peeked out of the cave to make sure they had actually gone, and once she saw they had she turned her attention back to Ezi.

"What is going on?" Ezi sat up, looking ready to bolt if Aiyre said run.

"I've been worried about you," Aiyre confessed.

"Why?" Ezi glanced down at her leg. "Eron says my leg is healing well. I don't think we have to worry about it."

"Not that." Aiyre came to sit close to her lifelong friend.

"What then?"

"Tor… he is your mate, and I wanted to make sure you knew what that meant." Aiyre cringed, not sure how Ezi would react. "I know we speculated on it earlier, but it's been confirmed by Daerk."

"I figured that much out while you all were gone. To say he was attentive would be an understatement." Ezi confessed. "Even before you mentioned it, I had to wonder if I'd been correct."

"Did he do anything?" Aiyre was ready to grab her spear and hunt Tor down.

Ezi raised her hands in the air. "He did nothing! I promise."

"Good." Aiyre calmed a bit. "How do you feel about it?"

"Having a mate?"

Aiyre nodded.

"Well… it's not an ideal time, obviously, but I don't know how to tell him that." Ezi nibbled her bottom lip as she turned her gaze to the fire burning brightly in front of them.

"It's probably better to do it sooner rather than later." Aiyre wondered if she was giving Ezi the best advice. "And as you know Daerk is my mate."

Ezi smiled. "Yes." She playfully punched Aiyre's arm. "Have you accepted his advances?"

"I have." She braced herself for Ezi's reaction, but again Ezi surprised her.

"He is a good catch and definitely a man who could provide for you."

Aiyre was stunned. "His clan attacked ours."

"Tor explained they weren't involved, and I believe him. Will it be hard to live among their people? Yes, but what choice do we have in the end?" Ezi tilted her head to the side as she thought about it. "Winter has set in, and it will be too difficult to travel for a long period, especially with my injury."

Aiyre nodded her head.

"I can't forgive what happened, but we can revisit leaving when spring comes. For now, we aren't in a position to leave."

"If you're fine with this, then I suppose I am as well, but do let me know if you need help with Tor."

"I will and thank you for your concern." Ezi patted one of Aiyre's hands and then squeezed it. "I may just take you up on that offer of help, if he continues to linger all the time."

"Is it safe to enter?" Daerk popped his head past the fur covering the entrance. "It's cold out here."

"It is." Aiyre rose and made her way over to where she usually sat near the fire.

All three of the men filed into the cave. Tor made his way over to the fire and placed all the bags near the heat of the fire, so the snow would melt, but not scorch the delicate skin bags.

"Have a good talk?" Daerk whispered in her ear as he plopped a seat next to her.

"I'm not repeating it to you."

He sent her a toothy grin, as he kicked his legs out towards the fire. Damn him for being so attractive. He was pulling her in despite her best intentions. That stubble was still growing on his face, giving him a roughness that appealed to her.

She watched as Tor made his way over to Ezi's side of the fire. Ezi seemed confident about everything when it came to telling a sabertooth to back off. She had guts, that one, despite her size and quietness.

They started speaking, and Aiyre wanted nothing more than to listen in and see if Ezi would be able to tell him that she just wasn't interested, but Daerk insisted on talking to her.

"Some meat?" He held out an offering.

"No, thanks." She waved it away, trying to return her attention to the couple across the fire.

"More for me then." He commented before asking, "What were the two of you talking about that required us men to leave?"

"What?" Aiyre finally gave him her full attention with an exasperated huff. He refused to just let her listen in to what Ezi and Tor were saying.

"What were the two of you talking about?" He asked again.

"Nothing to concern you."

His golden eyes moved over her. "It required me to leave the cave."

"Exactly. It's not something I wanted you to hear." He might be attractive, but she was beginning to wonder about his intelligence. Couldn't he hear what she was saying?

Daerk frowned at her but dropped the subject to her relief. She was sure he wouldn't understand her need to butt into another person's life. He was the type who thought instinct would make everything fine.

Ezi wasn't a child, but Aiyre was having a hard time leaving Ezi alone. Perhaps it was because she was afraid of becoming lonely. If anything happened to Ezi, Aiyre would have to face this life by herself.

Well… she glanced over at Daerk. Maybe not alone. She couldn't see that man ever leaving her side. He was addicted to her, and it felt nice.

Tor rose suddenly, barked something at Ezi, and then stormed out of the cave.

Aiyre was about to rise and go to her when Ezi motioned her to stay where she was. Then Ezi rolled over on her fur, giving everyone in the cave her back.

"What did you do?" Daerk asked, his golden eyes hardening as they narrowed at her.

She squirmed a bit. "Excuse me?"

"What did you do?" He asked, drawing out each word.

"Why do you assume I did something?" Aiyre leaned away slightly and pointed at her chest with a hand.

He crossed his arms in front of his chest, and she wished the furs weren't covering him so she could see his muscles bulge. He stirred her with the simplest movement. All those muscles were able to bring her so much pleasure, and her body responded to it instantly.

"I did nothing," she defended herself, "except talk to her about Tor's attentions. Nothing more, and nothing less."

"Perhaps you swayed her decision?" He raised an eyebrow.

"I did no such thing," Aiyre squeaked.

With a grunt, he rose.

"Where are you going?" She watched him pass by her.

"To remedy whatever you did." He made his way out of the cave shoving his shoulders through the fur flap at the entrance.

Her mouth dropped open. How could he not believe her? She'd done nothing more than make sure Ezi knew she needed to keep a little distance. But maybe she'd been wrong in doing so. Her eyes turned to where Ezi was laying and frowned.

Chapter 13

Daerk strode out of the cave, ready to find Tor and remedy any problems that had arisen between his friend and Ezi. He knew Aiyre must have talked to Ezi about Tor and dissuaded her from accepting Tor. Couldn't she just leave the two of them alone to figure it out on their own?

He easily found Tor's footprints in the snow and followed them down the hill. If there was one thing he'd learned, it was that Aiyre wouldn't just give up information to him freely. He'd have to work to get her to tell him anything.

Shaking his head, he hiked into the nearby forest, continuing to follow the tracks in the snow. He was glad he'd found his mate, but she was making his life a lot more complicated. More complicated than it already was.

He spotted Tor not too far ahead of him. "Tor!" He hollered out as he raised a hand.

Tor turned towards him. "What do you want?" He snapped.

Daerk tried not to take his tone personally. "No need to be angry with me." Daerk came up beside him. "What went on in there?"

"I'm just frustrated." Tor pushed his hood off and brushed his fur mitts over his black hair. "My mate is just pushing me away, and I have no idea why."

"I might." Daerk pursed his lips.

Tor's blue eyes pierced him with their intensity.

"I feel as though my mate is swaying yours."

Tor shook his head. "There's something else. I can feel it in my bones. Your mate might be helping to sway Ezi, but there is something else that is pushing her away. She won't talk to me though." He shook his head. "And it's more than our people killing her clan as well." He clenched a fist. "There's something she's holding back."

Daerk inclined his head. "You know your mate better than I do, but maybe giving her time would be best. She is injured and frightened after everything that's happened."

"I know." Tor looked completely dejected. "I wish she'd tell me more about herself so that I could understand. Right now, I am confused and... hurt she wouldn't at least try to trust me."

Daerk patted him on the shoulder. "I am still trying to convince my mate to accept me. You are not alone with this endeavor."

Tor smiled at him, a sad smile, but it was better than nothing.

"You'll win her over with enough time and patience."

Tor nodded. "I need to run in my sabertooth form and get out some of my frustration."

"I understand." And Daerk did. Running in their sabertooth form was freeing and relaxing.

Tor stripped off his clothes and shifted into his sabertooth form.

Daerk picked up his friend's clothing and watched Tor sprint off into the snow-covered forest. Tor would come back when he was ready, and until then Daerk would keep his clothes dry for him.

He trudged his way back to the cave and dropped Tor's clothes by the entrance once he entered the cave.

"Where did he disappear to?" Aiyre asked.

"He needed some time. It turns out you swayed Ezi's mind on having a mate." He glanced over to where Ezi was sleeping. He could hear the even breathing.

"There was no swaying needed." Her eyes narrowed at him. "She has been through more than you could ever imagine."

"Like?"

She glanced over at Ezi, and then back at him. "Want to go hunting?"

He grabbed his spear, and then tossed her spear to her once she was standing. He got the feeling she might talk to him once they went out hunting, away from any ears that might overhear their conversation.

Daerk allowed her to lead the way out of the cave, down the hill, and into the nearby forest. "The more we can bring back would be nice. My clan could use some extra meat for the winter. Prey has been scarce."

"I wish I couldn't say I didn't understand, but this winter has been harsh, and the prey has been scarce." Her soft brown eyes looked over at him past the fur of her hood.

"Unfortunately, I'm not sure killing your clan will do much for us."

Her eyes took on a sad look, as she nodded. "Unfortunately, it makes sense why your clan would want to believe your leader. He dangled hope in front of them. I want to hate them for what they did, but hunger and fear can be great motivators."

Daerk shook his head. "We shouldn't have done it. We will gain nothing, and now we have done something we can't take back. There is a reason why other clans fear predator shifters, because we react without thinking sometimes."

Again, she glanced over at him, and he felt hopeful blossom in his chest that he might just win his mate over. He found her to keep her expressions guarded, which made it harder to read her, but talking with her was getting easier with each day that passed.

"Your clan wasn't the only one having some trouble with collecting enough meat for this winter. For some reason, the mammoths haven't passed by our valley either."

They skirted past some fallen trees.

"All I can do is hunt what animals are left around our area for the winter and hope for the best outcome," Daerk said honestly.

"Good thing I'm handy with a spear." Aiyre tossed him a smile, and his heart warmed at the simple gesture. Everything she threw his way he would soak up with glee and eagerness.

"Perhaps we should see who can hunt down the most prey?" A little game that would both benefit them and lighten up the mood wasn't such a bad idea to him.

"I could out-hunt you even if I was blind," Aiyre challenged him.

"We will see about that," He challenged her back. "And don't expect me to go easy on you because you're my mate."

They loped off into the forest, separating slightly, but not enough to lose sight of the other. It could be dangerous to hunt alone, and even a sabertooth shifter would have to be careful.

Aiyre was the first one to make a kill, a small white rabbit, but Daerk wasn't going to let that shape the rest of the hunt. He was eager for the chance to show off, and he figured he had the upper hand since he was a predator twice over.

＊ ＊ ＊

Aiyre continued to put distance between them as they hunted, not because she wanted to, but because she wanted to come away the winner of their little game. The closer she stayed to him the harder it would be for her to get more game.

She walked further into the trees and heard something crunch through the snow over her shoulder.

Spinning around she found a small white rabbit shuffling around in the snow, looking for something to eat.

Aiyre reacted, letting her instinct drive her. The rabbit's long ears perked up, and then its head turned in her direction. They both darted, the rabbit trying to get away and Aiyre trying her best to predict its moves so she could add it to her stash.

Right as she leveled her spear at the zig-zagging rabbit something slammed into her, pushing her right into a tree. Her spear slipped from her hand, and when she glanced up, she couldn't believe who she was seeing.

"Girk?" Her mouth hung open despite her best efforts to close it.

"Aiyre." Girk smiled down at her, his brown eyes dancing with glee. "I never thought I would ever set eyes on you again."

"You're alive?" Aiyre wasn't sure if she was just seeing things or if he was really there right in front of her.

"My leg was chewed on by a sabertooth, but Bhirk and Drakk saved me. When I tried to rejoin them in the fight, I was knocked out. Then I came to, and everyone was dead or gone." He shrugged. "I dragged myself through the snow until I finally found somewhere to stay."

"You didn't come to the hunting cave?" She gazed up at him still stunned by what she was seeing. "The one to the east of the village?"

He shook his head. "In the chaos, I didn't think of it."

"I'm happy to see our clan wasn't wiped out." A smile spread across her face.

Girk backed away from her. "I'm just as happy."

Lower case

"Have you seen anyone else?" She asked, hoping there were more out there.

He shook his head as the smile slipped from his lips. "You are the only person I've encountered."

Aiyre wanted to tell him about Ezi, but she couldn't bring herself to do it. If she told him about Ezi, he would want to go back to the cavern with her, and she didn't need him trying to tear off Eron's head. He might be a sabertooth, but he wasn't a threat and nothing but nice.

"Same." She lied. She also didn't need him trying to move Ezi. Her leg was healing, and Aiyre didn't want Girk ruining that by insisting they leave and find another clan to join until spring.

"You must come with me." He grabbed her hand and began leading her away.

"I can't."

Girk turned and raised an eyebrow. "Why not?"

Her mouth opened and closed several times. She wasn't entirely sure what to say to him. How could she tell him about Daerk? He would never understand. Not after everything that had happened.

"Come." Girk yanked her behind him.

"No!" She yelled.

A roar vibrated off the trees shaking some snow off their green pine needles.

"Oh no," Aiyre muttered under her breath, knowing Daerk had heard her and was coming in his sabertooth form. "You have to leave. Now!"

"What are you talking about?" Girk turned but never let go of her hand.

Aiyre tried to get him to loosen his grip. "Go! Now!"

She heard something to her right, and when she turned, she found a sabertooth bearing down on them. "No!" She jumped to put herself between Girk and Daerk.

Daerk threw out his front legs and skidded to a halt before shifting back into human form.

"A sabertooth!" Girk yelled as he attempted to yank her behind him, but she wasn't having it.

Aiyre placed herself firmly between them as she yanked her hand away from Girk. Then she turned so they could both hear her as she held out her hands. "Let me explain."

"I think you should." Girk looked ready to grab her discarded spear.

"Agreed," Daerk growled, and she could tell he was barely containing his sabertooth.

"Daerk, this is Girk. He is from my clan."

Daerk's golden eyes never left Girk.

"Girk," she looked over at him, "this is Daerk, and he saved me."

"He's a sabertooth."

"I know." Aiyre realized that he might not understand why she was traveling with a sabertooth. "He's my mate."

Girk finally turned to glance at her. His eyes widened, and for a couple of seconds, he seemed lost for words. "Pronghorns don't have mates."

"She's my mate," Daerk growled.

He had to be freezing! He was butt-naked standing in snow that went mid-way up his calf.

Girk turned towards him, and she watched one of his hands open and close, and she knew he was itching to take Daerk on.

"I've accepted him as my mate."

Both of the men turned to stare at her.

"You can't be serious." Girk shook his head.

Aiyre understood his confusion. She'd refused his offer of joining and then accepted a sabertooth matehood. Of course, he'd be confused, and it was perfectly understandable.

"We've already joined." She said truthfully.

Girk shook his head as he backed away from her. "They destroyed our village, and you accept him over me?"

"He didn't destroy our village." She was slightly taken aback at her conviction when she said that.

"You'll take his word?" Girk seemed appalled by her actions.

"I've gotten to know him, and he hasn't done anything but help me." She was hoping Daerk wouldn't mention Ezi. She didn't need Girk insisting that he take Ezi with him, where ever he went, because she figured he wouldn't want to join the sabertooth clan.

"You can come with me." Girk offered her a hand.

Daerk growled.

Girk turned to glare at him.

Aiyre shook her head. "I'm going to stay here."

"You won't get a second chance to change your mind, Aiyre. I'm leaving the area to find another pronghorn clan to join." His eyes pleaded with her to choose him.

She couldn't though. Daerk was the man she could imagine standing by her side. He might be a sabertooth, but weirder things could happen. She was sure of that.

"I'm sorry." She took a couple of steps closer to Daerk. "I'm glad someone else survived, but I've found my place here."

Girk looked like he wanted to argue more, but he relented. He glanced over at Daerk and then back at her. "If you ever need me, I will try to make sure I keep an ear open at clan gatherings."

She nodded.

Girk looked back over at Daerk. "I offered her myself once, and she rejected me. Why she accepted you is beyond me. I only hope she knows what she's doing." Girk glanced over at her. "Goodbye, Aiyre."

"Goodbye." It was hard to say, and for a couple of seconds, she thought it might get stuck in her chest. She wanted nothing more than to have him stay, but he wouldn't be able to live among the sabertooths. She still wasn't sure she could live among the sabertooths.

Slowly, Girk backed away from her, and then he turned and loped off into the forest until he disappeared from sight.

Daerk strode over to her. "Are you alright?"

"I'm fine." She glanced at his naked body. "But you must be freezing."

"Stay here. I'll be right back."

"Okay."

She watched Daerk changed back into his sabertooth form and at first, she thought he might be about to hunt down Girk, but instead he bounded off in the direction that he'd first come.

It didn't take long before he came back in his human form, his clothing once more covering him.

He took her into his arms and ran a hand over her back. "You've accepted me as your mate?"

She pulled out of his arms and tipped her head back slightly so she could make eye contact with him. "Don't let it go to your head. I didn't want him fighting you, so I said what was needed."

"Afraid I might kill him?"

"Yes." She had no doubt Daerk would've easily been able to kill Girk. Girk was a good warrior, but Daerk had his sabertooth form, and she hadn't wanted it to come to blows.

"Will he truly leave you here?" Daerk asked as he gazed off in the direction Girk had disappeared.

"Yes." Aiyre nodded her head. "Girk isn't the type of man to play tricks with others. He gave me my chance, and then he left."

"And why not tell him about Ezi?" Daerk's gold eyes zeroed in on her. "You made it sound like you hadn't encountered anyone else alive."

"I didn't need him taking Ezi away. Her leg needs to heal, and I think the best place for her is here with me." Ezi didn't need Girk dragging her through the cold as he searched for another clan to join, not when they were already getting help. "Anyways," Girk was gone, and there was no reason for them to continue talking about it, "should we continue our challenge?"

He looked like he might want to argue, but he nodded his head. "Let's get back to hunting, but this time don't go far."

She nodded her head. Girk could have been something more dangerous. She wasn't planning on going anywhere far this time. Girk could have been a member of Daerk's clan, and there was no telling which of them would kill her before getting to know who she was.

By the end of the day, they had both collected a fair bit of small game. They met by a large pine tree.

Aiyre flopped her catch down on the ground next to his stockpile. He looked over at her pile. It did indeed look larger than his, but it was close.

"It looks like I have won," Aiyre announced with a triumphant smile, glad they were able to get past Girk's interruption. She'd been afraid Daerk might hunt Girk down, but he had surprised her. It helped her to believe Daerk had been telling her the truth that not all his people had been involved.

He returned her smile. "You're an impressive hunter. I never saw some of those snow rabbits that you killed." Which really was impressive, since he had better vision than she did and she couldn't help but smile at his compliment.

"If you had been in your sabertooth form, I'm sure you would have done a lot better."

"True." His other form would've given him a better advantage over her. "Let's get these back to the cave."

"I'm sorry about the interruption." She couldn't help but bring it up to see what he thought.

"You had no idea he was alive. I could pick up the smell of surprise on you a valley away." Daerk told her.

"Still, you won't" she couldn't believe she was going to ask this but, "you won't hunt him down, will you?"

"If he tried to take you away, then yes, but his scent is slowly disappearing from the area, which means that he is leaving like he said he would. I don't think there is any need for you to worry about us running into each other again."

"Thank you for not killing him."

"I wouldn't have killed your clanmate without cause." His gold eyes skimmed over her as he tried to read her. "I'm surprised you didn't go with him."

"As I said before, Ezi doesn't need the strain on her leg, and I figured you wouldn't just let me go."

He pressed her up against a tree. "Never." Then his lips came down and captured hers. After a couple of seconds, he broke away. Then he sniffed the air around them. "You can use Ezi as an excuse, but I can smell your desire. You want to stay."

Then he pulled away, and she was left to stare at him. He was correct though. She wanted nothing more than to stay with him. Girk hadn't been the right man for her, but Daerk was.

"Let's get back to the cave before they miss us." Daerk led her back over to their kills.

Space not needed

They each took a hold of their catch and made their way back to the cave, side by side. She could imagine more days just like this. It felt nice to have someone standing by her side, ready to back her if she needed it.

"It looks like that went well," Ezi commented from where she was sitting as Aiyre and Daerk strode into the cave, with their kills slung over their shoulders.

"We ended up making a better team than I would have thought." Aiyre looked over her shoulder at Daerk. She wondered if he would say anything about Girk, but she knew he had to be smarter than that. This was something she needed to tell Ezi without it being blurted out.

He tossed her a grin. He wouldn't say anything, and she knew he was still pleased that she'd chosen him over Girk.

She placed her animals by the fire and took a seat. It was time to clean and take care of the meat. Daerk took a seat next to her, and together they cleaned the animals.

She took hold of the feet and peeled off the skin. In the world that they lived, they tried to waste as little as possible. Once she was done with that, she took to gutting the rabbits and then placing them over the fire to smoke the meat without high heat.

"Tomorrow morning Eron and I will return to our village," Daerk told her as he placed a couple more rabbits over the fire. "There is only so long we can spend away from the village before drawing attention to ourselves, and I don't want someone growing curious and discovering you."

She nodded. "When can we expect you back?" And why was her heart longing for him to stay?

"As soon as I am able," Daerk promised. Then he turned his golden eyes on her and pinned her with an intense stare. "Please stay put this time. I don't want to chase you down in the snow because you are impatient for my return."

"I'll stay put this time." Mainly, because she had learned to trust him. As her mate, he would do anything to please her. She couldn't see him ever harming her. The one thing standing in the way was his clan. She wasn't sure they could figure that out, but she was willing to give it a try, mainly because she and Ezi would need to stay here for the winter.

"Good." Daerk's eyes relaxed a little bit with her promise.

Aiyre found it difficult to take her eyes off of him. He was so magnetic, always drawing her eyes to him. He would be a man she would welcome into her life with open arms if he weren't a sabertooth with a clan that wanted her dead. For now, she would take it day by day, but she wasn't sure she was ready for an entire life with him.

She glanced around the cave. If his clan didn't accept her, she wasn't keen on the idea of living with just him in a cave, or with a human clan where she wouldn't be able to shift.

Though she had to admit they'd been getting along and worked well together, but there were still a lot of challenges ahead of them, like a leader that would rather rip her throat out with his teeth than accept her into his clan.

Laying down she watched the rabbits cook from her position. So much had changed in her life, and she hadn't had the time to think about it. She missed her clan with all her heart, but sadly she had to move on and think of the future.

Aiyre rolled over, giving her back to the fire and watched the shadows dance over the crevices of the cave. Years of smoke had discolored the walls, and she wondered how long the sabertooth shifters had been using this cave.

"What are you thinking about?" Daerk moved behind her, laying down, and wrapping an arm around her waist.

She should push him away, but she needed the contact. Without a clan, she had no one else to turn to other than Ezi, but Aiyre couldn't burden her when Ezi had just as much to think about.

"If the mammoths had come on time, none of this might have happened." She confessed.

She felt him nod behind her. "The gods work in strange ways. I wish it could have been prevented."

"I believe you."

It shocked them both into silence. It was true though. She didn't get any evil intent coming off of Daerk, and she believed he and his friends were not involved in the attack on her people. She would save her judgment on the rest of his clan once she had the opportunity to meet them.

"Does this mean you will accept me?"

She could hear the emotion in his voice, the hope she would finally take him as her partner. She could still feel the area on her neck that he'd marked with a bite. A part of her had accepted him, but her mind wasn't quite there yet.

"No," Aiyre said. "I'm not ready to accept you. I told Girk what I had to so he'd go away without any threat of him coming back to rescue me."

"Why not?"

"I'm not ready. I need time."

He growled softly behind her, not threatening, but just irritated.

"What does this matehood entail? How do your people celebrate a joining?" She was curious to know what might be different between their people, and she was doing her best not to ask too many questions at once.

"I imagine it isn't too different from what your people do." His hand stroked over her belly playing with the fur of her shirt. "We have a cave system where we will go to join our bodies under the blessing of the gods. You'll be taken to the women's tent, and I will go to the men's tent before that. The day after, you and I will be joined, and our lives together will begin."

"It isn't much different then." It surprised her a bit to hear this. "I would've expected something different."

"What?"

"I have no idea what I would've expected to be different. I just figured it would be."

"The only difference would be our animal gods. We revere the sabertooth." He paused for a brief second. "If there is anything from your people you would like to do for the ceremony, please let me know. I would like to make you happy."

"I will let you know."

They went silent as he held her in his arms. She felt safe and happy where she was, but she still had to figure out what to do about his clan. They'd killed her people, and she worried about them finishing the job.

The crackle of the fire lulled her to sleep. When she closed her eyes, she could imagine herself back with her clan. Her dreams flooded over her. Naru and Bhirk welcomed her into their arms. Everything was back to normal, and she was going to enjoy the dream to its fullest.

Chapter 14

"Try not to be gone for too long." Aiyre looked over at Daerk, who was bundled up for the weather outside, and a spear gripped in one of his hands. The image he presented sent her heart skittering away inside her chest.

"I will do my best."

"How is Ezi's leg?" Aiyre turned to Eron. She was still concerned about her friend, who might be the only other survivor from the attack on her people, except Girk who was now gone. She had to remember to tell Ezi.

"It is healing nicely, and I don't foresee any issues with it." Eron gave her a broad smile, lines creasing over his weathered face. "I've changed the bandages again. If we can't get back within a couple of days, it would be wise to get her walking around. She'll need to strengthen her leg."

Aiyre nodded. "I can do that." She glanced down at her own leg.

"I wouldn't worry about your leg either," Eron told her.

"We will be back soon," Daerk promised again.

She nodded. "Don't worry about us. We know how to handle ourselves."

His eyes moved over her as if memorizing her form. With a nod, he and Eron headed out of the cave, letting the fur flap fall back into place behind them.

She let out a sigh, but instead of feeling relieved she actually felt like she was missing something. Daerk had made a place for himself in her life and heart.

"I hope I didn't hurt Tor by rejecting him," Ezi spoke up now that they were the only two in the cave. "He hasn't been back since he stormed off."

"He will get over it." Aiyre took a seat next to her friend. "Although it could be a good idea to let him know what is going on. He might understand if you let him know what you lost and what you might still gain." Aiyre made a point of looking at Ezi's stomach.

Ezi's hand rubbed over it. "It's still too soon to know."

"I know, but there is the possibility, and he'll have to face that." Aiyre wasn't sure how a mated species would take the hit that his mate was pregnant by another man. She hoped Tor would realize Ezi hadn't known him when she and Drakk joined together.

"Would he accept it?"

Aiyre could only shrug in response. "That is something you will have to discuss with him. I have no idea how a sabertooth would react to this."

Ezi nodded. "When he comes back, I will tell him why I can't accept his joining."

Aiyre frowned a bit. She felt like it was an if and not a when. Tor had been upset, and he hadn't been back yet. Perhaps he would return to the sabertooth village, and then he and Ezi could work out their differences, but she doubted he'd return to the cave.

"I have something to tell." Aiyre made eye contact with Ezi as she prepared herself.

"What is it?"

She sucked in a steadying breath. "I saw one of our clanmates while Daerk and I were out hunting."

"Who?" Aiyre was barely able to hear Ezi as she whispered the single word.

"Girk."

Ezi smiled, and then she glanced around. "Where is he?"

"I told him he was the only other clanmate I'd seen," Aiyre admitted not knowing what her reaction might be.

"Why?" Ezi twisted her hands in her lap.

"I didn't want him to come charging into the cave and demanding that you come with him. He could have made your leg worse while he tried to find another pronghorn clan."

"Probably for the best." Ezi surprised her.

"You aren't upset I didn't tell him about you?"

"Girk was a friend, nothing more. It was your decision on how to handle him. I just wished he could've stayed with us. It would've been nice to have another clanmate with us."

"He met Daerk."

Ezi's eyes widened as she leaned in. "How did that go?"

"Better than would've been expected."

"No fighting?"

"Thankfully, no."

"The gods must have been with you then."
Ezi leaned back against the cave wall. "Do you think
he'll survive and find another clan to join?"

"I think he will." Aiyre nodded her head as
she reached her hands out to the fire. "Girk is a fierce
warrior, and he won't let anything stop him once he
has his mind set on something."

Ezi closed her eyes. "Good."

Aiyre enjoyed knowing their clan would still
survive through Girk, because there was still the worry
that Daerk's clan would kill her and Ezi. But with Girk
out there, they still had a chance of their clan surviving.

When Daerk's village came into sight, he felt
his muscles tense a bit. It was back to being under
Brog's thumb.

"Be careful what you say." Eron cautioned as
they approached the edge of the village.

"I know." Daerk wasn't about to let anyone
know about his mate. There was no need to bring down
the wrath of Brog onto her head. Somehow, he would
have to figure out how to make his clan safe for her.

Eron headed off, most likely to get back to his
cave where he could commune with the gods and get a
fire roaring to life deep in the cave to heat his old
bones. He didn't like to leave the village or his cave
unless he had to, but Daerk was thankful he'd done it.

Daerk headed into the village, and it didn't
take long for people to notice his return.

Ryion walked over to him with a smile plastered all over his face. "Those rabbits for us?" He pointed to the rabbits draped over his shoulder.

"Of course." Daerk handed over the rabbits. He'd left several with Aiyre and Ezi and had taken the rest with him, so he could help to explain his disappearance. *haul. A haul is a large room!*

Ryion lifted the rope of tied up rabbits. "Looks like a good hall, but it won't take us long to go through it. Not with all the mouths we have to feed. Our clan is too big for our own good." *Not needed*

"I know."

Ryion looked at him, before clapping him on the back. "I didn't mean to bring you down." Then he looked around them, making sure no one was near. "I feel as though I should tell you something."

Daerk raised an eyebrow and leaned in. "What is it?"

"There have been a few grumblings since we attacked the pronghorn shifters. The clan is starting to think it may have been the wrong thing to do."

He nodded. "I am glad to hear that."

"Just be careful. These grumblings could reach Brog's ears, and if they do, he might blame you. He finds you to be a threat, and I hope he is right." Ryion slapped him on the back one last time and headed off.

Space not needed

Daerk felt his chest fill with excitement. His clan realized Brog had lied to them. His time might come. If his clan backed him, he would be able to challenge Brog, but it was a fine line. If he did challenge Brog, there was the possibility he might not survive, and he had a mate to think about now. It wasn't like Brog was old. Their leader was still in his prime and would be a formidable foe.

If Daerk died, she might not survive. He had to come up with a plan of what to do with her if he challenged Brog and didn't come out on top. Something that made everything a bit difficult was the fact that Tor was still gone, and he had no idea when his friend would come back. It meant there was one less person to back him up when he challenged Brog.

A couple of women ambled out of the hut of unmated females. Their eyes stroked over him, and he shivered in disgust. Now that he'd found his mate their appreciation only annoyed him to the core, but it wasn't their fault. They had no idea he was finally mated.

He wanted to tell everyone he saw but couldn't risk it. For now, he would keep his mouth shut and let everyone believe he was unmated, even his own mother and sister. They'd find out soon enough.

Mira sashayed her way over to him. "Why do you keep leaving the village?" She purred.

"To hunt for the clan. Perhaps you should think about doing that as well instead of staying here in the village." Daerk spat, baring his teeth, and he felt his canines lengthen slightly. He was tired of uselessness, and Brog seemed to think it was just fine to let his supporters sit on their butts doing nothing.

There was a reason their meat hut had a dwindling supply when only part of the clan was hunting, and the rest ate what they brought back.

Mira huffed. "It isn't a woman's place to provide for the clan."

Daerk snorted. "You're a sabertooth shifter, act like it." He stormed away from her. He didn't have the time nor the patience to go back and forth with her about this. She was a sabertooth, a natural born killer, and all she wanted to do was sit around the village while the threat of starvation hung over them all.

"You'll never find a mate with that attitude!" Mira called out from behind him.

He wished he could yell back that he had already found her, but he couldn't. Not yet at least.

What he needed was to find Rir and fill him in on everything that was happening.

"Daerk."

Daerk refrained from growling. It was Brog's voice calling out for him. Turning on his heel, he looked behind him to find Brog bearing down on him. He didn't look thrilled to see Daerk, but that was nothing new.

"Where have you been? And why did you take the healer?" Brog stopped in front of him, his chest puffing out imperiously.

Daerk took in Brog. He was of about the same size both in his human and shifter form. Maybe a challenge for leadership wouldn't be so hard, but he couldn't trust Brog to fight fair. This was a man who would do anything to keep his position.

"I was out hunting for the clan. You can ask Ryion about the rabbits I brought back." He couldn't resist adding, "Someone needs to hunt for the clan."

Brog's lips turned down in a frown, not missing the slight insult thrown his way. If Brog would get off his butt and go hunting, he would rise in Daerk's opinion, but he was lazy.

"As for the healer," Daerk continued, "I needed him to heal Tor."

"And where is Tor?" Brog raised an eyebrow as he looked around the camp. "No one's seen him for a few days."

Daerk loved the fact that he was having such an easy time of lying. Thank the gods. "Once Eron healed him, he took off in his sabertooth form. He needed some time on his own."

Brog studied his face, and Daerk hoped he wasn't giving anything away.

"I need to find Rir." Daerk excused himself.

Brog waved him away as if Daerk would've waited to be dismissed. Brog was getting too curious about Daerk, and he worried he wouldn't be able to keep his promise to Aiyre. If Brog continued to keep a close eye on him, he might have no other choice than to stay in the village until Brog's curiosity died down. Which meant he wouldn't be able to return any time soon.

"I'm worried about Tor," Rir spoke up from where he sat inside Daerk's tent.

"He will be fine." To be truthful Daerk was wondering if they'd ever see Tor again. He wasn't the type to run off and never come back, but he had been gone for a long time. Then again, he had a mate nearby, so Daerk refused to believe Tor would stay away for too long.

"It's been several days since you arrived back at the village. From the way you described how he stormed off, he could have done something stupid." Rir worried.

Daerk snorted. "Tor knows how to handle himself, and he isn't brash. His mate had just refused him. He needs time to cool down. Once he's calmed, he'll come back."

Rir shook his head. "What if he doesn't come back?"

Daerk looked up from where he was sharpening his stone spearhead for his spear. "He has a mate."

"Who rejected him."

Shaking his head, Daerk disagreed. "The mating drive will bring him back. Have faith in the gods to keep him safe and bring him back. It might take some time, but he will come back."

"You're probably right." Rir turned his attention back to the spearheads he was creating. "I can't help but worry about his mind. I have no idea how I'd react if my mate refused me." He slammed a rock down on top of another, creating flakes of the rock.

Daerk could understand that. Being so firmly rejected had to hurt. "I know how he feels. My mate is stubborn when it comes to rejecting me, but she accepts me between her legs. She is beyond confusing." And she was going to drive him insane. Now that he had a taste, he would never be able to let her go, not that he'd let her go either way, but now he was addicted.

"Both of you are making me feel lucky. I've always wanted to find my mate, but now I'm wondering…" Rir tossed him a smile. "Perhaps it isn't worth all the work and worry."

Daerk let out a bark of laughter. "My life would be easier, but I'm glad I found her. I just wish I could go back to see her."

Rir looked up, his expression gone serious. "The clan is unhappy with Brog."

Daerk shrugged. "We've always been unhappy with him."

"This time there is talk about supporting you as the next leader." Rir leaned in. "It's getting more serious, and it has to be the reason Brog is watching you like a hawk."

That caught his attention. Daerk placed his spearhead down. "I don't know if I'm ready. If he kills me in combat, my mate will be on her own in a dangerous world."

"If you die, which you won't, you can trust me to find and protect her," Rir promised with a firm nod of his head.

"Brog will make sure he wins. It won't be a fair fight," Daerk insisted.

"We will watch your back during the fight." Rir met and held eye contact. "If you won, you would be able to bring your mate into the clan. Here," he waved his hand around him, "into your hut. You can't tell me that doesn't appeal to you."

"Assuming she wants to join us. We did kill off her entire village." Everything was twisted around, and there were so many things up in the air. If only life wasn't so unpredictable!

Rir nodded. "It wasn't all of us though. Those people support Brog and will be cast out along with Brog, once you take over. They should have known better than to go along with our misguided leader."

Daerk shook his head. "Give me some time to think about it."

"Don't wait too long," Rir warned him. "The clan is behind you with this renewed anger at Brog. You'll want to use it before he gets them to fear him once more."

"You assume I will be a better leader than Brog." Daerk was afraid of letting his people down. Their expectations were built up, and he feared he wouldn't live up to those expectations. Brog had really driven them into a hard spot.

"We know Brog hasn't made the position an easy one, but if we survive until spring, we know you will set us right in the spring, and with the return of the mammoths."

Daerk nodded, a smile finally pulling at his lips. Perhaps life would turn around for them after all.

✳ ✳ ✳

Mira couldn't believe what she was hearing as she pressed her ear up against Daerk's tent the fur on the outside tickling her ear. He had a mate?! — ? only

She'd been sleeping with Brog because of his position and the need for protection. Brog would make sure those closest to him didn't die of starvation first, but she'd always hoped she would be Daerk's mate. There'd always been the hope as long as he remained unmated.

But he had a mate now… somewhere out there.

She turned to look at the forest surrounding their village. She couldn't help but wonder what his mate looked like.

Anger and jealousy boiled up inside her, and she felt her canines elongate. She wanted nothing more than to rip out the unknown woman's throat. But that wouldn't do her any good.

But Brog would reward her well if she took this information to him. It might hurt Daerk, but he'd just hurt her. He'd always rejected her advances, and now he had a mate! Now there was no chance for them!

With a frown firmly on her lips, she strode away from Daerk's tent and went in search of Brog.

It didn't take long for her to find him. Brog was inside his tent entertaining a couple of other women from the village.

Mira coughed, announcing her presence at the entrance to his hut.

Brog glanced up, a frown marring his face at the interruption. "What is it?"

"May I have a moment with you?" She smiled. "I have something you will want to know." She made sure to convey the importance with her eyes.

Brog waved the women away, and they scattered, leaving the tent in a rush. They nearly knocked her over in their haste. Brog wasn't known for being kind to anyone, especially anyone who didn't obey him. For a second, she wondered if she was doing the right thing. Daerk didn't deserve to have Brog breathing down his neck any more than he already was.

"What is it?" Brog snapped as he relaxed back against the pile of furs behind him. A large fire burning between them crackling happily as it ate away at the logs, but it did little to calm her.

"I…" Did she tell him?

"By the gods,woman! You better not have interrupted me to tell me nothing!" Brog barked irritably.

"Of course not," Mira rushed to say. She would have to tell him or face his wrath. "I came to tell you that Daerk has a mate."

"A mate?" Brog's brown eyes lighted up with the revelation. "Who is it?" He sat forward interested in the information.

"It isn't someone in the clan. It appears he met her outside the clan and has hidden her somewhere." Mira nervously shifted the fur coat on her shoulders. She felt ill. She shouldn't have told Brog about Daerk's mate, but it was too late. What was done was done and there was no going back.

Brog stood and smiled at her sending shivers of fear rushing over her skin. He rushed up close, cupped the sides of her face with his hands, and placed a kiss on her forehead. "I always knew you were my favorite. Thank you for this information. I will be sure to reward you."

He left the tent, and she was left to wonder if she'd done the right thing or not. It had been in the heat of the moment, and now that she was thinking properly she feared what Brog might do to Daerk. But if she warned Daerk, she feared what Brog might do to her. Mira worried she might have just gotten herself mixed up in something she should've left alone.

Brog gathered his men. It was time to find out where Daerk had hidden his mate. He gathered a few of his men and went out to see if they could track Daerk's smell from the village to wherever he had been going. *Lower case*

"Why are we trying to see where Daerk has gone?" One of the men asked as he looked around.

Another man was in his sabertooth form sniffing the ground helping to guide them over the expanse of snow.

"He found his mate," Brog informed them.

They went quiet for a second, and even the man in his sabertooth form froze before continuing to sniff for a scent to follow. *Lower case*

"What do you plan on doing?" One man asked.

Brog could clearly hear the apprehension in the man's voice. "Don't worry. We won't harm his mate, but this way I can easily control him. He won't give me any problems if I have control over something he loves and would do anything to protect."

The men nodded as they took in the information. He knew they wouldn't side with him if he threatened to kill Daerk's mate, but it was still an idea he was toying around with. If there was one sure way to break Daerk, it would be by killing his mate.

"Where do you think he's hidden her?" One of the men asked.

Brog shrugged as he hefted his spear. "I don't know. That's why all of you are here."

The man in his sabertooth form let out a growl and led the way as he found a scent to follow. Brog's chest filled with hope. He was going to control Daerk in just a matter of a day or two. He couldn't help but be excited about it. Daerk was the only threat to his leadership, and soon that threat would be eliminated.

Chapter 15

Aiyre looked around their cave. It had slowly transformed into their new home, but she found herself waiting to see Daerk again. It had been too long since he last visited, and she found herself wishing he would show up. Every time she heard a crunch of snow outside her ears would perk up, but every time she was left with disappointment.

"Are you thinking of him again?" Ezi asked from where she sat by the fire.

Aiyre turned her gaze away from the fur flap covering the cave entrance. "Sorry."

"No, please feel free to miss him." Ezi smiled over at her. "Just because I have something standing in my way of accepting Tor doesn't mean that you can't begin a new life with Daerk."

"But our clan…" Aiyre couldn't help but feel she was betraying all the people who had died.

"They wouldn't want us to stop living. They may have died, but we only have each other for a long winter if we don't go back to the sabertooth clan."

"Their clan killed our people," Aiyre insisted.

Ezi nodded her head. "But your sabertooth claims it wasn't the whole clan, just a few."

"True." It was a lot for her to think about. She would love to accept this matehood and have the hope for children. She just wished she didn't feel like she was betraying her people when she did it. "I will give it some thought," she said truthfully.

"To be honest, your sabertooth seems like a good man, and I believe he would keep you happy and safe." Ezi shifted as she stood up.

"Here, let me assist you." Aiyre came to stand beside Ezi.

"Let me stand on my own right now. I need to learn how to stand on my leg and put weight on it without help."

Aiyre rose her hands in the air as she backed away. "I will just be close enough to make sure you don't fall into the fire pit then."

Ezi sent her a broad smirk. "It was only once that I almost did that."

"Once is still too many times for my liking." Aiyre watched her friend hobble around the cave. She was glad Ezi's leg had healed. Ezi had a slight limp, but someone would have to look for it to see it.

Ezi slumped against a wall and slid down against it until she landed on her butt.

"Are you alright?" Aiyre was ready to rush over if Ezi needed her.

"Yes. It just takes a lot of effort."

A crunching sound outside the cave drew her attention.

"Did you hear that?"

"Hear what?" Ezi looked over at her, and then at the cave entrance. "I didn't hear anything."

Aiyre got the sense that something was outside. "I think something is outside the cave." She grabbed her spear. Call it instinct but her pronghorn was screaming at her to take shelter and not to make a sound.

"It could be Daerk," Ezi suggested. "Or maybe Tor is back."

"I want to be prepared in case it isn't." Aiyre crept towards the front of the cave. Her heart thundered in her chest like a herd of horses.

Men burst into the cave, several spears pointing in her face. She braced herself for a fight as she quickly backed up out of their reach.

"Do not resist us. We come from the same sabertooth clan that Daerk and Tor come from." A man stepped forward, his massive body covered by furs. A spear was gripped in one of his gloved hands ready to be used if necessary.

"That doesn't make me trust you any more than anyone else," Aiyre said honestly.

He motioned to the other men to lower their spears. "We could have come in here in our sabertooth forms and slaughtered the both of you, yet we didn't." He informed her like he'd done her a favor and that she should be thankful.

Aiyre's eyes narrowed. "If you come from their clan, why haven't Daerk, Tor, Rir, or Eron come with you?"

"Daerk and his friends are hunting for our clan, and Eron doesn't like traveling out of the village." The man's eyes skimmed over her as he assessed her. "Daerk wants us to bring you back to the clan."

She didn't trust these men, but she got the feeling she might have no choice but to go with them. "If we refuse to come with you?"

"I will have to insist." His brown eyes darkened.

Her jaw clenched. She wished her animal form was something more formidable than a pronghorn. "Who are you?"

"I am Brog, the leader of the sabertooth clan." He smiled waiting for her to cower in fear.

She kept her face neutral, but she heard a gasp come from behind her.

Brog's eyes looked behind her to where Ezi was seated.

"And which one of you is Daerk's mate?" Brog's eyes fluttered between them.

"Me." Aiyre didn't hesitate. She had the feeling Brog had something special planned for whoever ended up being Daerk's mate, and she didn't want to play games with him. If he needed to take his anger out on her so be it, but she wouldn't let him touch Ezi.

Brog's eyes scanned over her, and he shook his head, his dreadlocked blonde hair swinging around his face. "I will admit I do not like Daerk as much as some others, but I almost feel pity for him. To get stuck with a pronghorn shifter." He sighed. "He must have hidden you away to postpone his embarrassment."

Aiyre felt her face heat with indignation. "Doubtful."

"Why else would he hide you away in a cave?" She could see the intelligence gleaming in his dark eyes.

He wanted her to slip and give him a reason to kill Daerk. Good thing for Daerk she wasn't stupid. She knew when she was being baited.

When she didn't respond, he waved it away. "But none of that matters. He wants you to come back to the clan and be one of us, so he must not be that ashamed of you." Brog looked her over again, disdain clearly sprawled across his face. "Or he figures he has no choice."

She wished there weren't so many men with Brog, because then she might chance spearing him through his middle. He irked her with his cruelty. If he thought he was harming her by teasing her about being a useless pronghorn, he'd be dead wrong. If Daerk was ashamed of her, that was his problem, not hers, not that she thought he was or he wouldn't have introduced her to his friends.

"Gather what you need. We're taking you to our clan," Brog growled.

"Ezi will need to be carried. Her leg was injured the night your clan attacked ours." Aiyre couldn't help herself when she glared at him. This was the man responsible for killing her clan, and all she wanted to do was rip his eyes out. She sucked in a steadying breath through her nose.

He glanced over at Ezi. "Make something for us to pull her on." He turned on his heel to wait outside, while his men stayed in the cave to watch them.

"Don't help, then," Aiyre muttered under her breath. She set her spear down but made sure it was within arm's reach in case she needed it. Giving them her back went against all her instincts, but she knew she had to get on it, or Brog might lose the patience he was pretending to have.

She gathered up some furs and used two spears to tie the furs together. Within minutes, she had a sled ready to go. She helped Ezi onto it and then covered her with furs. If Ezi wasn't moving out there in the cold, she would freeze.

"How does it feel?"

"You did a good job." Ezi smiled up at her. "Although I don't trust these men." She whispered.

"Neither do I," Aiyre whispered back. "Unfortunately, we have no choice but to go with them."

"Don't let what Brog said get to you. Daerk clearly adores you and wants you as his mate. It was clear in his eyes every time he looked at you."

Aiyre smiled over at Ezi. "Do not worry about my feelings. I could care less if Daerk is ashamed of me."

Ezi cocked an eyebrow at her. "We've been friends for too long. You can't pretend you don't feel something for that sabertooth."

"Now isn't the time to discuss this. We've got bigger problems." Aiyre eyed the sabertooth shifters out of the corner of her eyes.

"We will discuss this later then," Ezi promised.

"Are you ready yet?" Brog entered the cave and sauntered over to them.

"We are."

"Good. I want to get back as soon as possible." He waved over a couple of men. "Carry this woman." He ordered them.

Aiyre backed away as she grabbed her spear. The men seized the ends of the spears and lifted Ezi off the ground. It looked like it was working. Good.

"Let's go!" Brog led the way out of the cave and into the winter wonderland that was their life, and Aiyre had no option to follow unless she wanted to face several sabertooths at once.

Walking into the sabertooth village had to be the most terrifying experience of Aiyre's life. The moment they walked into the village, a mass of people surrounded them as they wondered what their leader was bringing to them.

Aiyre made sure to stick by Ezi's side. She wasn't about to leave her friend when she was in such a vulnerable state. She reached out a hand and gripped Ezi's hand with hers.

"You will stay here in this tent with your clanmate." Brog motioned to a tent near the middle of the village.

"Thank you," Aiyre said as they entered the fur tent. She may not like the man, but she didn't want to anger him unnecessarily, not while she was still trying to figure out what he really wanted. She didn't believe his story about fetching them for Daerk, but she was sure Daerk would hear of this and come to her defense.

Brog's men dragged Ezi's sled into the tent and then left.

"I will let you get settled, but I want you to join us for our feast tonight." A gleeful light entered Brog's eyes, and her pronghorn screamed at her to leave the village and never look back.

"I thought your clan was having issues with your store of meat for the winter months," Aiyre said as she turned to look at him wondering what the sabertooths would be celebrating this night.

She saw his jaw tense as his eyes moved over her face. "I am clan leader, and I know exactly what my clan can and cannot do." He growled at her. "Keep to yourself, pronghorn." He spat with contempt.

Aiyre reminded herself to be more reserved. Brog wasn't the kind of man who liked being corrected, and she got the feeling he really didn't like it from a woman, much less a pronghorn.

She bowed her head demurely. "We look forward to joining your clan for the feast." It took all her self-restraint not to glare at him.

Brog left the tent in a storm.

"We better be careful around that one." Aiyre shook her head.

"I can see our lives flashing before my eyes right now." Ezi's eyes darted around the inside of the hut.

"I am as well." She wished she knew where Daerk was in the village. She might feel a little safer if she had him by her side. Aiyre couldn't defend them both against a whole clan of sabertooths, and she felt some fear trickle into her mind. Her pronghorn was still screaming at her to run away, but she couldn't leave Ezi.

Aiyre approached the front of the hut and noticed feet below the tent flap. They were being guarded, so she'd have to wait for Daerk to come to her.

* * *

Daerk stalked his prey from a distance. He'd stumbled upon a lone young stallion digging in the snow for any shoots in the desolate area. He was hoping for an easy kill to bring back to his people.

His fur boots let him glide over the snow with ease. Not a single sound came from him as he moved against the slight breeze. This stallion wouldn't know what had happened.

He'd chosen to hunt in his human form. His inner sabertooth grumbled with discontent at the choice, but he couldn't always rely on his sabertooth. He had to keep his human form honed.

Aiyre was still on his mind, but he focused solely on the stallion right in front of him. This beast would feed his clan for a reasonable amount of time. Once he was done with the kill, he could return to figuring out how to get back to the cave to see her again without Brog noticing.

All of sudden something crashed through the snow towards them. The stallion's head darted up, ears flew forwards, and then he darted.

Daerk tried in vain to send his spear flying through the air, but it landed in the snow with a hollow thump. The stallion had been spooked and gotten away.

With a growl, he whipped around to find a sabertooth bearing down on him. Then he recognized the form of Rir. He knew his friend wouldn't interrupt a hunt if it weren't something important... he hoped.

Rir pulled up beside him, barely stopping in time to prevent from plowing into Daerk. He changed into his human form.

"Brog... found... your mate," He panted, his hands resting on his knees as he sucked in much-needed breath.

Daerk's heart plummeted to the frozen ground under his feet. "How?"

"I have no idea, but he brought her into the village along with Tor's mate."

He had wanted to bring something back to the clan, but he couldn't leave his mate alone with Brog. Brog hadn't sought her out and brought her back to please Daerk. His leader was up to something.

Rir shifted back into his sabertooth form and darted back in the direction he had come from. Daerk didn't even waste time with shedding his clothing and shifted into his sabertooth form, ripping the clothes during the transformation.

He couldn't trust Brog as far as he could throw him.

Maybe it was time to see how much his clan would back him if he overthrew their leader. Brog may have just pushed him too far. He was willing to do anything for his mate's safety. And if that meant fighting to the death, then so be it.

His massive paws evened out his weight on the snow so he could fly over it with little to no effort. He dodged thick-trunked trees as he flew past them.

It took him a few hours to get back to the village since he'd been having a hard time finding anything decent to hunt near their village. Night had already fallen, and he could see a roaring bonfire in the middle of the village as he finally approached.

What did they have to celebrate? They had to hunt almost every day to keep their store of meat in stock. They never had a bonfire unless there was something to celebrate.

He changed out of his sabertooth form the moment he hit the edge of the village and kept on sprinting until he was fully in his human form. He had to find his mate and her friend. If something happened to Ezi, he knew Aiyre would hold him responsible. He didn't want to think about Tor's reaction, either.

Daerk found the whole clan gathered around the bonfire, enjoying the warmth and eating a lot of the stores of food.

"What happened to rationing the food?" Daerk grumbled in displeasure.

Rir rushed up beside him, undressed as well and still slightly out of breath. "We may have a more serious problem than food rations. I'm unable to find your mate among the clan. She and her friend must be in a tent, but we have so many tents to check."

"Stay with me. The moment I find Brog I get the feeling I will have to challenge him, and I need someone to guard my back." Daerk told him.

"The clan will be happy if you win."

Daerk frowned at his friend. "I have every reason to survive a fight, more reason than Brog. My mate is here, and if I die, she will follow closely after me."

They made their way through the village, searching every tent they could find and avoiding the crowd around the bonfire.

Mira strode out from behind a tent and blocked his way.

"Move," Daerk growled. He didn't have time for her and her games.

"I know where your mate is." She said.

Now she had his full attention. "Where is she?"

"Brog has them, and he plans on killing them tonight to put an end to the pronghorn clan once and for all."

Daerk let out a growl. "Where is she?"

The clan members around the bonfire went suspiciously quiet behind them.

"Is he doing it publicly?" Rir turned to take a look around all the tents. "Daerk!" Rir took off towards the bonfire.

Daerk took off after him. Mira was involved. Every fiber in his being screamed at him that Mira had done something. Guilt was flowing off that woman thick as ice. There had been remorse gleaming brightly in her eyes, like she may have done something she regretted. And if she had done something he was going to make sure she regretted it.

Brog's voice carried through the cold night air. "With the death of all the pronghorns, the gods will reward us with survival this winter!"

Daerk's blood froze in his veins as he came around the side of a tent and saw his mate all tied up. His eyes moved to where Ezi sat bound as well.

"I challenge you!" Daerk roared. The words were out of his mouth in a split second. It was one sure way of putting a halt to this. He knew what Brog was planning. He wanted to burn the pronghorn shifters alive.

"Daerk!" Brog's eyebrows rose in surprise.

"Wasn't planning on me showing up?" Daerk strode over to him. He was completely naked, and he could feel his mate's gaze on him. He was here to protect her and protect her he would.

"You challenge me?" Brog almost seemed taken aback by the declaration.

"Yes. Right now. Destroying the pronghorn clan has done nothing to help us. You would lead our clan into death based on wishes and fears. I declare you unfit to be our leader." Daerk growled his words, barely human. His sabertooth was clamoring to be released so it could rip out this foe's throat once and for all.

Rir came up and dragged the two tied-up women away from the flames of the bonfire, to Daerk's relief. He couldn't believe Brog would do something so viciously cruel. If he hadn't gotten here in time, he might have arrived to find a crispy mate. His heart faltered at that image before it began hammering away, ready to fight.

His skin crawled, his sabertooth ready to be released. He let out a growl as he shifted.

Rir finished removing the leather ties on Aiyre and Ezi and shifted into his sabertooth form to back him up in case Brog's men decided to intervene.

The clan moved away, each of them trying to get a good vantage point for the upcoming fight. They would support him if he won, but first, he had to do this on his own.

"Be careful, Daerk!"

One voice rose above the rest. His mother. There were a couple of other people in this clan he needed to fight for. Not only did he have a mate, but he had a sister and a mother still relying on him.

Brog smiled before shifting, letting his shift tear his clothing from his body. He was an impressively-built sabertooth, but Daerk had him when it came to motivation. This was his time to take control of the clan.

They circled each other, looking for any weaknesses in the other man. Brog let out a growl, and as they came around to complete the circle, one of Brog's men lunged for Daerk's leg.

Rir was quick to react, pushing the man away before his large canines could clamp onto Daerk's leg, but it distracted him, and Brog lunged for him in that split second.

As Daerk faced his opponent once more, he realized his mistake. He did his best to roll out of the way, but Brog's sharp teeth latched onto his leg. He growled in pain and twisted around enough to scrape his claws across Brog's face, causing him to pull back in a howl of pain.

Backing away, Daerk favored his leg. This wasn't going to plan. He'd been too eager, but if he hadn't challenged Brog, his mate may have been burned alive.

He reassessed Brog, watching for any old wounds he could take advantage of in this fight. Unfortunately, Brog presented him with no easy openings. They continued to circle as Rir kept anyone from the clan interrupting the fight.

Daerk darted forward, only to back away as Brog leaped to the right. This fight was going to come down to whoever could react the fastest, not who was the strongest, because they were evenly matched.

Brog rushed him, and they slammed into each other, driving each other onto their back legs. One of Brog's paws swiped past his face. Daerk opened his mouth letting a rumble escape his throat as he aimed for Brog's jugular.

Unfortunately, Brog ducked, knocking them both onto the ground before Daerk could land a blow to his throat. They rolled around on the ground, growling resonated through the air around them as the clan got excited by the fighting.

Brog's hind leg came up and scratched down the length of Daerk's hind leg. He let out a howl of pain but didn't let it distract him. He'd have time to lick the wound after he killed Brog.

He managed to get his two hind legs between them and pushed Brog off of him, sending Brog into the edge of the fire. Brog growled as his fur singed a bit but came roaring back at Daerk in a matter of seconds.

Ducking to the side, Daerk rounded and grabbed a hold of Brog's back leg, ripping into the flesh with his canines. Brog kept trying to swipe at him, but Daerk had him at a good advantage. Every time Brog leaped back at him, Daerk would pull on the leg and send Brog sprawling to the ground.

Then chaos broke out as Brog's supporters jumped to his aide. Daerk caught sight of Ryion, in sabertooth form, slamming into one of Brog's men. More sabertooth forms leaped into the fray, and Daerk felt a surge of warmth as he realized there were as many people fighting for him as for Brog. Now all Daerk had to do was finish off the threat once and for all.

Daerk was forced to let go of Brog's leg and focus on the ruckus around him. He didn't need one of Brog's men holding him down to give Brog an unfair advantage. Not when he was this close to victory.

"Daerk?" He heard Aiyre's voice break through the ruckus. His head shot up, and he saw her not too far away. Her eyes were focused on his thigh, and he looked down to see he was still bleeding from where Brog had gotten him.

Looking around, he found the clan in chaos, but Brog had disappeared. Quickly, he leaped over a couple of clanmates and sprinted over to Aiyre and shifted back into his human form.

"Are you alright? Did Brog do anything to you?" He checked her over pushing the pain in his leg to the back of his mind.

"No, we're fine, but if you hadn't arrived sooner we would have been…" She trailed off as her eyes looked over at the fire.

"I know. I'm sorry. I never thought he would find you both." But he should've known better. He shouldn't have waited so long to fight Brog. He just wished he could've gone back and changed the past so she wouldn't have been put through this trauma.

"You did come back to see us several times. It was only a matter of time before he became interested in what you were doing."

"But to kill you both, and in a fire?" Daerk growled. "I need to find him and put an end to this once and for all."

Aiyre glanced around. "He disappeared once your clan started attacking each other." She shook her head. "I lost sight of him."

"I'll find him. You and Ezi should stay near Rir." Daerk moved through the crowd before she could say anything else and found Rir. "I need you to stay with Aiyre and Ezi!"

Rir shifted into human form as another of Daerk's supporters filled in his space in the scuffle. "What will you be doing?" Rir asked.

"I need to find out where Brog disappeared while I was distracted. If I don't finish this now, he'll come back to be our living nightmare."

"I will stay with the pronghorns," Rir reassured him.

Daerk shifted and took one look back at Aiyre. She'd be safe with Rir, and he wouldn't be far if they needed him. He just needed to see if Brog was still in the area, and if he was, Daerk planned on ending his life.

Chapter 16

"Follow me."

Aiyre glanced up to find Rir standing next to them.

"Will you help me with her?" Aiyre assisted Ezi into a standing position before Rir swooped her friend up into his arms.

It was more help than she'd been anticipating, but she was glad he was so eager to assist them.

"Where are we going?"

"I'm taking you to Daerk's tent until he comes back. It will be the easiest place for me to protect you."

"Shouldn't you go with him?" Aiyre followed close on his heels as he led her through the calming crowd of sabertooth shifters. Brog's men had been chased out of the village or tied up like animals, and she worried Daerk might get teamed up on and killed.

Her heart puttered in her chest.

"You don't have to worry about him. He'll come back alive. He has a mate and a clan to live for, and he isn't stupid. Daerk will only search the immediate area around the village to make sure we don't have to worry about an attack by Brog's men."

"My leg hurts." Ezi looked over at her.

"I thought it was feeling better." Aiyre glanced over her friend.

"With the way they tied me up, I think they may have caused it to flare up." Ezi's face contorted as pain seared through her.

Rir guided them over to a tent. "You'll stay here." He pushed his way into the tent and placed Ezi down on some furs. "If I find Eron, I'll send him over here to help with Ezi's leg." And then he was gone.

"He doesn't know you very well, does he?" Ezi laughed from where she was lounging on the furs.

"Will you be alright if I leave you?" Aiyre glanced at Ezi.

"Daerk won the fight, and it looks like the skirmish is over. I doubt there's much for me to worry about in here." Ezi shrugged. "And Eron should be here in no time."

"I have to make sure Daerk doesn't get into something he can't handle. We don't need Brog coming back the winner."

"Go." Ezi waved her off. "I'll be fine."

Aiyre stripped off her clothing and shifted. It felt weird for her to shift into her pronghorn form in a sabertooth village, but there wasn't much she could do about it. The sabertooths would be able to scent the shifter smell on her, so there was nothing there to worry about... she hoped. A couple of flashbacks from the night her clan had been attacked tried to flood her mind, but she shoved them down. Now wasn't the time to let fear choke her.

She dashed out of the tent. As she twisted her long neck to glance behind her, she caught sight of the bonfire that had almost been the death of her, and the men that were now tied up beside it.

Turning on her four hooved feet, she skipped into the forest her hooves barely touching the snow-covered ground below them. She needed to find Daerk. He might be a sabertooth, but he'd worked his way into her life, and now she needed to make sure he didn't accidentally get himself killed.

"Aiyre!"

She stopped with a slight skid over the frozen ground as she turned to glance behind her. There stood Daerk in his human form. She shifted, the cold air rushing over her, but she could care less.

"Did you find him?" Aiyre walked over to him, hopping a bit as her bare feet protested standing on snow.

Daerk shook his head. "No. Brog got away with a few of his men." He growled. "I'd go after him but with my one of my legs chewed I don't want to challenge him alone."

She frowned. She was divided on how she felt about that. On one side it was good Daerk hadn't been in another fight, but at the same time, it meant Brog was still out there… and once he was done licking his wounds, he might be back.

She shivered and brought her hands up to rub her arms vigorously.

"Come here." Daerk coaxed her into his open arms.

Aiyre rushed into his arms and basked in the warmth radiating off his body. Then he stooped next to her and lifted her up in his arms.

"Let's get you back to my hut so we can get you warmed up͵" Daerk purred.

comma

"We can't warm up that much." She laughed. "Ezi is also in there."

"Eron collected her so he could personally watch over the mending of her leg."

"I just left the tent." She was stunned.

"He may be older, but he can still be fast on his feet." Daerk carried her into his tent and Ezi was indeed gone. "I saw him lead her away when I came back for you." Daerk placed her down on his bed of furs. "I've waited so long to get you here in my hut."

Aiyre glanced up at the mammoth bones that held up the covering of furs. "It's a large hut."

"Ready to be filled with children." His golden eyes gazed at her, and she could feel the love rushing off of him in waves.

"Even if they might be pronghorns?"

"I have no doubt they will be formidable hunters no matter what they shift into, if their mother is any indication."

Aiyre couldn't help but beam from the compliment. "And your clan?"

"Together we will show them that they have nothing to worry about. We will guide them through this lean winter." He sounded so certain.

Aiyre nodded her head. It would be more complicated than he was making it sound, but they could make it work. She was ready to give it a try. Nothing was perfect, and she knew their life would come with its fair share of problems, but she was willing to work them out with Daerk.

"Will you stay here with me?" His gold eyes were brimming with hope.

"I will."

A broad smile spread across his face as his head dipped down and he captured her mouth with his. His lips demanded her surrender, and she did just that. She melted underneath him as the warm air in the tent spread over her flesh.

Daerk ground his hard cock against the softness of her inner thigh. "I've waited so long to hear you accept me." He kissed his way to her neck and licked the area he'd marked her with his teeth.

"You never gave up." She panted as his hands wandered over to her breasts, and his fingers teased her taut nipples.

"Can you blame me?" He sucked the delicate flesh of her neck into his mouth and then released it with a pop. "My mate is something from a dream. She's the perfect match to me."

"What about your wound?"

"I'll have Eron take care of it the moment we finish here." He promised her.

Daerk continued to kiss his way down her body sending shivers of delight racing through her. As she glanced down her body, she caught Daerk looking up at her, his golden eyes glowing with the lust they were both feeling.

"Spread your thighs." The words sounded more animalistic, and she wondered if she was talking with his sabertooth side.

Aiyre did as he bid, and his eyes fell to between her legs. A long low growl rumbled through his chest.

"Better than a dream." He purred, and she blushed. He had a way of making her feel completely special.

His head dipped down between her legs, and he shocked a moan out of her when his hot tongue landed on her clit. "Daerk." She groaned as his tongue slid over her clit again.

"Does my mate like this?" His tongue circled her clit, and she nearly came right there as her thighs tightened around his face. ~~L~~ower case

~~comma~~ "More." She groaned, and he obliged her.

His tongue continued to circle and tease her clit while his hands pinched her rosy nipples. Her head fell back and her back arched as the pleasure built inside of her. Then his lips wrapped around her clit, and he sucked it into his mouth, and a pleasurable shock spread throughout her entire body.

"Daerk!" It felt so good, and she wasn't sure how much longer she would be able to last with him attacking her body like a beast. Her hands clenched into fists by her side as her head thrashed over the fur covers.

He growled in response, sending sweet vibrations soaring through her.

Moans escaped her mouth as the pleasure continued to build. She was going to shatter! "Daerk! More!" She bit down on her bottom lip as an explosion of color shot across her vision.

His fingers abandoned her nipples and instead shot deep into her sheath.

She broke.

Her body shuddered as her tight sheath tried in vain to draw his fingers in deeper. Panting her hips bucked as his tongue applied more pressure to her nub. His fingers never stopped pumping in and out of her.

Then she slumped as the last shudder of ecstasy flew through her.

Daerk pulled his fingers out of her and gave her one last lick before crawling back up her body.

"So responsive." He purred in satisfaction. "I could listen to you all day as you scream my name." He leaned down and planted a hot kiss on her lips, and she was able to taste her essence still lingering on his tongue.

His cock prodded her entrance. "Does my mate want more?"

Gods, did she want more. "Yes."

"Good." His hands landed on her hips, and he flipped her onto her hands and knees. "I've wanted to take you this way since I met you." He drew her back until his cock was once more pressing against her hot entrance.

"Yes!" She nearly screamed with delight but managed to restrain herself. "Enter me!"

Daerk couldn't believe he was about to take his mate in his hut and his village. Things were starting to look up for him. His sabertooth growled with impatience. It was done with his thinking. It wanted to take their mate and fill her with children.

Taking a firm hold of her hips, he guided his cock to her entrance and entered her in one fluid thrust of his hips. Her warmth immediately circled him, drawing him in further.

He began to thrust in and out of her. Then he reached for her hair, grabbed a handful and yanked back until her back arched. He groaned as pleasure built at the base of his spine.

After a few more thrusts he released her hair and let his hand find her nub. He began to rub it with the slickness that already covered her hot sex. The nub was swollen, and it didn't take him long to know she was getting close. Her sheath began to clench around his length.

A groan worked its way up his throat. "Aiyre." The pressure at the base of his spine built beyond his control. All it took was one more thrust until he felt the pressure release, and then he emptied his load into her.

Aiyre broke around him, her body shuddering, coaxing every last drop out of him until they both collapsed back onto the furs.

He gathered her into his arms and pulled her close, not wanting to lose contact with her lest she slip away like the dream he still thought she was.

"I love being here." She murmured as she snuggled into the furs. *comma* *lower case*

Daerk reached down and dragged a fur up and over her body. Then he placed a kiss on her cheek. "As much as I would love to waste away the night here in your arms, I must return to the bonfire. Now that I've won the fight, I need to lead my people."

She turned in his grasp. "Should I come out there with you?"

"No," he placed another kiss on her nose, "you stay here and warm back up. I'll join you as soon as I can."

"You won't hear me protest."

He smiled as he slipped out from under the furs and watched her curl up under the covers. He was so tempted to just slide back under the covers and take her back into his arms, but they would have plenty of time for that. Hopefully, a lifetime.

Daerk found a stack of clothing and slid a shirt and some pants on, and with one last look at her sleeping on his furs, he left the warmth of the tent and entered the chilly night air.

He walked over to the bonfire where most of the clan was still waiting to see what had happened.

"Did you find him?" Rir rushed over, his eyes bright with excitement from the events of the night.

"He slipped away," Daerk growled. Which meant trouble for them. Brog wasn't the type of man to just disappear without causing some sort of ruckus.

"So, we'll have to be concerned about him." Ryion sidled up beside them. "Brog won't let this go easily. He may have lost this fight, but he'll be itching to take control once more."

"Daerk?" A soft voice called out beside him.

Turning, Daerk was faced with Mira. What could she possibly want?

"I need to confess…" She looked between all three of them, her hands twisting in front of her. She'd done something, and she knew he wasn't going to like it. He could smell the fear flowing off of her in waves.

"What is it?" He urged her on.

"I… I told Brog about your mate." Mira never lifted her eyes, just stared at the ground below her feet.

A slow threatening growl rumbled out of his chest. He watched her flinch at the sound.

Rir threw out a hand, restraining him before he could pounce on Mira and tear her to shreds. His sabertooth wanted to watch her bleed for the danger she'd put his mate in.

"She's the least of our concerns," Rir reminded him. "What she did was…" he attempted to search for words, "something a clanmate should never do, but it wasn't like she harmed your mate."

"Still," Daerk ground out, "she should at least be thrown out of the clan." He watched Mira wilt even more under his anger.

"She will die out there in winter." Rir shook her head. "That would make you no better than Brog."

Ryion stepped forward. "In the spring, when the clans gather to trade and find mates, we can give her to another clan. Then she can be someone else's problem."

Rir nodded his head in approval. "It is the more sensible way to handle this situation."

"Fine," Daerk growled. "She can stay until spring and then she will be given to a different clan and be their problem." He ripped his gaze away from Mira. "But," he called out before she left, "if you come anywhere near Aiyre, you will be cast out sooner."

"I understand." And then he heard her walk away, her fur boots crunching on the snow.

"Now that we have that taken care of, what should we do with these men that support Brog?" Rir turned his gaze to the men who were tied up like animals in front of the bonfire.

"We could cast them out," Ryion suggested.

"And have them just rejoin Brog and attack us during the middle of the night?" Rir arched an eyebrow. "I think our only choice is to kill them."

Daerk shook his head, as he scrubbed a hand over his face shocked to feel the beard that was growing on his face. "We can't kill them. I won't lead our people with fear as Brog did. We'll banish them from the clan and send them on their way."

"What if they come back?" Rir glanced over at the men. "They could attack us in our sleep."

"So could Brog." Daerk reasoned. "For that reason, I will have sentries posted in the forest around the village. We'll know if someone is coming to attack."

Ryion nodded his head in agreement.

"I'll task you with sending them on their way and making sure they know they'll never be welcomed again." Daerk clapped Rir on the back.

"Now what about the women and many children Brog leaves behind?" Rir asked.

"We will continue to provide for them. They never did anything wrong. All they wanted was to be in a position of comfort and safety, which a clan leader would provide." Daerk couldn't hold that against them. It was much better to be on Brog's side than against it, as he knew very well. "You can send them to the women's hut until they find their mate or decide to leave the clan in the spring when we gather with the other clans."

Daerk glanced around the camp. "Has Tor still not returned?"

Rir shook his head, his eyes taking on a haunted look. "I'm beginning to wonder if he will ever come back."

It was completely possible Tor was laying somewhere out there dead, but Daerk had a hard time seeing Tor dying so easily when he had a mate.

"He'll come back. His sabertooth won't let him stay away for long. Ezi will continue to call to him."

"I hope you're right."

He hoped he was right as well because even he was beginning to wonder when they might see Tor once again. It didn't feel right that his longtime friend wasn't here to share in the joy of finally freeing their clan from Brog's insane clutches.

long-time

"Now that all that's taken care of," Ryion smiled over at Daerk, "when can we expect the joining ceremony to take place between you and your mate?"

Daerk's heart stopped in his chest before thundering away in excitement. "Hopefully, not long."

All the men chuckled before heading off to take care of different tasks. Now that he was the leader, he wanted to take a firm hold of their dwindling supplies and set them back in the right direction. He also needed Eron to take a look at his leg, which was pounding with pain.

✳ ✳ ✳

Aiyre held her breath as Ezi, who was seated behind her, braided her hair into one long braid.

"Are you ready to be joined?" Ezi asked, a hint of sadness marring her words, most likely remembering the one night she'd had with Drakk before he'd been cruelly snatched away by the gods.

"My hands are shaking, but I think this is the right decision. The gods wouldn't have brought him into my life if we weren't meant to be joined."

She could feel Ezi nod her head behind her in agreement.

"I only wish I could join you." Ezi finished tying off the end of her braid with a leather strap before motioning to her leg. "Eron wants me to let it heal before I take another step on it. When Brog had us tied up, they only caused more harm." Ezi patted Aiyre's shoulder signaling she was done with the braid.

Aiyre flipped around and took Ezi's hands in her own. "I wish you could come as well, but you need to listen to Eron."

"And I will," Ezi promised. "Now stand up and let me see you in this fur dress Daerk gave you for the ceremony."

Aiyre darted to her feet and spun around, loving the feel of the supple leather. Then she ran her hands over the white dress.

"Pretty." Ezi smiled up at her.

"Is she ready?" A now familiar head popped in from the entrance of the hut.

Ezi turned around and smiled broadly. "She's ready to be taken by the women."

Tira came in all the way, several women following after her. "Our ceremony will have to be changed since you're not a sabertooth."

Space shouldn't be here

This was Daerk's mother, and she felt nothing but joy flowing off the woman. Aiyre had been nervous how his family would react to her, but this matehood had meant more than her being a pronghorn shifter. She and Ezi had been welcomed with open arms.

"Daerk told me." Aiyre watched the women gather around her, all of them wearing the brown leather dresses and shoes to match. And they were all decorated with colored beads that were made from wood and stone, and some even made from bone.

A couple of them held bowls of red dye in their hands.

Aiyre held still as the women began to spread designs over her exposed skin. Tonight was the night she and Daerk would join together, and she couldn't be happier. If she didn't need to hold still for all the women painting designs on her skin, she might give a small jump in excitement.

When the women finished, Tira came up with a bundle of smoking herbs and waved them around Aiyre. She sucked in a deep breath, the subtle smoke penetrating her lungs, and she felt herself relax as the colors around her seemed to glow brighter.

"Now you're ready to be brought to the cave." Tira led the way out of the hut, and Aiyre followed, the other women following close behind her.

They directed her through the forest as they headed for the sacred cave. It would be the place where she and Daerk would be joined. The jitters entered her once more. She was both excited and alarmed by this new adventure she was about to take.

They entered the cave, and Tira led her through the inky darkness until they broke into a large warm chamber where a fire was roaring in the center. The flames leaped up into the air, eating hungrily at the wood that sat in the firepit.

Tira walked over to the fire, stuck another bunch of herbs into the heat of the fire until it began smoking. Then she withdrew the bunch and began chanting as she walked around the chamber, and then walked around the women who were gathered inside.

Aiyre watched the trail of smoke curl in the air behind Tira. Slowly, the grey smoke faded into the air around them, making its way into all their lungs.

"Now we wait for the men." Tira directed them to take a seat around the fire on furs that were already spread out.

They each sat down, and Tira produced a wood pipe. She stuffed it full with some dried herbs, lit it, took a couple of puffs, her cheeks puffing out with the effort, and then she blew a stream of grey smoke into the chamber.

"For you." She handed it over to Aiyre, who took it.

Aiyre placed the wooden pipe to her lips and slowly breathed in the smoke. She choked, her eyes watering as she handed the pipe over to the next woman.

Tira chuckled. "It takes a few times to get used to it, but it will enhance your joining with my son. Together the both of you will make our clan strong and ready to face whatever challenges come our way. The gods will make sure of that."

Aiyre smiled at Tira. She was ready for whatever came.

Within minutes the pipe had made a couple rounds around the women, and Aiyre was beginning to feel the full effects. She felt like she could see animals dancing around in the flames of the fire.

And then she heard it.

A light musical voice. It was Naru's voice, calling to her, singing. It sounded peaceful and content and gave Aiyre the much-needed hope that Eron had assisted her clan in their journey to the Eternal Hunting Grounds.

Men chanting could be heard echoing down the rock corridor.

Tira stood and motioned for the rest of the women to stand, except Aiyre. "You and Daerk will finish the ceremony with Eron."

Nerves once more raced back into her body as she watched the women file out of the chamber. Tonight was the night. She just hoped she'd chosen the right man.

Daerk followed the men in his sabertooth form, excited for the night that laid ahead of him. He and Aiyre had already shared pleasure in his furs, but this was the night where they would be joined formally before the gods.

His sabertooth purred its approval. It was just as eager as he was to set his eyes on Aiyre. His back leg limped a little as he walked, but Eron had done his best to help it heal after Brog had bitten it.

As they entered the dark cave, the lights the men around him were carrying lit up the space. His nails scraped the stone floor underneath him, and then the men around him began chanting, letting the waiting women know they were coming.

Soon he could hear light footsteps making their way towards him. They passed by the women, and then the men joined them. Now it was just Eron and him who would continue.

Eron's torch cast light over the rough cave walls all around them, making the stone appear to come to life. Each jagged edge looked like it was trying to reach out and touch them.

His cat eyes focused on the light coming from in front of them. It was there that he would find Aiyre, and he wasn't entirely sure he would be able to wait for Eron to finish the ceremony before he jumped his mate.

They broke into the main cavern, and there she was.   *Presumably meant to say 'air'*

Aiyre was sitting beside the fire, and when he lifted his nose and sniffed the warm hair, he could smell the sweet scent of her body as well as some apprehension flowing off of her, which was to be expected.

Even he was nervous about what the future might hold for them. The clan had barely any time to process the fact that their leader was mated to a pronghorn shifter. So far, they'd been accepting, if a bit surprised.

His sabertooth only had eyes for Aiyre and no thought about the future. Quickly, Daerk reined in his sabertooth. If he broke tradition, Eron would have no qualms about whipping him with a sapling branch like he was a naughty cub.

She was wearing a brown fur from a deer he'd killed a few years back. He'd saved the fur, not sure what to do with it until he met his mate, and then he knew it would be her dress for this night.

And he was right.

His mother had been kind enough to sew on a lovely pattern of beads.

The dress highlighted the slender shape of her body and highlighted her alabaster skin and dark hair. The firelight flickered over her, drawing his eyes to the light gleaming in her eyes, her small nose, and those luscious lips of hers that called his name.

Daerk let the shift overcome him until he was back in his human form.

"I don't think I'll ever get used to your sabertooth form." Aiyre breathed.

He sat beside her. "As long as you never fear him, because he would never do you any harm."

"I know that now." She whispered back, and her eyes briefly flickered over his wounded leg, and concern shown bright in her eyes.

"Don't worry about my leg. It is the least of the concerns we will need to worry about once we are joined."

Eron began chanting over them as he asked the gods to bless them and the clan. Daerk reached over and gripped her hand with his. They were in this life together now, and he couldn't be happier.

Epilogue

Birds sang happily in the trees high above them, as Aiyre and Daerk strode through the forest. The snow was now gone, and the animals had once more returned to their area. The clan's meat hut was filled to the brim, and the mood was now lighter. The worry of winter was gone.

"We're close," Daerk told her.

"Thank you for doing this." Aiyre's heart thudded in her chest as they approached her village.

"My clan was happy to do this. They felt it was the least they could do for you and Ezi." Daerk frowned. "All of us wish we had handled Brog differently before he'd the chance to kill your clan."

Aiyre sighed. "I've come to realize that I can't dwell on the past and what could have been. Now that winter is gone, and the animals are back, I am looking to the future and what it will hold for us. I know Naru would have wanted me to continue to live life."

"We're here."

They broke out of the trees to see her decimated village, now uncovered for the world to see. Her throat threatened to close up as her eyes scanned over all the toppled huts.

Thankfully, there were no bodies strewn about like the last time she'd visited all those months ago.

"Would you like some time, or should we head over to the burial?" Daerk placed a hand to the small of her back, giving her reassurance.

"Let's head over to the burial." Aiyre led the way past the village and then over to the burial that wasn't far away. The green grass under her fur-booted feet felt good. The snow was gone, and now they would have a few blissful moons of no snow.

They stopped by the edge of the large burial site, and she pulled up beside Ezi, whose stomach had grown significantly. She'd been right about Drakk leaving her with a part of himself.

"How are you feeling?" Aiyre asked her longtime friend.

"Very well." Ezi rubbed a hand over her stomach. "This little one keeps kicking though, and I still throw up every once in a while." Ezi smiled. "But I'm happy."

"You deserve to be happy after everything that's happened."

"Thankfully we made it to spring."

Aiyre nodded her head. Her eyes skimmed over the burial area. The bodies had already been covered up, but the brown spot of recently turned soil stood out in stark contrast to the green blades of grass waving in the light wind.

"Are we worried about Tor?" She asked Daerk as Eron took his position at the burial and lit some incense.

Daerk heaved a heavy sigh. "There's nothing we can do. Rir and I already searched for him, and we haven't found a single sign to indicate he is anywhere near the village."

Aiyre glanced over at Ezi. The clan would provide for her, but she worried Ezi might have missed an opportunity for the happiness Aiyre had found with Daerk. She couldn't help but wonder if pushing Tor away had been the right decision, but at the time she hadn't known what the right course would be.

Eron's chanting drew her attention back to the ceremony. Unfortunately, some animals had found a few of the bodies of her clanmates before them, so they were missing a few clanmates, but there'd been nothing they could do about it.

She closed her eyes and took a steadying breath. After this ceremony was finished, she could think fully of the future and only the future.

Printed in Great Britain
by Amazon

12868475R00181